"Isn't that something, Will?" Vivian asked. "The man we talked to on the phone last night was from Canada, too."

The back of Graham's neck started to tingle. "Who did you talk to last night?"

"I called the Santa Trackers." Will looked embarrassed.

"I answered phones last night for NORAD. I answered so many calls, they've kind of run together, but I'm pretty sure we talked, Will. You told me about your dad, right?"

Will stared at him like he'd just turned into Santa Claus himself. "That was you? You're the hero on the phone?"

"I don't know if I'm a hero, but I definitely remember talking to you."

Vivian was staring at him in shock. "This is unbelievable. I mean, what could be the odds?"

"Probably pretty great. I guess we were meant to meet in person."

The soft smile that had been playing on her mouth lit her eyes. "I guess so."

Dear Reader,

A series of events served as the inspiration for this novel. First, I spied a pair of Canadian servicemen at the BMV in Colorado Springs. When I first saw them, I was surprised to see a maple leaf on each of their uniforms. I couldn't help but wonder what their lives were like, since they were obviously stationed so far from home.

Later that week, the local newspaper published a story about COVID restrictions forcing members of the Royal Canadian Air Force to spend Christmas in Colorado instead of going home for the holidays.

Soon after that, one of my neighbors mentioned that he'd been a Santa Tracker for NORAD several years earlier.

For some reason, those three small things caught my interest and held on tight. After a lot of notes and more research, I eventually came up with this story.

As you might imagine, this novel was a bit out of my usual comfort zone—but in all the best ways. I loved the opportunity to feature a military hero. It was fun to reach out to my husband's Canadian cousins for research help, too. But most of all, I loved the opportunity to write a Christmas romance featuring a little boy in need of a hero...and a lonely hero in need of a Christmas wish or two.

I hope you will enjoy this story! Happy Christmas!

With my blessings,

Shelley Shepard Gray

HEARTWARMING

The Sergeant's Christmas Gift

———

Shelley Shepard Gray

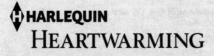

HARLEQUIN®
HEARTWARMING™

ISBN-13: 978-1-335-58471-7

The Sergeant's Christmas Gift

Copyright © 2022 by Shelley Sabga

For questions and comments about the quality of this book, please contact us at CustomerService@Harlequin.com.

Harlequin Enterprises ULC
22 Adelaide St. West, 41st Floor
Toronto, Ontario M5H 4E3, Canada
www.Harlequin.com

Printed in U.S.A.

Shelley Shepard Gray writes inspirational and sweet contemporary romances for a variety of publishers. With over a million books in print, and translated into more than a dozen languages, her novels have reached both the *New York Times* and the *USA TODAY* bestseller lists. Shelley's novels have also been featured in a variety of national publications.

In addition to her writing, Shelley has hosted several well-attended Girlfriend Getaways for Amish reading fans. Her most recent Girlfriend Getaway, hosted with several other novelists, was highlighted on Netflix's *Follow This* series.

Before writing romances, Shelley taught school and earned her bachelor's degree in English literature and later obtained her master's degree in educational administration. She now lives in southern Colorado near her grown children, walks her dachshunds, bakes too much and writes full-time.

Books by Shelley Shepard Gray

Inspirational Cold Case Collection

Miniseries

Widow's Secrets
Amish Jane Doe

Visit the Author Profile page
at Harlequin.com for more titles.

For all the volunteers who graciously become Santa Trackers on Christmas Eve. Thank you for helping to make many wishes come true.

Acknowledgments

As usual, I am so grateful to the many people who helped to make this novel a reality. Thank you to the fabulous team at Harlequin. Each person works so hard to make every novel something to be proud of, and I'm so grateful for both their dedication and their expertise.

Next, I owe a great deal of thanks to my Colorado Springs neighbors for sharing their stories about being Santa Trackers. Thank you for always answering way too many questions about military life!

In addition, I'm also so grateful to my husband's cousin Carron for kindly sharing lots of very fun stories about spending Christmas in Windsor—including letting me know about the "right" way to order a coffee at Tim Hortons. Carron, next time I ask for a "double double," I'll think of you!

Last, but not least, I am so blessed for the opportunity to work with my editor, Johanna Raisanen, on this book. Johanna, thank you for very kindly sharing some of your favorite Canadian Christmas memories, helping to explain exactly what a "tourtière" is...and for not laughing out loud at my shameful hockey ignorance. Here's to one day going to Tim Hortons together! My treat!

CHAPTER ONE

Colorado Springs, Colorado
Christmas Eve

"HEY, SERGEANT, ARE YOU doing okay? Need a break?" Brad, the American airman Graham was sharing a table with, asked.

Graham Hopkins glanced up from his phone's screen. "Thanks, but I'm good."

A line formed between Brad's brows. "Are you sure? Some of the Santa Tracker calls can get kind of stressful. I had a kid start crying on me last year. I didn't know what to do."

Graham had signed up to be a Santa Tracker for NORAD—the North American Aerospace Defense Command—on Christmas Eve. Every year, dozens of volunteers gave up hours of their time to post information about Santa Claus's route—and answer calls from excited children around the world.

Kids weren't really his thing, but helping out his colleagues when he could was. Since Graham was single and in town, he'd signed up so everyone who had family nearby could spend time with them.

He hadn't exactly been dreading the evening, but he had thought that he was going to be watching the clock the whole time. He couldn't have been more wrong. It had turned out to be one of the most enjoyable Christmas Eves he'd ever had. The kids were cute, and their questions and eagerness about Santa's visit kept a permanent grin on his face. His scheduled time was flying by.

The whole experience was a whole lot better than moping around his apartment wishing he was sitting in front of a roaring fire in his parents' living room back in Windsor, Ontario. "I'll let you know if I need anything, Brad."

"I hear ya, but there's no shame in taking breaks. You ought to go grab something to eat, too." He held up a fried chicken wing. "These things are great."

Graham chuckled. So far, Brad had eaten two plates of wings, a huge slice of chocolate cake, a bunch of chips and salsa, and a plate of barbecued ribs. The guy either had an iron stomach or was going to be sick as a dog in about four hours. "I'll get some food in a while. Promise."

"Okay. If you need anything, just let me know."

"Will do."

Brad looked doubtful but wandered back toward the huge spread of food that the bigwigs at NORAD had put out for the volunteers.

Graham chuckled to himself. This was only Brad's second year volunteering, but all night long he'd been happy to mentor Graham through the ins and outs of answering the phones. Graham had been grateful for all the tips, too. Being a Santa Tracker was a pretty big deal.

Every Christmas Eve for over sixty years, volunteers with the North American Aerospace Defense Command had taken a break from their normally stressful jobs monitoring the skies of the continent to track Santa's progress across the globe.

Though this was the fourth year Graham had been stationed at the Cheyenne Mountain base with other members of the RCAF—the Royal Canadian Air Force—he'd been fortunate to always get to go home at Christmas.

Feeling like some of the others needed a trip home more than he did this year, Graham had volunteered to stick around. He was glad he had, but that wasn't to say he didn't miss Christmastime in Canada. It had been an unusually warm December in Colorado Springs, and there had been little to no snow so far. For some reason, the sunny days made his longing for all things Canadian even more pronounced. He'd give a couple of toonies for a bag of all-dressed Ruffles chips right now.

When Graham's phone rang again, he shook off his doldrums. "Hello, you've reached the NORAD Santa Tracker."

"Hi," a young boy's voice replied. "Are you really watching Santa's sleigh?"

Graham relaxed in his chair and glanced at the large lit screen that took up at least half the wall in front of him. "Yep. He's over Newfoundland right now."

"Where's that?"

"Newfoundland is in Canada. Above Maine. Do you know where Maine is?"

"Kind of. I don't think it's very close to me. Canada's real far away, right?"

"That depends on where you're calling from. And, maybe, who you're talking to."

"Oh." After a pause, the boy added, "What do you think?"

Graham grinned. He was getting a kick out of this little guy. "Well, I think Newfoundland isn't all that close to most people in the world. Where do you live?"

"In Colorado Springs. Do you know where that is?"

Graham's grin widened. "I sure do. I live there, too."

"Really?"

"Really. What's your name?"

"Will. What's yours?"

"Graham."

"Oh."

Since Will didn't seem in a big hurry to get off the phone, Graham leaned back in his chair. "What have you been doing tonight, Will? Getting excited for Santa's visit?"

The little boy sighed. "We're not doing too much. We don't have any guests this year. It's just my mom and me, and she's always too tired to do anything."

Graham could practically feel the little guy's disappointment over the phone line. Thinking about the large family gathering he was missing back home, he said, "I'm sorry about that. Do you usually have a bunch of family over?"

"We live in a B&B. My mom runs it." He paused. "Do you know what that is, Graham?"

"I do. I bet living in a bed-and-breakfast is fun."

"Sometimes," Will replied. "It all depends on who's staying with us. Some people are nicer than others, you know."

"I guess that would be the case."

"Uh-huh. When they aren't so nice, it's not that fun living here." Will lowered his voice. "I used to ask my mom to make them leave. It never happened, though."

It was all Graham could do not to start laughing. "I don't think your mom would be a very good innkeeper if she asked her guests to leave."

"My mom says the same thing. She says that we have to be nice to everyone staying here. You know, treat others like you want to be treated and all that."

"The Golden Rule."

"Yeah. Do you have to do that, Graham?"

Trying to keep up, he asked, "Do what? Be nice to people, or treat others how I want to be treated?"

"Both, I guess."

Graham chuckled. "I try my best. I'm a sergeant in the air force. It's kind of expected that we don't smile too much, and some people confuse that with meanness." Beside him, Brad grinned.

"Oh."

Realizing that they'd been talking awhile, Graham figured it was time to wrap things up. "So, I bet you can't wait to open your presents tomorrow."

"Yeah."

"What do you hope you'll get?"

"I don't know. Just some toys, I guess."

There was a wistfulness in the boy's voice that got to him. "You don't sound too excited."

"It's not like Santa can bring miracles or anything. Only Jesus does that."

Graham swallowed back the lump that had just formed in his throat. "That is true. Miracles are hard to come by."

"I know. My mom always says that when I tell her I wish my dad was still alive. She says I should just be grateful that he was such a good man and that I had him for a little while. But I don't know about that. I mean, I was only three when he died, and I'm six now." Lowering his voice again, he added, "I don't see why I'm supposed to be real grateful for him going to heaven before I could even ride a bike. I mean, I'd rather he lived a lot longer."

Graham felt as if he had been kicked in the gut. "I'm sorry about your dad, buddy."

"Me, too. He died in a car accident."

"I'm sure you miss him."

"My mom does." He paused, and then said, "I don't really remember him, though. Sometimes I even forget what he looked like. Do you think that's bad?"

Graham was beginning to realize that there was a whole lot more to being a decent Santa

Tracker than simply telling callers where the flashing Santa icon was in the world. "I don't think that's bad at all," he replied, taking care to make sure every word was from his heart. "I think forgetting some things about someone who's gone is normal. Time makes a lot of things fade."

"I have a picture of Dad in my room so I never have to tell my mom that I don't remember much about him. I just pretend I do."

"I'm sure your dad loved you a whole lot."

"That's what my mom says. Oh, hold on. Hey, mister, what's your name again?"

"Graham."

"Graham, my mom wants to talk to you. 'Bye."

After a couple of whispered words, a woman came on the line. "Hello?"

Her voice sounded stressed and distracted. Imagining her home alone with her son, and how different their evening was from the loud, chaotic Christmas Eves of his childhood, Graham felt his heart ache. "Hello, ma'am. This is Graham over at the Santa Tracker headquarters."

"Graham, yes. I—I just wanted to apologize. I had no idea that Will called you. I also just realized that he's been talking your ear off for ten minutes. I'm so sorry that he kept you on the line so long."

"That's why I'm here, ma'am. To chat with people who call." Realizing that she still might feel like he was annoyed, he added, "I enjoyed talking to your boy. He's a very nice young man."

"Thank you. I don't want to keep you. I just…well, I overheard you talking to Will about missing his father—" she lowered her voice "—and I just wanted to thank you for being so nice and patient with him. This has been kind of a tough December for us."

"I'm sorry for your loss, ma'am."

"It was three years ago, but thank you. And thank you again for giving up your time and being on the phones tonight. I think you helped him."

"I'm glad to do it. Like I said, he seems like a good boy. You should be proud."

Her voice warmed. "He is a good boy. I'm blessed." She took a breath. "So, I know a little bit about the Santa Trackers, and I know most are in the military. Are you in the service?"

"I am. I'm in the RCAF, ma'am. Royal Canadian Air Force."

"You're Canadian! You're far away from home, aren't you?"

"I am, but that's all right." And for the first time all night, Graham realized that was the truth. Somehow, talking to a little boy about his late father had made up for the emptiness he'd been battling for days.

"Oh, gosh. Here I was apologizing for my son keeping you on the line, and now I'm doing the same thing. I'll let you go. Thank you for your service, Graham. And merry Christmas."

"Happy Christmas—I'm sorry, I didn't catch your name."

Her voice warmed. "It's Vivian."

"Happy Christmas, Vivian."

"You, too, Graham."

After hanging up, Graham felt like he needed to move around a bit. He glanced over at Brad, who was talking on the phone next to him, then stood up and walked to the back tables. There were four of them pushed together, covered with white tablecloths. A variety of sandwiches were heaped on platters. There were also Crockpots filled with soup, chili and Brad's favorite fried chicken wings. It all looked amazing.

Piling a couple of sandwiches on his plate, he took a bite of ham and looked through the glass at the snow that had just started to fall.

The flakes were thick and fluffy. It was beautiful. Almost like home.

"Look, it's finally snowing," a woman wearing lieutenant's bars said. "We'll have a white Christmas after all."

"That's good."

Taking notice of his Canadian uniform, the woman said, "It will almost be like home for you, huh?"

"Almost." He smiled.

Staring out the window at the snow blowing, he knew that his barracks weren't anything like being in his parents' cozy home in Windsor, and the spread of food nothing like his mother's traditional Christmas Eve tourtière.

But, as he thought of that little boy and his mom, he realized that was okay. For some reason, he felt like he'd needed to be the one to speak to Will and his mother tonight. Each of them had sounded a bit lost. He hoped that, in some small way, he had helped them to feel a little less alone.

Graham closed his eyes and said a quick prayer for them. Then he popped a couple of chicken wings on his plate and headed back to his chair.

Santa Claus's sleigh was now over Pennsylvania. It wouldn't be much longer before the big guy would be alighting in Colorado Springs.

CHAPTER TWO

Christmas Day

THEY'D DONE IT. They'd survived another Christmas morning. Looking around at their beautifully decorated living room, the dining room table still littered with the remnants of breakfast casserole and chocolate chip muffins, and the gently falling snow outside, Vivian Parnell smiled. It had been as perfect a Christmas as she'd been able to manage.

Not that she always strove for perfection, of course. But since there were so many days when she felt completely imperfect, this morning's success mattered.

Sipping her coffee, she checked on Will again. He was happily playing with his new Legos while watching *Elf*. Things were good. She drew a sigh of relief.

For a while, she'd been afraid that this Christmas was going to be even worse than the first one after Emerson passed away. Back then, Will had been a three-year-old toddler with a fondness for both the word *no* and *Dora the Explorer*. As long as he'd had a couple of cardboard boxes to play in, Will had been fine. That year, she'd been the one who had barely been able to hold it together.

This holiday season hadn't been all that easy for her, either. She'd been feeling restless and out of sorts for weeks. Vivian wasn't sure if she was still struggling with widowhood or if it was merely a matter of not being used to relaxing. Their old, sprawling house seemed too empty and too quiet without the usual throng of guests parading through.

Who knew? Maybe they were both experiencing some growing pains. Will had been restless for weeks. He'd been having trouble sleeping and had even pulled away from her a bit. She hadn't known what to do. Talking with him about his father didn't seem to help.

The night before had changed everything, though. When she'd first heard Will on the phone, Vivian had thought he was talking to his grandparents. Emerson's parents, Beverly and Phil, called often and loved to chat with him about everything under the sun.

She'd been surprised to discover that her son had called the NORAD Santa Tracker— and shocked to realize that he'd felt comfortable enough with the man on the other end of the line to pour out his heart to him.

When she'd finally gotten ahold of the phone and talked to Graham, she'd understood why Will had been so chatty. The man's calm voice and genuine interest in their lives had coated her frayed nerves like a soothing balm. Somehow, during their brief conversation, this stranger had made her feel more optimistic for the future than she had felt in ages. Vivian never would have imagined that was even possible.

After she'd hung up, she'd sat with Will and they'd talked late into the night. Vivian had patiently chatted with him about his father, the Santa Tracker volunteers and Jesus's birthday. It was after midnight when she'd helped him get into bed—far later than he usually stayed up, but so worth it. For the first time in weeks, her son's angst and sadness seemed to have eased.

After she'd gotten him to sleep, Vivian had stayed up for another hour. She'd sipped tea, revisited their conversation and thought about Emerson. Eventually, she'd flipped through a couple of magazines in an attempt to clear her mind. Finally, just after one in the morning, she pulled out the presents she'd wrapped weeks before and placed them under the tree.

Their morning had been good, too. Will had been excited about his new Lego kits and seemed much more like his usual self. Maybe they were both finally on their way to moving on. She sincerely hoped so.

When her phone rang, Vivian put down her cup of coffee and picked up her cell. Checking the screen and seeing that it was her parents, she mentally braced herself before answering. She was going to need to sound like she was the happiest woman in Colorado Springs or she'd be stuck answering fifty questions about things she didn't want to discuss. "Hey, Mom! Merry Christmas!" she said in her most cheerful voice.

"Hi, sweetheart, it's your dad. Merry Christmas to you, too. How's your day going?"

Smiling at her father's gruff voice, she said, "It's going all right. So far Will and I have opened presents and had a big breakfast. Now we're just relaxing. What about you? How is your Christmas going?"

"We're in sunny Mexico, so it couldn't be better."

"I bet." Her parents were in the middle of a two-week cruise through the Panama Canal, followed by stops in various ports along the Pacific coast. It was one of many trips they took during the year. Long ago, Vivian had resigned herself to the fact that Will wasn't going to have two sets of hands-on grandparents.

Emerson's parents were that set. Her parents? Well, they sent gifts, called every couple of weeks and enjoyed dispensing unsolicited advice.

"Where's that grandson of mine?"

"I'll get him." She covered her phone. "Will, come over here. It's Grandpa Jim."

Will took the phone eagerly. "Hi, Grandpa! Guess what? I talked to a Santa Tracker last night. He told me all about Santa, and I told him all about how I don't have a dad."

Vivian winced but didn't dare interrupt her son's story. No, it wasn't easy to hear him talk about life without a father. But it was good to hear him sound a whole lot more at peace.

"Hi, Nana. Uh-huh. I liked it a lot. I miss you, too." He frowned as he listened, then said, "He was nice. He told me about Newfoundland and we talked about Daddy being gone and miracles." He paused, listening hard. "Oh, okay. Here, Mom." He passed the phone back to her. "Nana wants to talk to you."

To Vivian's amusement, he rolled his eyes before returning to his Legos. Getting settled on the couch again, she leaned back and watched the snow fall outside. "Hi, Mom. Merry Christmas."

"Merry Christmas, dear. What's this about Will telling strangers about his father being in heaven?"

"It's a long story, but I promise it wasn't as weird as it sounds."

"It doesn't sound weird, it sounds worrisome."

"Um, I don't know about that. I think it's normal to want to talk about missing his dad every now and then. You know how it is at school."

"Do you need to go back to the grief counselor?"

Vivian picked up her coffee cup, frowned when she saw it was empty and set it back down again. "I don't think so. We only see her a couple of times a year now."

"It's been three years, dear."

She bit her tongue to prevent a sarcastic response from escaping her lips. "I know. But we really are okay, Mom." Before her mother could argue, Vivian added, "Thank you for the packet of gift cards you sent. They'll come in handy."

"You're welcome. We liked the Amazon gift card you sent. Now don't forget to put them to good use soon."

"I will. It will be fun to have a reason to drive to Denver to shop."

"Nothing wrong with spoiling yourself a little bit, dear. Oh! We've got to go. Your father says international calls get expensive. We'll be home after New Year's. I'll call you then."

"Sounds good. 'Bye, Mom. Love you."

"Love you, too. Chin up, sweetheart. Merry Christmas!"

When she disconnected, she leaned back in her chair and chuckled.

Will, who was back on the floor building some kind of spaceship, grinned. "Nana and Grandpa sure are different from Gran and Pop."

"They are. But they love you just as much."

"I know." He paused. "Hey, Mom?"

"Hmm?"

"Graham said he lives in Colorado Springs, too."

"I didn't know that, but it does makes sense. NORAD is here, and they're the ones who track Santa Claus every year."

"Do you think we'll ever run into Graham?"

His voice sounded so hopeful, it was hard to keep her own voice steady. "Maybe, though even if we did, I don't know how we would know it was him. We only got to hear his voice, not see his face, right?"

"It would be cool if we did meet him in person. Graham sounded nice. And he had a funny accent because he's Canadian."

"He did sound nice. But, honey, don't get your hopes up, okay? Just because he was nice on the phone doesn't mean that we'll ever get to talk to him again."

Some of the light left her son's eyes as he nodded.

It was almost worse that he accepted that so easily. "It's enough that you got to speak to him last night."

He gazed at her for a long moment, then nodded. "I guess you're right. I mean, just because I want something, it doesn't mean I'm going to get it."

Her mouth went dry as the words she'd said slammed back in her face. She'd said that to Will when he'd asked for an iPad for Christmas. She'd never meant for it to take on a greater meaning for her son.

As she struggled to come up with a response, she realized that he'd already left the room. Ah. So he hadn't expected her to say anything more about not always getting what he wanted. She'd taught him that lesson well.

Unfortunately, she didn't know if that made her feel better or even worse.

CHAPTER THREE

THE GIFT CERTIFICATE that lay on Graham's desk was taunting him. Every time he passed the thing, it felt like it was screaming at him, the way older cadets were fond of doing to younger classmen. Although he was noncommissioned and Canadian, instead of an officer commissioned at Colorado Springs' famed Air Force Academy, he'd been on both the dispensing and receiving end of his share of mockery.

But even all that experience wasn't making his Snow Drop Inn gift certificate any easier to receive. The second lieutenant had smirked when he'd handed it to him, too. "Here you go, Sarge. Mrs. Howard told me that she asked the proprietor if you could stay there soon. I guess she's waiting for you to call."

Graham cringed. "Are you kidding me?"

All traces of amusement vanished from the junior officer's face. "No, Sergeant Hopkins."

"I can't believe this," he muttered under his breath.

"I hope you have a real good time there."

When Graham had glared at him in return, the kid backed away fast.

When he was standing alone, he read over the note, thought about the lieutenant's words and groaned.

The cardboard certificate was green and red and white and in the shape of a snow-covered bungalow. It looked like something you'd see in a Disney cartoon. It was cute and, he imagined, the product of a lot of effort. That said, he had no desire to spend any time in anything called the Snow Drop Inn.

He definitely was not the type of man to hang out in a bed-and-breakfast. Especially not one in Colorado Springs. Why couldn't the B&B at least have been in a mountain town?

To make matters worse, his new buddy Brad had received both a gift card to a chicken joint and a three-day ski pass to Winter Park. Graham liked both chicken and skiing. He would've loved to be getting ready to spend three days in the mountains instead of two nights at a girly inn.

When Brad had seen Graham's colorful certificate clutched in his hand like an unwanted sock, it was obvious that he'd been trying not to laugh. "If I were you, I'd get it over with," he'd said. "It's not like you can't go."

"Yeah, you're probably right." His American CO's wife had—for whatever reason—specifically gifted the Snow Drop Inn certificate to him as a thank-you for volunteering, and Graham knew he had no choice.

He was going to have to go or risk appearing rude.

Unless there was maybe someone still around who looked in worse need of a B&B vacation than he was? With a little bit of effort, he could probably spin his passing on of the gift certificate into some kind of good deed.

Feeling pleased with that idea, he stuffed the certificate in a pocket and headed to the commissary. After pouring himself a cup of strong coffee, he looked around for someone who seemed in need of a pick-me-up.

The only other people there were Bing, who Graham knew was working on a classified project with no end in sight; a pair of female junior officers, one of whom had a major chip on her shoulder; and two privates who looked scared to even be in the same room with him. Everyone else was either on duty or on leave.

It was a sign. No doubt about it.

Walking to his quarters, he squared his shoulders and finally accepted his fate. He'd received his orders and there was no alternative except to do what he was expected to do. He was going to the Snow Drop Inn.

He made a mental note to pick up a couple of books from the lending library before he left. If he had to hang out there for forty-eight hours, at least he'd have something to do.

When he got inside, he sat at his desk and pulled out his cell phone and the gift certificate and dialed the number. He'd never been the type of man to put off what had to be done.

"Snow Drop Inn," the woman on the other end said. "May I help you?"

He thought her voice sounded vaguely familiar but brushed off that notion. A lot of Americans' voices sounded the same to him—especially when he was feeling lonely and nostalgic for home.

"Yes, ma'am. I received a gift certificate to your establishment. For two nights."

"That's wonderful. I hope you'll visit here soon."

Still staring at the certificate, he said, "That's why I called, ma'am. I'm inquiring to see if you have any vacancies."

"Let me see." He could hear the click of computer keys. "For which dates?"

"Tonight and tomorrow night. Leaving the twenty-seventh."

"You'd like to check in tonight?"

Feeling good about getting the visit over with, Graham nodded as he leaned back in his chair. "Yes. Would that be possible?"

"Well…"

"I know it's late notice, but it's kind of important. I, um, don't have a lot of other days off."

The woman hesitated again. "Well, I guess that would work. What time do you plan to arrive?"

He looked at the clock. "It's fourteen hundred hours. How does two hours from now sound? Sixteen hundred?"

"Do you mean four o'clock?"

"Sorry. Yes, ma'am."

Her voice gentled. "Are you in the military?"

"I am. Air force."

"Now I understand about you not having a lot of time off. I think four o'clock will be just fine. Do you and your guest have any special needs or requirements?"

"No." Feeling more awkward, he added, "And it's just me. I'll be arriving alone."

"I see." She paused, then added in a softer tone, "I look forward to seeing you then. Mr.…?"

"Hopkins." He purposely didn't correct her use of "Mr." After all, there had to be more to him than being a sergeant.

"I'll see you this afternoon, Mr. Hopkins."

"Thank you. 'Bye." He hung up, feeling satisfied that he had made progress.

Ninety minutes later, only after he'd noticed how empty all the city streets were, did he realize what he'd done. He'd just booked himself into the woman's inn on Christmas Day.

No wonder she'd sounded so confused—and maybe even a tad reluctant. He was likely arriving in the middle of her holiday dinner.

"You've turned into a Scrooge, Graham," he said out loud.

"And likely a bit of a jerk, too."

Maybe he needed this break more than he realized.

CHAPTER FOUR

GRAHAM HAD BEEN driving in circles for the last ten minutes. For a place that was supposed to be a well-known B&B, the Snow Drop Inn was sure hard to find.

He was still feeling guilty about calling on Christmas Day and then practically forcing his way over. His mother would shake her head if she ever heard that he'd been so clueless. Of course, once he'd realized how rude he'd been, he couldn't think of a way out of it. Calling the lady back to say he'd changed his mind felt even ruder. After turning right and then reaching a dead end, he scanned the street and the addresses one more time. Of course, half of the house numbers were either covered with snow or hidden in odd places. Why did every other house on this street look like something out of a nursery rhyme, anyway?

When he saw a blonde woman walking her beagle, he broke his usual code to never ask for directions and slowed down beside her.

Unusual streets called for unusual circumstances. Rolling down his window, he called out, "Excuse me, ma'am?"

She stopped and looked at him warily. "Yes?"

"I'm sorry, but I'm trying to find a place called the Snow Drop Inn." He held up the torn piece of paper on which he'd written the street address. "Have you heard of it?"

"I sure have." She rubbed her beagle's ears. "Ziggy and I were just over there having a cup of coffee. Now, to get there, you need to go one street over. It's actually on Alpine Circle, not Drive. You can't miss it, though. There's a cute sign in front of it."

"Thanks. That should be easy to find."

"Hope you enjoy your stay. Vivian is a doll. She's sweet as can be."

"Thanks." For a second, he was tempted to tell her that he wasn't the type of guy who usually stayed in quaint inns but figured it didn't matter. He was staying in one now. "Happy Christmas."

The lady's smile brightened. "Happy Christmas to you, too."

Sure enough, when he turned right and then right again, he located the Snow Drop Inn immediately. It looked like something out of a Hallmark movie set, with its alpine-style architecture, Christmas lights, red door and cutesy-looking wooden sign in the front yard with each letter designed to look like a fat white raindrop.

Just as he was about to turn into the parking lot, his phone rang. When he saw it was his sister Meredith, he decided to head back to the park he'd just passed. All things considered, he'd rather wait a few more minutes instead of knocking on the inn's door too early.

Clicking on his cell, he grinned. "Hey, Mer."

"Graham! I can't believe we got you. Happy Christmas! Are you busy?"

"Not at all."

"No? Well you're in trouble, then, because everyone wants to say hello."

Putting his car in Park, he chuckled. "That's good, because I want to hear from everyone, too."

"That's wonderful! Okay, it's such a madhouse here, I'm going to talk last." Raising her voice, she called out, "Who wants to talk to Uncle Graham first?"

His heart lifted and he leaned back as he heard a chorus of munchkin-sounding voices call out.

"Hi, Unca Gam!"

"Hi, Chloe. Happy Christmas."

"Happy Christmas!" As his tiny niece jabbered in his ear, he felt everything inside him click into place. No, this wasn't his best Christmas ever, but it sure wasn't horrible.

All things considered? It was absolutely good enough.

LOOKING OVER AT the tan Jeep Cherokee in the parking lot next to Sherman Park, Maisie Arnold wondered what was keeping the young man she'd just talked to from going on in. There had to be a story there. He most definitely didn't look like the usual guest who stayed at Vivian's quaint inn.

She looked down at Ziggy, her three-year-old beagle. "What do you think his story is, Zig? Is he meeting a girl there? Or…maybe his girl told him that she's staying there when she's not, and he's going to catch her in a lie!"

Ziggy barked and wagged his tail.

With a chuckle, she started walking again. "You're right, buddy. That is probably too far-fetched, even for me. Let's get you home."

Obviously recognizing that word, Ziggy increased his pace, his white-tipped tail pointing up as he trotted toward his house, which was just four houses down from the inn.

Maisie increased her pace as well, pleased to put the handsome stranger out of her mind…and return to concentrating on the man who had taken over most of her thoughts these days: Lawson Greer, PI.

Five years ago, still reeling from both her husband's indiscretions and the subsequent divorce that cost her most of her savings, she'd taken a leave from her job at the bank and started writing a book, mainly as a form of therapy. It had turned out that she'd loved writing, especially since she'd made up her perfect man, in the form of Lawson Greer. Lawson solved murders in Cedar Springs, a made-up small town in Colorado. Of course, Lawson's first case was to solve the murder of one philandering husband who'd been stabbed in the heart.

Oh, that had felt so good.

What she'd never expected was to actually finish the book within the year. Or that the one person she'd dared to show it to would encourage her to enter it in a mystery contest. Or that she would win the contest, get the book published and then get a three-book contract, followed by another multibook contract.

It had all been very, very wonderful—especially since it had all happened after the divorce. Now she lived in the perfect small house, wrote full-time and had a dear, quirky roommate named Audrey who was young enough to be her daughter.

It was only on holidays, like Christmas, that she let her mind wander, wondering what her life would've been like if Jared had loved her enough to stay faithful.

When Ziggy started barking, she frowned and then noticed that Audrey was standing in the driveway next to a very tall, very well-built man who looked old enough to be her father.

"Maisie, I was about to get in the car and start looking for you," Audrey said.

"I told you that Zig and I were going for a walk."

"I know, but I didn't think you were going to be gone so long." She smiled at the man standing by her side. "I've been waiting to introduce you to my uncle Clay."

"Hi," he began, and then did a double take. "Wait a minute. Are you Maisie Arnold?"

"Yes?"

He held out his hand. "I'm Clay Stevick." His smile turned into a broad grin. "I'm also known as Clayton Stevick."

She blinked. She knew that name, but... "Wait a minute. You're Clayton? *My* next-door Clayton?"

His expression warmed further. "Yep."

She grasped his hand and then hugged him. "I can't believe it's you! This is wonderful."

Stepping back, she boldly looked him over from head to toe. "Clayton, I have to say that you look completely different."

He laughed. "I hope so. I mean, we were only thirteen when I moved away." Bending down, he scratched Ziggy between his ears. "What's her name?"

"Ziggy. He's a boy." Noticing that Ziggy was already looking at him like they were best friends, Maisie added, "He's really friendly."

"He's adorable, Maise."

"Thank you. I…" For a person who worked with words all day, she was finding herself completely tongue-tied. Then something else finally clicked. "Wait a minute. Audrey, did you say that Clayton is your uncle?"

"Yes." Audrey looked as stunned as Maisie felt. "I was sure that you two would like each other, but I can't believe this. Boy, talk about a small world."

"I agree. As surprises go, this is a pretty big one. A great one, though," she added as they walked inside the house, Ziggy looking pleased to finally be released from his lead.

Clayton was standing with his hands behind his back, assuming a parade-rest stance. His eyes were focused on her. "Maisie, you're going to have to tell me everything that's been happening to you. Audrey told me you're a writer."

She nodded. "I write mysteries."

"I want to hear about them."

"I'll be happy to chat about whatever you'd like, as long as you do the same." Hearing the flirty tone in her voice, Maisie felt her cheeks heat. Talk about acting completely awkward!

The three of them were still standing in the foyer of the house, each obviously attempting to come to terms with the startling coincidence.

Or maybe not. Audrey seemed stunned and she was blushing, but Clayton didn't seem to be anything but pleased. He kept staring at her as if he liked everything he was seeing.

Maisie cleared her throat.

"You know what?" Audrey asked. "I think I'm going to bring over some hot drinks while you two sit down and get reacquainted."

Feeling guilty—especially since Clayton had come over to see Audrey and not her—she said, "I can get the drinks."

"No way. Go sit down. It's obvious that you two have a lot of catching up to do."

Smiling at her, and at Ziggy, who had just hopped up on the couch next to him, Clay murmured, "We sure do."

Gingerly, Maisie sat down as well.

And wondered what in the world had just happened.

CHAPTER FIVE

WHY HAD SHE answered the phone? Vivian was usually very good about ignoring her business line when she and Will were doing something important. But she had answered it—and then had even gone one step further and allowed the guest to book a room that very evening.

She'd known it was a mistake, too. From the moment she'd encouraged him to come on over, she'd wanted to tell Mr. Hopkins that she'd changed her mind.

But of course she hadn't.

And because of that…well, she was pretty sure that she'd just ruined Will's Christmas.

Arms folded across his chest, he was glaring at her like she'd just broken a cardinal rule.

Maybe she had.

"Mommy, I don't understand why we have to have him here tonight."

"I know."

"It's *Christmas*."

It was now official: she had ruined Christmas Day.

Will was unhappy, and he wasn't afraid to show it. He wasn't happy that they had sat inside most of the day, that none of his grandparents were in town and that he didn't have a father. But most of all, he was really unhappy that she'd gone back on her promise of not having anyone stay at the house until December 27. Vivian didn't blame him.

Actually, she still wasn't sure why she hadn't told the man that she was closed until the twenty-seventh. She couldn't put the blame on him being in the military, either. He hadn't told her that until she'd already agreed.

So, neither answering the phone nor accepting his reservation made sense. But there had been something in his voice that had sounded lonely—and that loneliness had evoked a reaction from her that she hadn't been able to deny. She knew all about feeling lonely on Christmas Day, even when she had the best little boy in the world by her side.

She just wished he wasn't on the verge of having an honest-to-God little-boy fit.

"Will, we've already discussed this. I know how you feel. But the decision has been made. There's no need to discuss it again."

"Who says?"

"Me, obviously."

He jutted his chin out. "Well, I'm part of

this family, too. There's two of us, remember?"

She nodded. "I haven't forgotten."

He pressed on. "That means I get to make decisions, too."

"You do, but only about things you can control. This isn't one of them." When he continued to stare at her with a mutinous expression, she added, "Will, for the last time, you need to stop pouting. You might be upset with me, but it isn't our guest's fault. If you can't be nice to him, then you're going to have to stay in your room."

Will's blue eyes filled with tears. "You'd make me do that on Christmas Day?"

Vivian hated this whole conversation. She would've loved to be able to promise him a dozen other things. Things like a fun evening playing games with his siblings or cousins or someone besides her. She'd love to have taken him to the mountains to go sledding. And, yes, she wished that his father could be there and that their lives would suddenly be much different.

But of course that wasn't the case. "I don't want you to go to your room, but I'll send you there if I have to." She reached out and ruffled her fingers through his blond mop of hair. "Listen, there has to be a reason this man called and asked to come this evening. He must be feeling very lonely. Maybe we could cheer him up." She smiled encouragingly.

Will did not take the hint. "Maybe he's mean. Maybe there's a reason he's alone on Christmas and it's because no one wants him at their house."

Okay, so that avenue of reasoning had failed. "I hope he's not a Scrooge. But no matter what, he's only going to be here for two nights."

"And then?"

He'd lost her again. "And then what?"

"Do we have more people coming?"

"If you mean, will we still be living in a bed-and-breakfast, the answer is yes. I told you that we have a big family arriving on the twenty-seventh."

Now he looked even more irritated.

She carefully bit back her first instinct, which was to apologize for their way of life. This was something she'd learned in the last year, when she'd started going to therapy once a week because she couldn't sleep and had been besieged by bursts of guilt.

During her third visit, Abby, her therapist, had looked her in the eye and asked if she felt guilty for wanting to be happy again.

The question had taken her off guard. At first she'd been defensive and had given Abby a piece of her mind. Abby had sat back and let her fume and rant. And cry. Boy, had she cried.

But eventually, after she'd gone through a handful of tissues, Vivian had realized that Abby had hit the nail on the head. She had felt bad because Will wasn't having the easy, carefree childhood she thought he deserved. She felt guilty for working too much. Sometimes she even felt guilty for temporarily forgetting about Emerson. Or for simply being happy.

Though nothing about their circumstances had been her fault, even though she'd been suffering the consequences and had been experiencing every sort of reaction imaginable in the privacy of her bedroom and bathroom in the middle of the night, she'd never allowed herself to express those emotions to anyone else.

It had been hard, but in the middle of the fourth session, when she'd admitted that she did feel guilty, Abby had smiled. And Vivian had at last started to heal. Of course, it wasn't an immediate change. But she'd started to make progress.

All that was why she was usually able to hold firm when Will kept glaring at her like she was ruining his life by running a bed-and-breakfast. And why she knew she needed to stop apologizing.

"Will, you have a choice. You can either help me prepare for Mr. Hopkins and make the best of things, or you can go to your room and sit by yourself. What you may not do is continue to complain and glare at me."

Her son got to his feet. Seemed to struggle with his decision. Took a breath.

She tensed, hoping he, too, was making progress and would respond the way she'd prayed he would.

"I'm going to my room."

Watching him turn around and walk down the hall, Vivian bit down on her bottom lip. She was disappointed but knew she had to come to terms with it. Will was just a little boy. Only six years old. He wasn't twelve or sixteen or twenty-six. Even a child living in the most ideal situation was still just a little boy. He wasn't capable of dealing with adult situations like an adult.

So, it was understandable.

But, boy, at this minute? His reaction still hurt.

It hurt a lot.

"It looks like you and Abby are going to have a lot to discuss at your next session," she mumbled to herself. "Starting with why you decided to accept a guest on Christmas Day."

When the doorbell rang, she felt like crying. Praying that her guest hadn't decided to come an hour early, she opened the door and breathed a sigh of relief. "Hi, Maisie. Merry Christmas!"

Her friend and neighbor Maisie and her dog, Ziggy, were a welcome sight after the last couple of hours. "Come on in."

"Are you sure you don't mind? I just wanted to drop off a Christmas gift for you and Will."

"I don't mind at all. I could use a bit of beagle love."

Maisie chuckled. "It sounds like we came at the right time, then." After she closed the door and unhooked Ziggy from his leash, she looked around the living room. "Where's Will?"

"He's in his room. He's, uh, not very happy with me right now." Bending down, she gave Ziggy a hug. He responded by licking her cheek. "Would you like a cup of coffee?"

"I'd love one. We'll follow you to the kitchen."

Vivian loved how easygoing Maisie was. Maybe it was because she was older and had experienced her share of heartache, too, but whenever she was around, Vivian felt like her blood pressure lowered.

When Maisie sat down, Ziggy curled in a ball next to her feet. His eyes were closed by the time Vivian set two cups of coffee on the table.

"Now, what's going on?" Maisie asked.

After peeking out the doorway, Vivian said, "I think I ruined Will's Christmas."

"Because…"

"Because I accepted a reservation. He's going to arrive within the hour." Taking a fortifying sip, she added, "I don't blame Will for being upset with me. It's just…the man sounded lonely, you know?"

"That's the worst, isn't it? Being alone or sad on Christmas Day is really hard. I wouldn't wish it on anyone."

"What do you think I should do?"

Maisie shrugged. "What can you do? Welcome your guest and hope he's not a jerk."

Vivian giggled. "You certainly have a way of putting things in perspective."

"I think we both know that you aren't the first innkeeper to welcome a stranger into your house on Christmas Day."

Vivian thought she was pretty far from being like that innkeeper long ago, but she was suddenly glad that she hadn't told Mr. Hopkins that there was no room at the inn. "What are you going to do today?" She gestured to the counters, which were covered in casserole dishes. "Would you like to join us for dinner this evening?"

"Thank you, but Audrey and I had a big dinner last night. I'll probably talk with my girls, then I'm hoping to simply chill out on the couch and binge movies."

"That sounds so nice."

"That also sounds like I have a far more relaxing day coming up than you do." Standing up, she hugged Vivian close. "Chin up, dear. I have a feeling everything is going to work out just fine."

CHAPTER SIX

The Snow Drop Inn was just as cute and kitschy-looking as Graham had imagined. It looked like an Swiss Alpine chalet—it had white stucco siding, a dark tile roof, matching dark wooden trim and a bright red door. Surrounding it were a half dozen white pines and blue spruces on one side and some craggy-looking scrub oaks on the other.

In addition, there were white twinkling lights on the whole structure and on the trees. The wooden cutouts of smiling reindeer and snowmen on the lawn were the finishing touch.

It was honestly his worst nightmare. He was a simple guy and liked things clean and sparse. Parking his Jeep in the small parking lot to the side, he pulled out his duffel bag and backpack, locked his Jeep, and then braced himself for living the next two days in what would likely be the most uncomfortable place he'd ever stayed at.

Graham allowed himself to imagine whom the owners might be. An older couple with a little extra padding around the middle and a penchant for ugly Christmas sweaters came to mind. He hoped they weren't the type who liked to chat incessantly about nothing.

On the heels of that thought, a wave of guilt crashed over him. Here he was, not only being ungrateful for a gift, but now finding fault with the place where he was blessed enough to stay for free, a place that was someone's livelihood. It wasn't the owners' fault that he would rather be in Windsor for Christmas.

They sure didn't deserve such unkind thoughts.

Reminding himself that he'd stayed in far worse places than a too-cute grown-up gingerbread house, he walked to the front door and rang the bell.

The door was opened almost immediately by a young woman with dark brown eyes, a pert nose and beautiful auburn hair that reached the middle of her back. Her hair was shiny and thick and lightly curled. She was wearing a pair of faded jeans, suede clogs and a dark green sweater with an embroidered collar—something that looked like it came from Germany or the Swiss Alps and matched the whole chalet vibe.

When she met his gaze, she smiled. "Hello. You must be Mr. Hopkins."

"It's Graham, miss."

Her smile widened. "Come on in out of the cold. Welcome to the Snow Drop Inn, Graham."

When she closed the door behind him, he noticed a tall tree, lit with multicolored strands of lights, garland on the mantel, poinsettias in the center of a dining table and two red candles burning on either side. He was instantly surrounded by the scents of evergreen, vanilla and peppermint. And—if he wasn't mistaken—roast turkey. His mouth watered.

It was calm and elegant inside. Not packed to the gills with Christmas chaos at all. "This wasn't what I expected."

"Oh?" Her smile dimmed. "Is something wrong?"

He wished he had just kept his mouth closed. Meeting her gaze, seeing the way her brown eyes were imploring him, obviously waiting for a response, his mouth went dry. He was in a rough spot. What was he going to do now? Say that both she and the house were a lot better than he had anticipated?

"No, not at all. It's all good." He rolled his shoulders like they were stiff. "Sorry, it's been a long couple of days."

"I bet you're exhausted, and here I am, talking your ear off." She nodded. "Let me show you to your room, and then you can relax."

"Thanks." He followed her through the living room, up the wooden stairs—also festooned with green garland—and down the hall.

She paused at the door at the end of the hall. "That leads to my suite. My son and I live there." Her expression dimmed a bit as she continued. At the opposite end of the hall, she paused in front of an open door. "This will be your suite, Mr. Hopkins. I mean, Graham."

"Thank you." He followed her inside and did his best to control his expression. Because it wasn't Christmas crazy. Actually, it was the exact opposite. Calming. Tranquil. Decorated in shades of pink and gray and ivory with touches of beige. The cinnamon-colored wooden floor was covered with thick area rugs. A gray love seat was centered in front of a gas fireplace. Behind it was a queen-size four-poster bed covered in crisp white sheets, four pillows, a duvet and a light brown cashmere blanket. On a table were several water bottles, a glass and even a bucket of ice. "This is really nice."

She perked up a bit. "Let me show you your bathroom, then I'll get out of your hair."

He followed her to the doorway of the en suite bathroom and grinned when he saw the shower. It was massive, with two showerheads. A claw-foot tub sat on the other side of the room.

Vivian opened a closet. "Towels are in here." Walking to the counter, she pointed to a basket. "Shampoo, soap and lotion are in here." Facing him again, she added, "I'm hoping you'll have everything you need in order to feel comfortable."

"I'm used to barracks showers, Vivian. This might just be the best Christmas present I've ever had."

She chuckled before sobering again. "I certainly hope not."

"Seriously, this is great. It's a treat. Really."

"It's my pleasure." She smiled. "Will and I would love to have you join us for Christmas dinner."

Though his mouth watered, it felt like an imposition. "Ma'am, that's very kind of you, but I don't want to be a burden."

"I don't know if you heard, but a whole turkey usually serves more than one woman and a little boy." Her cheeks pinked. "Plus, I've also made stuffing, yams, beans, rolls, potatoes and a pie."

He chuckled. "You made a whole feast."

"I'm afraid I only know one way to make a Christmas dinner, and that's going all out."

"It would seem so."

"So, see? You'd be doing me a favor. There's only so many days of leftovers a person can handle."

Graham was tempted to ask where her husband was. Where her family was. Why this attractive woman and her son didn't have a group of people anxious to ask them over for a meal.

Why she'd even allowed him to be there on Christmas Day.

He inclined his head. "If I can help you out, I'll be happy to do so. What time will you be eating?"

"Is six too early?"

"Not at all. I'll look forward to it."

Looking relieved, and maybe even pleased as well, she smiled at him again. "I'll let you rest for a bit. Come downstairs whenever you want."

"Are you sure you don't need any help? I can boil potatoes or something." He wasn't much of a cook, but her menu seemed like a lot for one woman to handle.

Her brown eyes lit with humor. "I'd never ask a guest to cook. Please, relax and enjoy yourself. I've got it."

Just as he was about to tell Vivian that sitting alone in his room wouldn't exactly be relaxing for him, a little boy's voice called out. "Mom?"

"Oh! I better go see what he needs." She smiled at Graham again before darting out the door and closing it behind her.

Leaving him alone in the fanciest bedroom he'd ever stayed in in his life.

He sat down on the love seat in front of the fireplace and pulled off his boots just as his phone rang. Seeing who it was, he grinned.

"Hi, Mom. Happy Christmas."

"Happy Christmas to you, too, Graham. How are you?"

She sounded breathless and excited. She sounded like his mother on Christmas Day. His heart warmed as he thought about his home. This wasn't where he wanted to be, but it was okay. At least his mother was where she needed to be, which was home, with the rest of her family there.

"I'm fine. What about you?"

"No, no, no, dear. This time you are not going to get out of this so fast. I want to hear about everything. Did you get my box of presents?"

"I did. You know that because I wrote you about it. I loved the sweater, the gift card. Thank you. Thanks for the money, too. But you know it wasn't necessary."

"We want you to be able to get anything you

need whenever you need it. That's important to us." Her voice lowered an octave. "What are you going to do for supper? Is your CO taking care of you guys this year?" Sometimes the senior officers invited the other Canadian airmen to their homes for Christmas dinner.

"He is, but I won't be there."

"Oh, no. Did they assign you to duty?"

"It's the air force. It's kind of my job to be on call. But no, I'm not on duty. I'm actually at a bed-and-breakfast."

There was a significant pause while his mother obviously tried to put two and two together. "Graham Hopkins, are you on a getaway with someone special?"

And just like that, he was bright red and feeling like he was fourteen and had just asked Allie Beekman to be his girl. "No! Jeez, Ma."

"Who are you there with, then?" Before he could answer, she covered the mouthpiece and said, "Graham's not alone in his barracks. He's at a B&B." Another pause. "I don't know, Doug. I'm asking now."

"Mother, I'm alone. And no, don't start broadcasting that throughout the whole house. Who's there, anyway?"

"Your brother, Doug, and Susan. Your sister Eileen, Kevin and their kids. Aunt Claire and Uncle Paul. Meredith and Tom are coming over later. Oh! And Bonnie and Rick from next door."

"So everyone." He could see them all now. The whole group, with various stages of interest, were now edging toward his mother, who was no doubt sitting on a stool in the kitchen.

"Not everyone, Graham. Now stop being so testy and answer my question. What is going on?"

"I'm thirty-five years old, Ma."

"I haven't forgotten how old you are."

"I'm a sergeant in the Royal Canadian Air Force."

"I realize that, too. Now what is going on?"

"I won a gift certificate to a B&B and didn't feel I could get out of it, because the CO's wife gave it to me."

"Ah." She sounded deflated. "How is it?"

It was good. It was turning out to be better than good. But Graham knew if he said such a thing, it would be an invitation for his family to ask even more questions. They'd also likely bring up everything he said for the next five years to come. "Fine."

"Fine?"

"Yes, ma'am. Now, can I please speak to Eileen or Doug?"

"Fine. Here you go."

"Graham. Happy Christmas!" his brother boomed.

"Happy Christmas, Doug." Graham smiled to himself. "How are things going?"

"About like you would expect. Mom's ordering us all around, the kids keep spilling stuff and there's way too much food."

He grinned. "So, it's good."

Doug chuckled. "Yeah. I don't know what I'd do if it was any other way. Hey, sorry you're not here, but we're proud of you."

He said that every time. "Thanks."

"Look, I'm going to pass the phone on, because Susan has her hands full. You take care now, yes?"

"You, too."

"Here's Eileen."

"Hey, you."

"Hey, Graham. Sorry you're not here, but you should be kind of glad. Aunt Claire is acting as petty as ever. She's already complained about there not being any mincemeat."

"We all hate mincemeat."

"We might… Turns out Aunt Claire and Uncle Paul love it." She lowered her voice, and it was obvious to him that she'd walked farther away from the rest of the family. "And… Rick from next door is even more unfiltered than usual."

"No way."

"Way. Mom looks tempted to put a gag on him. He started telling stories about when he was in the navy."

He chuckled. "Again?"

"Oh, yeah. And they get raunchier every year."

Leaning back against the couch, he murmured, "Text me if anything good happens."

"Will do. I'm going to pass the phone on to Kevin now. Love you."

"Love you, too, Eileen."

"Hey, Graham," Kevin said. "How goes it?"

Kevin was Eileen's husband and a successful financial planner. Everyone liked to joke that Eileen and Kevin were the successful branch of the family—Eileen owned a popular clothing boutique in town with two of her girlfriends.

And so it continued. Graham chatted with everyone there, laughed with his siblings and did his best to keep conversations with extended relatives short. It was familiar and awkward and funny, and made him feel like he was right there with them.

To his surprise, it also made him kind of glad he wasn't. Next year he would be.

By the time he got off the phone, almost an hour had passed. The silence that greeted him felt a little jarring—but also curiously good.

He was left with a feeling of being loved by his family but not being entrenched in the thick of it. Experience had taught him that wasn't always a bad thing.

CHAPTER SEVEN

BY THE TIME dinner was ready, Vivian was such a ball of nerves she doubted she'd be able to eat a single bite. When Will had called out to her while she was showing Graham his room, she'd rushed to see what he'd wanted. She'd been sure he had felt bad about his behavior and wanted to say he was sorry.

Instead, he'd asked when they were "finally" going to eat. She'd been so irritated, she'd almost said he could eat when he had a better attitude.

Of course, Vivian hadn't done that. She'd told him they would eat around six, that their guest, Graham, would be joining them, and if he was really hungry he could join her in the kitchen and she'd give him a snack. Five minutes later, obviously feeling bored and lonely, Will had followed her there.

"Would you like an apple, some carrot sticks or peanut butter and crackers?"

"Peanut butter and crackers."

Vivian fixed him a small plate, poured him

a glass of milk and turned up the Christmas music station she'd been listening to for the last hour.

"You sure love that hippo song, Mommy."

"I know. I like silly Christmas songs."

"That's because you're silly, Mom." Finally in a better mood, Will stayed by her side. Sometimes singing with her, sometimes helping her prepare one of the dishes.

An hour later, Will started eyeing the stairs. "Are you sure he's nice?"

"I thought so. Plus, he's in the air force. I bet he knows a lot about planes and helicopters."

His curiosity piqued, Will looked toward the stairs again. "When is he gonna come down?"

"Whenever he's ready, I suppose. Don't forget, being here is a vacation for him. He's supposed to be relaxing."

"It's almost six o'clock."

"And the dinner is almost ready. We just have to wait for our turkey to rest a little bit longer."

Her boy wrinkled his nose. "How much longer does it have to sleep?"

She couldn't help it. Vivian burst out laughing. "Oh, Will."

"What? Isn't that what he's doing?"

"Not exactly." Just as she paused to explain,

they heard Graham's footsteps coming down the hall.

Will turned to look, his eyes growing bigger as Graham entered the room. Vivian didn't blame him. Their guest had put on a pair of worn khakis, a formfitting navy Henley and what smelled like some kind of woodsy cologne.

Vivian suddenly felt frumpy in her jeans, Christmas sweater and stained white apron. Why hadn't she at least taken a couple of minutes to brush her hair and put on some lipstick? And maybe worn a sweater that didn't have a smiling reindeer on it?

"Hi," Graham said. Smiling at them both, he added, "I hope you don't mind me joining you a little early, but I couldn't help but follow the laughter."

"I'm glad you joined us. We were just laughing about something Will said."

"Mom was laughing. I wasn't," Will corrected.

"Sorry, but he asked something that I thought was so cute. Will asked when the turkey was going to be done sleeping."

Graham's eyebrows lifted. "Sleeping?"

"He meant resting." She pointed to the big bird on the platter.

Graham's puzzled expression eased into a

smile. "Sorry, Will, but that is kind of cute."
Turning to her, he said, "What can I do to
help?"

"Nothing. You're our guest."

"That might be true, but I'm used to helping my mother prepare the big meal. My father would've had something to say about me
and my siblings sitting around while she did
all the cooking." He pointed to the sink. "At
the very least I can wash dishes."

Vivian was tempted to still refuse his offer,
but from the way Will was watching Graham,
she realized that this was an important mile-
stone for her little boy. Here was a handsome,
able-bodied man with a good job, and he was
willing to lend a helping hand in the kitchen.

"Come to think of it, I'd love it if you could
stir the gravy. Maybe you could also help me
get the rest of the dishes out of the oven in
about five minutes? They get pretty heavy."

"Of course. I'll be glad to do that."

"Thank you." Hardly able to look away from
his dark brown eyes, she added, "The gravy
is right here."

When he reached for the whisk she was
holding, his fingers brushed against hers.
Catching another whiff of cologne, she lifted
her chin to meet his gaze. He was tall. At least
a few inches over six feet. And so solid, too.

How much did a man have to work out to have a chest like that?

"Thanks," he said.

Quickly averting her eyes, Vivian stepped away. "So, um, I think I'll check on the turkey now. Will, please fill three glasses with ice and water."

"Okay."

Soon the three of them were working in unison. They maneuvered around her lovely, expansive kitchen as if they'd prepared meals together dozens of times. Will darted back and forth from the kitchen to the dining room, carefully filling each glass and walking it out to the table. She checked the rolls, put them off to the side and asked Graham to help pull out the dishes from the oven.

Finally, it was time to carve the turkey. She eyed the bird with a bit of trepidation. She always hated making that first cut.

Graham noticed her hesitation. "I'd ask if you'd like my help, but I'm sure you can handle carving a turkey just fine."

A lump formed in her throat. Emerson had thought she was a good cook, but he'd also found fault in a lot of things she'd done. His fiercely competitive nature found it difficult to take a back seat, even when it came to food preparation. Graham's belief in her was a balm to her confidence.

"Have you carved many turkeys?"

"Not a one." He winked at Will. "I might be thirty-five years old, but it's always been my brother's job, since he's the oldest."

Will's eyes widened. "Your brother still won't let you carve it?"

"Oh, I think he would if I really wanted to, but I know my place. Even when you're as old as me and have been all around the world, when it comes to carving turkeys on Christmas Day, when you're the younger brother, you're always the younger brother."

"Since I don't have a dad anymore, my mom does all the carving."

"I'm sure she's a pro."

"I'm adequate. At least I hope so," Vivian joked.

Graham eyed the bird with a look of appreciation. "Your turkey looks like it came out of a magazine. I'm sure it's terrific."

Feeling a bit on display, Vivian picked up both a serving fork and the knife she'd sharpened that morning. "Here goes nothing," she said as she sliced a piece of turkey neatly and placed it on the platter. Not only had she sliced it easily, but the piece was cooked perfectly and not dry. She breathed a sigh of relief.

"It looks fantastic," Graham said.

She couldn't resist feeling a small burst of pride. "Thank you. We'll see how it tastes."

"Do you like everything on the table or served here in the kitchen?"

"When it's just Will and me, I usually make two plates. When we have a full house of guests, I put the serving bowls on the table."

"And then Mom and me have to eat in here," Will said. As if he was just realizing that they were handling everything in a different way, he blurted, "What happens today?"

"I'm hoping that even though Graham is our guest, he won't mind you and me sharing a Christmas dinner with him—or filling his plate in here."

"It wouldn't want it any other way," Graham said with a smile.

Unable to help herself, Vivian smiled back. She wouldn't want this dinner to happen any other way, either.

CHAPTER EIGHT

GRAHAM HAD GROWN up eating a big meal on Christmas Day. He and his sisters and brother would all help prepare it, there would be a mad dash in order to have everything ready at the same time, and then there'd be a good amount of teasing and laughter as they sat at the table. His mother was a good cook, too, so dinner was always delicious and something to savor. He treasured the memories.

However, he was starting to wonder if he'd always look back on this meal with fondness, too.

Vivian, dressed in her jeans, sweater and white apron, did everything with an economy of motion and little fuss. At least at first glance, it seemed that way. Only when he looked a little more closely did he notice that the muscles around her mouth seemed stiff and her eyes looked a bit worried.

Graham wondered if that was the way she usually reacted when serving a big meal or if he was the reason.

Her little boy was adorable as well. But he, too, seemed a bit on edge.

Still feeling like the interloper that he was, Graham tried to set them both at ease after they'd said a brief prayer and dug in.

"This is really wonderful. It's the best meal I've had in months." It wasn't an exaggeration, either. Not only was the turkey moist and flavorful, but the corn bread–and–sausage stuffing was perfectly seasoned, the green beans not too soggy, and the yams with the crunchy topping were tasty as well. "I don't even like yams, and I love these."

"Thank you. I'm glad you are enjoying it."

"Is this *really* the best meal you've eaten in months?" Will asked.

"I'm afraid so. Since I'm not a very good cook, I eat most of my meals on the base. Those cooks do a good job, but not like home or like this."

"Where's home for you, Graham?" Vivian asked.

"Canada." He smiled. "I grew up in Windsor, Ontario. Just on the other side of Lake Erie."

"You're from really far away," Will said.

"Not so much. Windsor is just an hour or so from Detroit." Thinking that Detroit must seem pretty far away to a little boy living in

Colorado, he added, "Detroit is in Michigan. It's about a three-hour flight from Denver."

Vivian gave him a sympathetic smile. "I'm sure you're missing home today."

"I am, but we always have turkey dinner on Christmas Day, too. So this feels familiar. We eat something you've probably never heard of on Christmas Eve, though. It's called tourtière."

As he'd hoped, Will perked up. "What's that?"

"It's like a meat pie. My mom and sisters make it every year. It doesn't feel like Christmas without it."

"Isn't that something, Will?" Vivian asked. "The man we talked to on the phone last night was from Canada, too."

The back of Graham's neck started to tingle. "Who did you talk to last night?"

"I called the Santa Trackers." Will looked embarrassed.

"I answered phones last night for NORAD. I answered so many calls, they kind of run together, but I'm pretty sure we talked, Will. You told me about your dad, right?"

Will stared at Graham as if he'd just turned into Santa Claus himself. "That was you? You're the hero I talked to on the phone?"

"I don't know if I'm a hero, but I definitely

remember talking to you." Unable to believe that it had taken him so long to figure it out, he added, "We talked about the bed-and-breakfast, didn't we?"

Vivian was staring at him in shock. "This is unbelievable. I mean, what are the odds?"

"Probably pretty great." He was feeling kind of rattled. "I guess we were meant to meet in person."

The soft smile that had been playing on her mouth lit her eyes. "I guess we were."

Everything about the little boy had seemed to warm up. "How long are you gonna stay with us?"

"I'll be here tonight and Boxing Day. I've got to go back to the base on the twenty-seventh."

"What's Boxing Day?" Will asked.

"It's what we call the day after Christmas in Canada. And in a couple of other places around the world. What do you all usually do the day after Christmas?"

"Will usually plays with his new toys and I start taking all the decorations down."

Graham was surprised. "You take everything down on Boxing Day?"

Vivian nodded. "Why? What do you do?"

"We eat leftovers, stay in our pajamas and

watch movies. We certainly don't clean the house on Boxing Day."

Looking pleased, Will said, "We should do that, Mom. We could wear our Ernie the Elf pajamas all day."

Graham couldn't resist. "Ernie the Elf?"

Looking slightly flustered, Vivian explained, "Ernie the Elf brings us new pajamas on the night before Christmas Eve."

"He wraps them up in goofy Christmas paper and leaves them on the ends of our beds, because he doesn't want anyone to think Santa comes early."

"Boy, I wish I would've known about that. I would've come here on the night before Christmas Eve. I could sure use some new pajamas. The ones the air force gives you aren't very cozy," he teased.

Still looking serious, Will nodded. "It's too bad that you missed out."

"I have some sweatpants, so I can wear them tomorrow while you wear your new pajamas," he said. Realizing he'd just insinuated himself into yet another one of their special days, he added, "Or, if you'd rather, I can give you two some privacy."

Looking even more flustered, Vivian shook her head. "I don't want you to be alone. If you'd like to join us, we'll be glad to have you. Right, Will?"

Will nodded.

"And, um, as much as I'm glad you're joining us for our first Boxing Day, I don't think I'm quite ready for you to see me in my pajamas. I'll be wearing sweats, too."

A sudden vision of Vivian looking soft and sweetly rumpled in the morning filled his head before he carefully removed it. "Looks like you're going to be the only one wearing pajamas tomorrow afternoon, Will."

"That's okay. It's still gonna be fun, 'cause you'll be here."

"I could try to make tourtière, too, if you'd like," Vivian offered.

Thinking of all the work it was, he put his fork down. "That's kind of you to offer, but there's no need to go to all that trouble."

"It's no trouble. Besides, I'm always up for trying out a new recipe." Her eyes sparkled.

"All right, then. But only if you'll let me help you make it."

"Absolutely. You can find the recipe, too."

"I'll call my mom or one of my sisters tomorrow."

"That's going to be a lot of fun," Vivian said, before her cheeks bloomed again. "I mean, calling home for the recipe will work out just fine. Will and I can run to the store to get all the ingredients."

"All three of us should do that."

Will was practically bouncing on the edge of his seat. "I can show you all around our grocery store, Graham. I know where everything is."

Graham gave Will a fist bump. "We have a plan."

"Now, may I offer you seconds?" Vivian asked. "There's lots of food left in the kitchen."

His first plate had been heaping. "Thank you, but I had enough."

"It's really all right. You saw how much we had. With just Will and me, we're liable to still be eating turkey sandwiches until January."

He got up. "In that case, I'll be glad to help you out."

As he walked to the kitchen, he couldn't help but reflect how life really did have a way of working out. One minute, he was mourning the fact that he wasn't going home for Christmas. The next, he was thanking his lucky stars that everything had turned out the way it had.

He couldn't think of anywhere else he'd rather be than at the Snow Drop Inn.

CHAPTER NINE

AFTER HELPING THE young man find the Snow Drop Inn, and then being reunited with Clayton, the rest of Maisie's Christmas Day passed in a blur of emotions. Truth be told, she had found herself staring at her old neighbor a little more than she intended. That had led to feeling a bit giddy every time he smiled at her.

She succumbed to embarrassment when she realized that Audrey had taken note of it all. Her darling housemate was no doubt wondering what had happened to her fifty-five-year-old divorced friend.

That would make two of them.

After staying two hours, Clay traded phone numbers with Maisie, exchanged Christmas gifts with his niece and finally was on his way. Not long after that, Audrey went over to visit with a couple of girlfriends she knew from college, leaving Maisie alone for the first time all day.

At first she'd tried to pretend she wasn't curiously deflated by the quiet. After taking Ziggy for a short walk, she'd sat in front of the fire and attempted to work on her current book's plot. Unfortunately, all she'd actually done was think about Clay—and wonder why his reappearance in her life had affected her so strongly.

After a night of tossing and turning, she'd woken up early. Determined to stop wondering if Clayton was actually going to call her, she'd made a long to-do list. By eight, she got straight to work hand-washing the last of the dishes in the sink. By nine, she was at her desk, finally writing the chapter that hadn't been written on Christmas Day. She typed and plotted and edited and soon had enough done to attend to the next thing on her list: laundry.

Audrey had other plans.

"Maisie, stop working and come sit down," she called out.

"Sorry, but I'm pretty busy." She wasn't, of course, but she sure didn't want to discuss Clayton with his niece.

"Please?"

"Fine." After pouring herself a cup of coffee, Maisie sat down next to Audrey. Her housemate was still in pajamas and sipping a homemade cappuccino. "So, what's going on?" she asked Audrey. She really, really hoped she sounded breezy instead of worried.

"What's going on is that I've given you

almost a full twenty-four hours to recover from the shock of seeing Uncle Clay, and you haven't said anything to me about your reunion."

"I was asleep when you got home, and you just got up."

"I still think you're avoiding me. What gives?"

Ugh. She knew she'd been too flirty with Audrey's uncle! "What gives is there's nothing to tell. Clayton used to be my next-door neighbor. We were happy to see each other again. That's it." She sipped her coffee, hoping she sounded calmer than she felt.

"Come on, Maisie. The two of you could hardly take your eyes off each other. I could've left the house and you probably would never have noticed."

"I would've noticed."

"Maybe. Maybe not, though." Leaning back in her chair, she sipped her drink with two hands. "I know Uncle Clay only had eyes for you."

"Well, I am irresistible," she joked.

"I'm being serious."

"I know. I'm just, um, finding it a little hard to believe." What if Clay really had been looking at her like she was something special?

"How come?"

"We haven't seen each other in years, for one thing. Not since I was thirteen."

Audrey picked up the piece of pumpkin pie she must have already sliced and stabbed the end of it with a fork.

"You two must have been quite the teenage couple."

"I wouldn't go that far."

"Come on, there must have been something between you two for there to still be something lingering now."

Her sweet roommate's grumble was just whiny enough to pull Maisie from yet another round of introspection. "You, my dear, are a nut."

"I'm not! I'm serious."

"Well, there is nothing between me and your uncle to get all serious about. First of all, I had forgotten all about Clayton Stevick until he was standing in the driveway, so there wasn't anything to tell you about. Secondly, how was I supposed to know that he was your favorite uncle?"

"I guess you have me there." Audrey ran a hand through her blond curls that always looked to be in perfect disarray. "He's great, though, right?"

Maisie nodded. The fact that Clay was great couldn't be ignored. While she'd stayed in

Colorado Springs, married, started working at a bank, got divorced and at last had become a writer, he'd entered the army, married, had two kids, divorced somewhat amicably, transitioned out of the military after twenty years and now did a bunch of contract work for the army. He had lived all over the world and was currently living in San Antonio.

He was also the same very nice guy she'd once been so close to. Thinking about their friendship, and the way she used to watch for him out her bedroom window, Maisie sighed. Clayton really had been the focus of so many hopes and dreams back then.

"I'm glad Clay turned out so well." That comment sounded a bit flat, but Maisie wasn't sure what else she was comfortable saying. She certainly wasn't going to tell Audrey that Clayton had been her first kiss. When Ziggy padded over to join them, she reached down to run a hand along his soft ears.

Ziggy sighed in contentment before sprawling under the table.

It was better to keep her feelings to herself. Clay's sudden appearance in her life had been a shock. The way he'd seemed to have set every nerve on end? More so.

"I can't believe you didn't recognize him."

"We were thirteen, Audrey. You can't hold that against me."

"Uncle Clay recognized you right away."

"I don't know how. However, I do have to tell you that he looks nothing like the boy I used to walk to school with."

Audrey sat down on the overstuffed couch and tucked her legs underneath her. "Are you trying to say that he didn't always look like a power lifter?"

"He did not. He also had thick glasses, was shorter than me and had a lot more hair." The Clay Stevick she'd spent two hours chatting with the day before looked like he should be on the cover of some kind of sporting magazine. He was that attractive.

Obviously attempting to look nonchalant, her roommate added, "You know, Uncle Clay said he's going to be in town a lot. Probably every other week for the next year."

That meant she could possibly see him at least twenty-six times. If they just spent three hours in each other's company, that was seventy-eight hours together. More than enough time to get to know each other well.

Little butterflies might be thinking about dancing in her belly at the thought of seeing him so much, but Maisie firmly pushed them away. "I know you're busy, but I imagine you'll still be able to see him from time to time."

"I'm sure you'll see him, too."

"I won't be able to help that, given that I'm your housemate." And yes, she sounded ridiculous.

Audrey rolled her eyes. "You know what I meant. I was sure Clay was going to ask you out for tonight."

She'd gotten the feeling he'd been thinking about it, too. Though it might have just been wishful thinking. "He said he'd call."

"I bet he will, then," Audrey said as she returned to the table with her cup of coffee. "If Clay says he's going to do something, he will."

"You sound awfully sure about that. Are you really that close?"

"I think so." After taking another bite of pie, Audrey said, "Maisie, you know how my family is. They're great, but they're also a lot."

"I know." Audrey's parents owned a number of properties in the state and spent the majority of their time either checking on them or checking on their only child. They were both meddling and emotionally distant, which Maisie always considered a dangerous combination.

"Clay is my mother's youngest brother, and

he's always been awesome. He's helped me through a lot of long holidays over the years."

"I'm glad he's been there for you. Now I am, too, you know."

Audrey smiled. "I know. I think that's why I was so excited at the thought of you two seeing each other. Then, two of my favorite people in the world will be happy."

"I wouldn't hold your breath about Clayton and me becoming a couple. But you can be sure that both he and I will always be in your life. That's also a good thing, you know."

"I know."

"So, are you working today?"

Audrey nodded. "I don't have to be at the store until one, thank goodness." She glanced at the clock. "Before that, I'm going to go for a run, shower, then maybe do some laundry."

"I'll put a few Christmas things away and start dusting."

"And wait for the phone to ring?"

Probably. "Of course not. When you get to be my age, you don't let little things like phone calls bother you much."

Audrey raised an eyebrow. "Whatever you say, Maisie. See you later."

Only when the girl was out the door on a three-mile run did Maisie put the phone out where she could see it. Ziggy stared at it and tilted his head. "I know, Zig. I'm being silly, but don't tell Audrey, okay?"

Ziggy wagged his tail. Maisie hoped that meant yes.

An hour later, when Clay's name flashed on the screen, she couldn't help but answer immediately. "Hello?"

"Maisie, it's me. Is it too early to call?"

"Not at all. I've been up for hours."

"Me, too. I went for a run this morning and was planning not to do much besides watch football on the couch when work called. So I'm on my way to work now."

"I'm sorry about that."

"Me, too." He sighed. "It's fine, though. I might not be in the army anymore, but I haven't forgotten how things work."

"I hope you have a good day and they don't keep you too long."

"That's why I was calling, actually. Would you be free tomorrow evening? Say, around six? I'd love to take you to dinner. We still have a lot to talk about."

"Yes," she said before realizing that she should have probably sounded a little less eager.

She smiled at herself. Oh, who was she kidding? She was too old for silly games. Chuckling, she said, "I meant to say that dinner tomorrow night sounds good. Thank you."

"Great. See you then, Maisie."

"See you then."

"Hey, Maise?" he said, using his pet name for her.

"Yes?"

"I...well, I just wanted to tell you again that I'm really glad our paths crossed. I'm looking forward to getting to know you again."

"Me, too, Clay."

She could hear the blaring of a car horn and a muffled curse out of his mouth. "Got to go. Half the drivers here don't know what a red light means. 'Bye." He hung up.

She laughed, thinking he had a point. But maybe she was simply laughing because it was so great that he'd called and that they had a date tomorrow night.

Or maybe it was because she was starting to realize that she wasn't too old to still have a crush on Clayton Stevick.

CHAPTER TEN

BOXING DAY GREETED them with freshly fallen snow. The meteorologists were reporting that some parts of the city had gotten almost a foot, and more was expected. Since the Snow Drop Inn was near downtown, they received about seven inches. It was more than enough to coat everything with a good amount of white fluff. Being from Colorado, snow didn't faze Vivian too much, but even by her standards, it was a lot.

She'd take it, though. Since her only guest was Graham, Vivian enjoyed a rare lazy morning. She'd slept in until six. Pleased not to have to set up coffee service in the living room, she slipped on a robe over her new pajamas and padded downstairs. Soon, she would have to get dressed and run to the grocery store. For now, though, all she wanted was a hot cup of coffee and a few precious minutes to relax before she officially started her day.

Vivian was halfway down the staircase when

she realized that she wasn't the first one up. The aroma of coffee had drifted up the stairs.

She skittered to a stop when she caught sight of Graham sitting on one of the big easy chairs next to the fireplace. He had on a pair of navy sweatpants and a snug-fitting gray T-shirt. His hands were curved around a big stoneware mug, and his eyes were on her.

His presence wasn't unwelcome, but it did make her feel flustered. Honestly, she had no idea what to say. Thank him for starting the coffee maker? Apologize for not being the first one awake? Simply tell him good morning?

Graham, on the other hand, didn't appear to have any worries. Grinning, he said, "I guess I get to see your Ernie pajamas after all."

The comment was too funny for her to be embarrassed, especially since her pajamas were obviously Ernie-the-Elf Christmas ones. For no other reason would she buy navy flannel pajamas with black Labradors wearing red Santa hats.

Playfully, she covered her face with a hand. "If I could erase this from your memory, I would. I didn't think you would be up."

"There's no way I want to forget this moment. You look adorable." He pointed to her feet, snugly encased in red-striped socks and sheepskin slippers. "Your feet look cute, too."

She wasn't sure how to take that. She felt a little tingle of appreciation from the compliment, coinciding with a burst of confusion that she was so happy to receive it.

What was going on with her?

"Um, thanks," she said at last. "I'll be right back." She hurried to the kitchen, filled her largest mug with coffee, sugar and cream, and sipped gratefully. Then took another long sip.

Graham appeared in the doorway. "Hey, I'm sorry if I embarrassed you. You'll have to forgive my manners. I've lived in barracks for so long, I'm afraid I've gotten a little too used to communal living. I think I forgot that not everyone wants their privacy invaded."

"No, that's all right. You're not invading my space or anything. I'm glad you made yourself at home."

"Sure?" He still looked worried.

"Positive. I… I'm just one of those people who is worthless before my first cup of coffee."

"My sister is the same way."

Since she'd been guzzling that cup of coffee like it was her last one on earth, she poured herself another cup and then turned to face him. "Not you, though?"

He shook his head. "Nah. I like a shot of caffeine, but I don't crave it. Not like exercise. If I don't get at least a run in every day, I feel sluggish."

"Exercising is no doubt better for you."

"My CO seems to think that, too."

They shared a smile. She could practically feel the warmth lingering between the two of them. It was a tangible thing—and so confusing.

Or maybe not. Graham Hopkins was a handsome, athletic man with a great smile who volunteered to do things like be a Santa Tracker. He was definitely a man in a million.

Realizing she was feeling a bit too comfortable around him, she said, "I better go get dressed."

"You sure? You look comfortable. I don't care if you wear that all day."

"I would if I could, but I have things to do."

"Such as?"

"A trip to the grocery store. We've got to find a good recipe for tourtière and then go get all the ingredients."

"There's a saying that there are as many recipes for tourtière as there are cooks in Quebec."

"I'm anxious for you to show me how it's done."

"I'll be happy to help you as much as I can, but like I said, my mom is the pro at making it."

"For breakfast, I'm going to make eggs in a hole and bacon. It's Will's favorite. Is that okay with you?"

His brown eyes met hers. "Anything you want to make is good with me. Promise."

Why did his words make her feel warm all over? Flustered, she poured herself more coffee. "As much as I wouldn't mind hanging out in my dog pajamas, I'd better go change. I'll be down soon to feed you. Stay put," she teased as she headed upstairs with her cup of coffee.

She was halfway up the stairs when he replied, "Take your time, Vivian. I promise, I haven't been this relaxed in weeks."

Funny, she'd just been thinking the same thing.

NEVER WOULD VIVIAN take a solitary trip to the grocery store for granted again. Her plans had been to cajole Will to accompany her by promising that he could get a carton of peppermint ice cream and hot fudge, but then everything changed when Graham asked if he could go as well.

She hadn't known how to tell him he wasn't

invited, so next thing she knew, she was wandering around King Soopers with one handsome Canadian airman and one very talkative little boy.

Both acted as if a visit to the local grocery was an exciting adventure and insisted on walking down every aisle. By the fourth aisle, they'd also taken to teasing her about her shopping methods. Graham happened to think Will's stories about her being picky with her fruits and vegetables were hysterical.

His laughter was loud enough to echo through the entire store. The other shoppers, many of whom looked frazzled and tired on the day after Christmas, seemed to look at him with relief. Vivian wondered if he was known for his easygoing manner among his unit in Cheyenne Mountain.

Vivian had done some homework on tourtière and had discovered that either ground pork or beef, or a combination of the two, could be used in the meat pie. Since she didn't have much experience with ground pork, other than in sausage, she planned to only use beef. In an adorable show of concern, Graham had pulled out his phone and called his mother in Windsor to ask her opinion on the matter. She'd answered on the first ring.

Standing next to the butcher, Vivian folded

her arms over her chest and listened as Graham discussed the pros and cons of pork, beef and a combination of the two. She'd begun to smirk—honestly, his confusion was so cute—when he handed the phone to her.

"Ma said she'd talk to you about this."

"Oh, all right." Adjusting the phone on her ear, she murmured, "Hi, Mrs. Hopkins. This is Vivian."

"It's Gwen, dear. And I remarried after Graham's father passed away, so it's actually Gwen Evans. Happy Boxing Day."

"To you, too. I hope you had a nice Christmas."

"We did. It made it better to know that Graham was at your house eating a turkey dinner."

"I'm glad he joined us. Both my son, Will, and I enjoyed his company."

"He does have a certain charm about him," she joked. "Now, on to tourtière. Graham is right. I usually do use a combination of pork and beef, but either works just fine. Whatever you do, it's the spices that make the difference, right?"

Vivian knew that the recipe had called for allspice, cloves and paprika. "It's an unusual combination, but I'll do my best."

"I'm sure it will be wonderful. You know

how boys are—they're always sure that their mother's version of something is the best. They forget that it's just one version."

"Yes, ma'am."

"Also, Graham really loves to eat brussels sprouts with that."

She wasn't a whiz with brussels sprouts, either. But since she was determined to give Graham his Boxing Day meal, she said, "Gotcha. I'll make him some."

"'Bye now."

She smiled. "Yes, goodbye."

"Well?" Graham asked. "Do you feel better now?"

"Your mother gave me a lot of good tips." She inhaled. "I think I'm ready."

Looking down at Will, Graham said, "What do you think, buddy? Do you think the three of us are going to be able to make this dish?"

"Yep." He nodded earnestly. "My mom is a really good cook. People come from all over to eat her breakfasts."

"You're right. She's talented in the kitchen, for sure." Smiling at her softly, he said, "I do believe we have faith in your ability to make a successful tourtière, Ms. Parnell." He winked. "Especially since my mother gave you some good tips."

Graham might be charming, but he was a

man through and through. She'd yet to meet a man who didn't think his mother's cooking was the best. "Oh, for heaven's sake! I should've known that was coming."

This time, it was Will's giggle that drew all the other customers' smiles and curious glances.

Vivian didn't blame them one bit. Her little boy's exuberant laughter ringing throughout the store was wonderful to hear, especially after some of the sad Christmases they'd had in the past.

So wonderful. Really, so everything.

CHAPTER ELEVEN

GRAHAM KNEW HE would never forget this particular Boxing Day as long as he lived. After the three of them arrived home from the store, they unpacked all the ingredients for the tourtière and arranged them on the counter per Vivian's surprisingly specific directions.

Next they had lunch. Graham was put in charge of pulling out leftovers from the spare refrigerator while Vivian made a small plate of turkey, gravy and stuffing for Will. After Will finished and went off to play with his Legos, he and Vivian ate their meal. When they were done, he went outside to shovel the driveway again while Vivian washed the dishes and made a to-do list for the upcoming week.

An hour later, they were all back in the kitchen. Vivian clapped her hands together. "Well, shall we begin?" she asked.

He and Will were quickly relegated to sous-chef positions, and Vivian proceeded to order them about. Graham soon discovered that Will didn't usually spend too much time cooking with his mom. The little boy seemed excited to be helping so much.

His mother knew how to handle his exuberance. She gently cautioned him to settle down, then handed him some bars of margarine and a container of flour. Graham helped him measure the flour but otherwise kept to his job, which was cutting up onions and carrots.

"Am I doing this right, Graham?" Will asked from his perch on the step stool.

Peeking into the bowl, Graham thought the dough looked a little rubbery but shrugged. "I'm not sure about the dough. That's a question for your mom."

"Mom!"

Vivian laughed. "Still here, dear. You don't need to shout in my ear."

"I wasn't shouting. I mean, not exactly."

"Speak more softly, if you please. What if we had other guests here?"

He sighed. "We don't, though, Mommy."

Graham was curious. "When do the next guests arrive?"

"Tomorrow."

"So soon?"

"This was more time off than I usually give myself. Will and I decided that we needed a break this year, so I blocked off some time to ourselves. It's been nice."

"And here I came and joined you. I'm so sorry."

"I'm not sorry," Will said quickly. "You're fun, Sarge."

Vivian hid a smile. Will and Graham had gone back and forth with what would be the best way to refer to him. She hadn't loved Graham's first suggestion, which was for Will to call him by his first name. After that, they'd tried "Mr. Hopkins," "Sergeant Hopkins" and "Mr. Graham" on for size. At last they'd decided that Will would call Graham "Sarge." Will loved that idea, and even Vivian had admitted that the name did sound pretty cute coming from a six-year-old's lips.

"Thank you, Will. Don't tell the men who report to me that I'm fun, though."

"How come?"

"You'll ruin my reputation. I have a pretty good reputation for being tough as nails, you know."

Will's eyes widened. "I won't tell any of them that I think you're fun."

"Good job." Turning back to Vivian, Graham added, "What I was saying is that I'm sorry I called and you felt obligated to let me be here."

Vivian had been boiling the potatoes and

had just heated up a skillet for the pork and beef. "I feel the same way as Will. Your company has been very welcome. I've enjoyed it a lot." Glancing his way, her expression warmed.

Graham felt that same pull toward her that he'd been trying to ignore for the last twenty-four hours. He was starting to wonder if maybe he wasn't the only one who was feeling that something special was taking place between them. "Me, too," he said at last.

Vivian's smile grew. "Besides, if you weren't here, Will and I wouldn't be getting to make tourtière today."

"And I wouldn't get to tell people happy Boxing Day," Will added.

"I'm delighted to share some of my Canadian traditions with you. Next thing you know, you'll be wanting poutine and wearing a toque."

"What's poutine?" Will asked.

"Gravy and cheese curds over fries."

Vivian wrinkled her nose. "I think I'll stick to tourtière for now. Okay, gentlemen. You two work on the dough, and I'll brown this meat and add the spices."

"Roger that."

Carefully, Vivian measured the correct amounts of spices and garlic and added them to the mixture while Graham and Will rolled out the dough and put part of it in the pie dish. The dough still looked to be on the gummy side, but Vivian didn't say a word. Maybe that was how it was supposed to look?

When the mixture had simmered down and some of the liquid had evaporated, she handed Graham a spoon. "It's up to you to tell us what it needs, Sergeant."

Playing along, he nodded. "My pleasure, madam." Carefully he dipped the side of the spoon into the meat mixture, gathered about a tablespoonful and, after a quick blow, popped it in his mouth. He closed his eyes, ready to love the traditional, rich taste.

It tasted nothing like it.

Knowing that Vivian was watching him carefully, he worked to keep his expression blank.

"Graham, you're driving me crazy! Say something. What do you think?"

Vivian had been smiling and joking for the last two hours. Will had just hugged his leg and told him that he liked today better than Christmas. There was no way he was going to tell them the truth. "It should work."

She looked perplexed. "What does that mean?"

"It means that it doesn't taste like I remember, but it doesn't taste exactly wrong, either." And that was as diplomatic as he could be.

"So you're being as clear as mud."

"I'm being honest." Kind of.

She popped a hand on her waist. "Are you really?"

"I'm a sergeant. We're used to telling the truth no matter what." Of course, he was also great at telling his superiors what they wanted to hear, but she didn't need to know that.

"Huh. Well, let's put it in the oven. Some things don't taste the same until they're completely done."

"Like banana bread," Will said.

Graham laughed. "Is that true?"

Before Vivian could answer, Will nodded. "When Mom's banana bread comes out of the oven, it's sweet and yummy. When it's just batter, it's kind of gross."

Graham glanced her way. "He's a tough customer, hmm?"

"Yes, but at least he's an honest one." She picked up the heavy pie dish and slipped it into the oven. "Well, gentlemen, we now have about forty minutes until Boxing Day dinner."

Will tugged on his arm. "Let's go play outside, Graham."

"Hold on, buddy. We need to help your mother clean up."

"But you said that we could go out in the snow."

"We can do both. But first we're going to help your mother."

"It's okay, Graham. Will doesn't, um, get to spend much time doing guy things. I can clean up the kitchen on my own. Believe me, I'm used to a bunch of dirty dishes."

"See, Graham?" Will reached for his coat from the hook by the door. "Let's go."

"No. We're going to help her, Will. Take off your coat. If your mother was kind enough to make this dish for me, I'm going to help her clean up the mess."

"Thank you, Graham."

"You're welcome." Ignoring Will, who seemed to be trying to decide what the consequences would be for pouting, Graham snatched a dish towel from Vivian's hands, tucked it in the waistband of his jeans and turned on the faucet. Next, he squirted a bit of dish soap into the sink, picked up the sponge and started cleaning the pot she'd made the filling in.

"Mom, I'm gonna go to the bathroom."

"Fine. You can help dry when you come back."

After the boy left, Graham said, "I think he just dodged KP."

"Probably so." She lowered her voice. "Don't

tell him, but I'm okay with that. I can usually get the dishes done a whole lot faster without him."

Realizing that she still looked a little hesitant, Graham glanced her way as he reached for another pot. "Are you thinking the same thing? That it would've been easier to clean up without me?"

"No. I was actually thinking about my husband. Emerson helped me around the house, but he was never the one to suggest it. I would always have to ask him."

"Obviously, I've never been married. But in the air force, everyone learns which guys shirk duties and which ones are always ready to lend a hand. I never wanted to be in the first group."

"I can't imagine you being in the first group. I bet you're a fantastic sergeant."

He laughed. "I'm far from that, but I love my job." Spying Will lurking just outside the kitchen, he called out, "You going to help me dry, Will?"

Will picked up the towel and started wiping down the big pot. When he finished, Graham motioned for him to put it on the counter and grab another freshly washed pot.

After putting away the flour and some of the spices, Vivian looked like she was at a loss about what to do. "I guess I could go set the table now."

"You could," Graham said. "Or you could even make yourself a cup of tea and relax for a spell. We've got this. Right, buddy?"

"Yeah, Mom. We've got this," Will said.

"Well, um, all right."

After she left the room, Will smiled up at him. "Now it's just us guys."

"It sure is. You're going a good job. I'm proud of you."

"Is this what you do up on Cheyenne Mountain?"

"Nope. When I first entered the service I spent some time washing dishes. Now, though, I spend most of my time behind a computer or ordering guys around."

"Really?"

"Yep. My rank means I've been in the air force a long time. I work with the officers and help the men who report to me learn what to do."

"And you run a lot, right?"

He grinned. "Right. If you're a soldier, you've got to take care of yourself so you can take care of others."

"Maybe I want to do that, too."

"Maybe you will. Though you're only six, so you've got lots of time to decide." He handed him a wooden spoon. "Here's the last thing to dry."

"Good. I'm getting tired."

"That's too bad, because I was thinking about going out in the snow."

"You still want to do that?"

"I told you I would, remember?"

Will smiled at him like Graham was a superhero. "Maybe we can make a snowman."

"I bet we could, Will. That sounds like a lot of fun."

Later, as he helped Will put a carrot on the snowman's face, Graham knew he was going to have to figure out a way to spend more time with Vivian and Will. He already couldn't wait to see them again.

CHAPTER TWELVE

GRAHAM COULD JUMP from a helicopter, march for miles without stopping, analyze data coming in from multiple sources and make mere corporals shudder in their boots.

He was also pretty good at soccer, playing poker and fly-fishing.

He was not good at making tourtière.

Or, it seemed, at faking his opinion of the version that was on his plate. His first bite had been a shock. The second one had made him want to call his mother and apologize for taking her expertise for granted. Both of those things had absolutely been on his mind.

He sure didn't have to display his opinion so blatantly, though.

Looking into her pretty brown eyes, Graham felt shame wash over him. Vivian had tried so hard to give him a piece of home today. She'd taken him to the store, discussed the filling with his mother and done everything she possibly could to give Graham the meal he'd talked about with such longing. Those things were amazing.

The least he could have done was kept his opinion to himself.

"It's really that bad?" Vivian asked.

He swallowed, trying to buy himself some time to find the right words. "No…"

She sat back in her chair and raised an eyebrow. "Someone told me recently that sergeants have no trouble stating the truth."

Graham supposed he deserved that. "I promise that it's not horrible."

"It's not horrible?"

He inwardly winced. "I mean, it's edible." Kind of. Like, if one was starving or in prison. Graham was just about to stuff another forkful in his mouth when he noticed then that her plate was still full. All Vivian had done was move the meat around on her plate.

Realizing that she likely felt the same way, he added, "It's, uh, just not like I remember."

"I see."

Graham realized he was sitting ramrod straight. Practically at attention, like a crotchety general was sitting to his left. He needed to relax.

He had no idea what else to say, however. Seconds passed.

Vivian put her fork down. "Will, what do you think?"

"I don't like it." Frowning, he added, "It tastes like Christmas."

"What does that mean?" Graham asked.

"I don't know," Will said quickly. He looked at his mother for help.

To Graham's amazement, she was chuckling. "I'm really confused now. Is 'tastes like Christmas' some secret code you two have?" he asked.

"I think my son means that we went pretty heavy-handed on those cloves," she explained. "It does kind of make this dish taste a little bit like a gingerbread cookie."

"Does it?" He had thought there was something off about the taste.

Looking at him warily, she blushed. "Sorry, I don't mean to offend you. Some people really like gingerbread."

"Not meat that tastes like it! I think my older sisters would be grinning ear to ear at my attempt to make this."

"It's more like my attempt." She wrinkled her brow. "I'm not quite sure where I went wrong. I followed the recipe exactly. I don't suppose Canadians have different words for teaspoon and tablespoon?"

"Nope. I'm afraid we're all the same in that regard."

When Will started playing with his food, Graham decided to put them all out of their misery. "Turkey sandwich, anyone?"

"Yes, please!" Will said.

Vivian grinned. "Go get out the bread. I'll be right there." When they were alone, just him sitting at the end of the table and her sitting on his right, Vivian lowered her voice. "I'm sorry about this. I wanted you to have something special."

She *had* done that. It had been years since someone had done so much to make him happy. "At the risk of sounding sappy, even making a bad version of tourtière is special. I appreciate you going to so much trouble to help me feel a little less homesick today. You didn't have to do that."

She smiled. "I enjoyed our project. Even if it didn't turn out the way we expected, I'm still glad we gave it a try."

"Mom, what's this?" Will called out.

"What's what?"

"This." He thrust a bag of all-dressed potato chips on the table. "I've never seen these before."

Glad to have something to break the tension, Graham picked up the bag and quickly tore open the top. "This, Will, is why Canadians are manly men." He reached in, picked out a chip and handed it to the boy. "Try a taste of this."

Will reached for it and glanced at his mother. After she nodded, he put half in his mouth. Seconds later, the whole chip was consumed and he was holding up the bag and staring at the front of it. "These are really good."

Unable to help himself, Graham popped two chips in his mouth and grinned. "They sure are. These are the most popular chips in my town. Everyone loves them."

"Did you bring your own potato chips over from the base?"

"I did not." He raised an eyebrow. "Vivian, any idea how they came to be here?"

"I might have sneaked some in the shopping cart while we were at the grocery store," she said.

Her eyes were bright with amusement. She looked adorable—so much so, he didn't feel like he could look away.

Or maybe he just didn't want to.

"Thanks," he said. "That was really thoughtful of you."

"It wasn't anything much. I just wanted to make you feel a little more at home today."

"If that was your goal, then your mission was accomplished. It means a lot. Everything you did meant a lot."

Her gaze softened before she seemed to collect herself. "Well, I suppose we had better clear off these dishes and make ourselves some turkey sandwiches."

"Can we have those chips, too?" Will asked.

"It's up to Graham. They're his."

"Will you share them, Sarge?"

"Of course, buddy. Come on. Let's get to work."

After they ate, the three of them went outside. It was after six, so the sky was essentially dark. Vivian had turned the Christmas lights on, though, and those, plus the blanket of snow, made everything shiny. Almost luminescent. "This is perfect," he said.

Looking at Graham, dressed in his jeans, boots, Henley and a thick coat, she couldn't help but agree. For the first time since Emerson had passed, she didn't feel awkward and alone. It was as though she and Will had had a third family member with them today. It had been great to have someone to laugh with, to help do chores. He'd even nudged her son to help, too.

As hard as it was going to be to tell him goodbye in the morning, she knew she wouldn't regret their time together. Not for a minute. Graham had reminded her that she wasn't just a mother and an innkeeper. No, she was also a woman with a heart and a soul and a lot of living left to do. Somehow she'd all but forgotten that.

Will brought over a football someone had given him for Christmas. "Hey, Graham, want to play catch?"

"Yep. Do you know how to throw a football?"

"Not really."

"I'll show you." After demonstrating where to position his fingers, he tossed it to Will, who carefully placed his hand on the ball's stitches, stepped forward and threw.

When it sailed three feet in a pretty good line, Vivian clapped.

Will acted like he was embarrassed, but he got a new swagger in his step.

After a couple more tosses, Graham went to sit next to Vivian on the steps. "That kid of yours doesn't like to sit down much, does he?"

She chuckled. "Sometimes he does...but not if there's a real, live Royal Canadian Air Force sergeant in our midst."

When she turned to watch her son, who was now chatting with one of her neighbors, she felt Graham's attention stay on her. "What?"

"Oh, nothing. I was just looking at your hair."

"Hmm?" Reaching for her ponytail, she realized that at some point since they'd finished their sandwiches, she'd loosened her hair from its elastic and it now fell down her back. "There's a lot of it, right?"

"I was actually looking at all the different colors. The lights are making them all stand out."

"I used to hate my red hair when I was younger. Now I kind of like it because it's different."

"I think it's gorgeous."

She felt her mouth go dry. "Thank you."

"You're welcome," Graham said, still finding it hard to look away. Vivian had on thick black leggings, leather L.L. Bean boots and an off-white fisherman's sweater. Every bit of her was lovely, but it was the way she gazed at her son that drew his heart toward her. Everything about her look said that she was a woman who loved. It beckoned his heart and made some of the loneliness he'd been feeling for so long dissipate.

"Oh, no. Do I have something on my cheek?"

He blinked as she swiped her fingers over her cheekbone, attempting to remove a flaw that hadn't been there to begin with.

"Not at all. I'm sorry, I guess I was staring at you." Her eyes widened, but she didn't say a word. Of course, what could she say? He shook his head. "I'm sorry. I meant, I just realized you weren't wearing a coat and was wondering if you were cold."

Her body relaxed. "Oh, no." She pinched a few inches of the extra bit of wool of her sleeve. "This is so thick. It's one of those Irish wool sweaters. Gorgeous and usually too heavy to wear indoors."

"I have one of those, too. It's so heavy, I never wear it." Wondering where it was back at home, he added, "I've gotten hot wearing it outside in January."

"If it was too hot for a Canadian winter, I'm guessing that says everything."

"I had forgotten about it, to tell you the truth. It's too nice to give away but too hot to wear."

"I've had mine forever. I'm not a knitter, but even I can appreciate the workmanship." Looking a little embarrassed, she added, "I'm not sure why I put it on. I just decided to get cleaned up a bit after we got the kitchen put back to rights."

"Well, it looks pretty on you…um, now that I know you're not freezing." Mentally, he slapped his palm on his forehead. He'd give just about anything to be even half as smooth as some of his buddies were when they went out to the bars.

She smiled again. "Thank you."

He looked for Will and found him in a neighbor's yard. He was petting a beagle and talking to the woman who had directed him to the inn two days ago. "It doesn't seem like your boy has ever met a stranger."

"That's my friend Maisie and her dog, Ziggy. But you're right, Will is pretty outgoing. I think part of it is because we often have strangers in our house. But it also has to do with the fact that he's so comfortable here in our neighborhood. A lot of our neighbors helped us out when his father died. He trusts them, you know?"

He nodded. "Trust means a lot at any age."

She wrapped her arms around her knees. "You do understand."

"Vivian, everything you've accomplished? Well, it's impressive."

"Not really. I've only done what had to be done. Nothing like you. You've fought in wars and likely done a thousand things most people will never know about. You're even living in another country in order to do your job."

"Maybe, but you're giving me more credit than I deserve." When she was about to interrupt, he waved a hand. "Here's the thing. A lot of folks thank me for my service and act like what I've been through over the years is something to be proud of."

"That's because it is."

"What I'm trying to say is that you've been courageous, too, Vivian. What you've done— pulling yourself together, raising this boy, starting your own business…and still being able to smile? Well, it's something to be proud of, too."

Little by little, her bright smile faded. She swallowed, as if she was trying to catch her breath. "Sometimes, I think all it takes to be strong is finding the will to get up in the morning."

A lump filled his throat. She really was something. Beautiful, sweet, hardworking. She was so much of what he used to think he was looking for…until he realized that he might never be what any woman was looking for.

Then, of course, there was the fact that he wasn't going to be in Colorado much longer. His CO had told him earlier this week that there was a good chance Graham's latest request to return home would be approved.

"Did I say something wrong?" she asked. "You look upset."

That's because he actually was. It didn't make sense. How could one Christmas weekend change his perspective about so much?

Fumbling for words, he shook his head. "No, it's just that I, uh, just realized that I'll be leaving here soon."

"I've thought the same thing. But you do live close by, you know. Maybe one day we could meet for a burger or something."

"No, Vivian. I meant that I'm pretty sure I'll be heading to another base soon. One up in Canada."

"Oh."

Graham could swear that he spied a glimpse of disappointment in her eyes before she composed herself. "I'm sorry. I should have broken the news a little less bluntly."

"No, no. Well…" She swallowed, pinned on a smile. "I'm surprised, but of course I understand. Colorado Springs is a very long way from Canada. I bet you can't wait to go home." She stood up. "I better go get Will. If I'm not careful, he's going to visit with the whole neighborhood!"

Watching her walk off, Graham found himself thinking about two things. One, that he'd managed to ruin the best Boxing Day he'd had in years. Maybe ever. The other?

He was disappointed that she hadn't admitted that she would have liked the chance to get to know him better.

How self-centered was that?

CHAPTER THIRTEEN

LOOKING AROUND THE fancy restaurant, with its white linen tablecloths, sparkling silver and dim lighting, Maisie realized that it had been quite a long time since she'd been out to such a fancy dinner.

And, perhaps, since she'd felt as cared for.

On the drive over, Clay had told her an amusing story of how he'd asked a couple of people at work about the best place to take a woman on a first date. The responses had run the gambit, from hole-in-the-wall Mexican restaurants to sushi in Colorado City to the four-star steakhouse up in Flying Horse.

"So, all of that good advice was useless," he'd declared with a laugh. "I had no idea if you liked Italian, were allergic to shrimp or if you had a gluten-free diet. I'm sorry, I should've asked."

He'd been making fun of himself and his lack of dating experience. Maisie had thought it was the sweetest thing. "Let's see, yes, no and no again."

"I'll keep that in mind for next time."

She'd smiled politely, but inside, she'd been doing a little happy dance.

"For the record, I think you made a great choice. I haven't been to McKenzie's Chop House in ages," Maisie said now.

"That's a relief." He chuckled. "There it is."

"There's what?"

"That *Mona Lisa* smile. You're the only person I ever met who can smile like that." He waved a hand. "You know, without hardly curving your lips."

That sounded weird to her. "I don't know if that's a good thing or not."

"It's a great thing. I used to think about that smile a lot back in the day."

After the server brought them glasses of wine, Maisie said, "If I have the same smile, you still have the same ability to catch me off guard."

"Like now?"

She nodded. "I… I didn't know you used to think about me."

"Come on. Back when we were thirteen, you were already gorgeous, and I was a foot shorter than you." He rolled his eyes. "I thought it was the worst thing in the world. I thought you'd never give me the time of day."

"Obviously you were wrong." She paused.

"And, just for the record, I think you turned out pretty nice." He had, too. He was now a good five inches taller than her, had filled out and had obviously turned into a good man. That said, he still had a sweetness to him that she'd always been drawn to.

"So, have you decided what you're going to order yet?"

"Not yet." He chuckled. "I guess I got lost in this menu. It's way too big."

"I was thinking the same thing. There are a lot of choices."

"I think I'll probably get a steak. What about you?"

She bit her bottom lip, thinking. "I was leaning toward either the salmon or the chicken. Or the filet mignon." Realizing how silly she was being—it was a meal in a restaurant, not a matter of national security—she put her menu down. "I guess I've gotten lost in this menu, too."

"I'm sure you know this, but McKenzie's is known for their steaks. If you like beef, I think you should get one. What have you gotten here in the past?"

"I don't remember."

"It's been that long?"

She lifted a shoulder in an attempt to brush off the burst of sadness. "I'm afraid so. Jared stopped taking me out to nice restaurants years ago. He used to say that it was a waste of a good paycheck."

"I'm sorry. I hate that he treated you like that."

"I'm sorry, too, but I've learned that it takes two people to make a marriage work and two people to help it fall apart. I can't let him take all the blame." She sipped her water. "Divorce happens, right? Even to you."

"Pam and I drifted apart. I was gone all the time, and she missed having someone who put her first. When we were married, Pam used to say that she sometimes felt as if the army was my mistress." He looked Maisie in the eye. "I wouldn't have called it that, but I can't deny that I always, always put the army first. I don't blame her for wanting something more."

Clay didn't seem bitter at all. It was surprising. Had he really been able to come to terms with both his marriage and his divorce?

"Is it really possible to be as calm as you seem to be?" she asked.

"I'm not trying to prove anything. It was hard. I had plenty of bad days. Guilty days. But I didn't cheat on her, and she didn't cheat on me. We just drifted apart. So much that when I knew I should devote more time to making things work, maybe go to counseling, I didn't want to. Pam didn't, either."

"And that was that?"

"Pretty much. She and I have talked about it, believe it or not. We're both a lot happier now." He gentled his tone. "What I'm trying to say is that your ex was a fool. You're gorgeous and have a lot to offer." When she continued to stare at him in wonder, he waved a hand. "Maise, you're a famous mystery author. You're incredible."

"You're going to make me blush."

"If I do, I'll be pleased. You need someone to make you blush more often. It might as well be me." He grimaced. "I'm sorry. I bet I sound like a worn-out valentine. Am I coming on too strong?"

Feeling amused, she shrugged. "I'm not sure if you did or not. Right now I'm trying to figure out how our discussion about the menu turned into a Maisie pep talk."

He grinned. "Put that way, I don't know. I guess we should make up our minds, though." Seeing the server approach, he said, "Would you like more time?"

"No, I'm ready."

"Me, too." After the man told them about the specials, Maisie ordered the salmon, while

Clay ordered his steak. When they were alone again, he smiled at her. "Decision made."

"Yes. It took me so long to like salmon, I figured I might as well put all that work to good use."

He tilted his head. "Sorry, but I'm not following."

"Oh. Well, everyone always talks about how good it is for you. I never cared for it much, though. I found it too strong. But then, when a girlfriend invited me over for some kind of special salmon that she'd actually had flown in, I decided I'd better start liking it."

"And it was as easy as that?"

Feeling sheepish, she shook her head. "It wasn't easy like that at all. I had to try it until I liked it."

He laughed. "*That's* why you started eating salmon?"

"Yep. Now I choose salmon over steak. However, since I like it with butter or a glaze or even hollandaise on it, I don't know if it's a win in the health department, but I accomplished my goal. I really do like it now."

"I'd say that's a win."

Taking a sip of her sparkling water, she smiled again. "I was hoping you'd say that."

"This is nice, Maisie."

"I was just thinking the same thing." Honestly, she realized that she hadn't felt so charmed or been so relaxed in a very long time. Maybe not since she was thirteen.

He sipped his wine again. "So, are you ready to tell me how you started writing mysteries about a guy called Lawson Greer?"

"I am, as long as you promise to tell me when you get bored. I tend to go on and on about Lawson like he's a favorite uncle."

"I'm not going to get bored, Maisie."

The way he looked at her made her feel all flustered inside. It seemed her teenage crush was alive and well.

CHAPTER FOURTEEN

IT FELT LIKE an eternity had passed since she'd sat on the front porch of her house with Graham. If Vivian's life had been different, she'd have happily spent the majority of that time lazing on the couch, eating leftover Christmas cookies and watching old Midsomer Murders episodes on television.

She hadn't had days, or evenings, like that in a very long time.

Instead, after saying goodbye to Graham on the twenty-seventh, she'd cleaned the living and dining rooms and divided her time as best she could. She took Will to the movies, cleaned Graham's room and bath, did a bunch of laundry, and took down a few of the loudest Christmas decorations in the house. Finally, she did everything she could to prepare for the Vanderhavens' arrival.

The Vanderhaven family consisted of Donna and Frank—the grandparents—Evan, Kyle, Craig and Mimi—their four grown children—their spouses, and assorted grandchildren all under the age of sixteen. They'd arrived in a stream of vehicles late in the afternoon on the twenty-eighth.

Vivian was fairly sure she'd counted eighteen people at breakfast that morning, but she might have missed a baby. The Vanderhaven crew had booked the entire inn for several days, which was such a blessing.

Not only was their booking providing a healthy addition to her bank account, they were relatively easy guests. It turned out that each of the grown children was in charge of a day's activities, so the entire group was really only around for breakfast. The last two nights, they'd straggled in at different times. So far, all anyone had needed was some hot tea or coffee, or a fresh bucket of ice for one of the rooms.

Vivian had sent up Will with the ice bucket. He'd had so much fun talking to the family, she'd begun to wonder what had kept him.

Workwise, it almost felt like she was having her own vacation. She was used to preparing big breakfasts, and she'd baked many items in advance and frozen them two weeks ago, afraid that she would be overwhelmed by the group. It was a nice surprise to realize that she actually had time on her hands.

But, in the way things always went, her extra time happened to have some unanticipated consequences—which was that she now had far too much time to think about Graham.

After his big announcement about moving to Canada, Graham had declared that he was going to get ready for bed, because he planned to get back to the base early the next morning. Will had been dismayed and had even asked if Graham wanted to play a game of cards first.

Graham's expression had softened, but he shook his head, saying that he really couldn't.

The sergeant had been good to his word, too. Graham was gone by 6:00 a.m. He'd been wearing his uniform and had his phone in his hand when she'd hurried out of her room to see if he wanted a cup of coffee before he left.

He hadn't, claiming that there was a Starbucks on the way to the base that he liked to hit whenever he had a chance.

She had been disappointed for sure. Will's gloominess, however, was starting to feel unbearable. He'd been bored, listless and a bit of a handful while she'd been getting the house ready for the next guests.

It was obvious that his mood hadn't improved when he wandered into the kitchen right now. His hair was rumpled, there was a smudge of dirt on his cheek and she was pretty sure that his long-sleeved T-shirt was inside out. "What'cha doing now, Mom?"

"The same thing I was doing an hour ago," she said lightly. "I'm working on our dinner."

Will wrinkled his nose as if the chicken and broccoli casserole on the counter offended him. "How come we always have this?"

"Because we like it." And it was easy.

"I don't like it that much."

She focused on grating the last of the cheddar cheese for the topping. "It's been noted, but it's still dinner."

He folded his arms over his chest as he lifted his chin and glared at her—his favorite stance when he'd been four. "Why don't we ever go out to dinner, Mom? Maisie and Audrey go out all the time."

"They probably go out all the time because they don't own a B&B."

"I saw Audrey and Ziggy yesterday. Audrey went to Denver for the whole day yesterday."

"Uh-huh." She kept grating cheese.

"She said Maisie went skiing!"

"Did she, now?" More than once, they'd encouraged Vivian and Will to get out to the mountains more often. "Well, I hope Maisie had a good time."

Will sighed. "I bet she did. And I bet she isn't eating a chicken casserole for dinner tonight, either."

Vivian mentally counted to five. The last

thing she wanted to do was berate her son for being a little boy. Then she got to thinking that she might not be able to take off to either Denver or on a ski trip…but getting out of the house for a meal absolutely was possible.

"You know what? You're right." Reminding herself that the casserole could easily be saved until tomorrow night, she asked, "Where would you like to go out to eat?"

Will's eyes widened. "We can go out for dinner? Really?"

"Yes, *really*." Reaching out to ruffle his hair, she added, "You are exactly right, too. We don't go out to dinner very often. It's time we did."

"Maisie's gonna be really happy when I tell her."

"I bet," Vivian teased. Half speaking to herself, she murmured, "The Vanderhavens are doing fine, too. I don't think they'll be upset if I slip out for a while. So…what sounds good?"

"Tacos or chicken fingers."

"I think tacos sound terrific. We'll go to Acapulco Joe's."

Her little boy bounced on his feet. "Okay. When?"

"How about ten minutes? Go wash your hands and put on a clean shirt that is outside out."

"Can't I just switch this one?"

"Nope. That's the deal. If you want to go out to eat, you're going to look like a clean Will Parnell, not a grubby one. Clean hands, clean shirt and brush your hair."

"I'll be right back." Watching him run down the hall, Vivian smiled. She didn't have the heart to remind him to be considerate of their paying guests.

Not for the first time, Vivian wondered when she was going to decide that being home all the time just wasn't worth it. She might always be physically present for Will, but she was starting to realize that there were many other times when she was so concerned with their guests' needs that Will's were relegated to the back burner.

"Whatever you're feeling, take a deep breath."

Vivian turned in surprise to see Donna Vanderhaven watching her from the corner of the room. "I'm sorry. I didn't see you there."

Donna smiled softly. "You are the ultimate innkeeper, dear. So polite." Walking toward her, she added, "I promise, I wasn't eavesdropping—well, not on purpose. I was coming to ask you a question but didn't want to interrupt you two. It sounded like a pretty important conversation."

"You shouldn't have worried about that."

"I guess most guests don't?"

She had to be honest. "Some do, some don't. Most are very considerate of the fact that I'm a mother of a little boy, though." She mentally shook her head. "What may I help you with, Donna? Does anyone need more ice?"

"Actually, we were wondering if we could have a little birthday party in the living room this evening. Would you mind if we did that?"

"You're not going out?" She hoped she kept the dismay from her voice but doubted it.

"We are going out to eat, but we're going to come back and have cake, ice cream and such."

Vivian could practically feel her date with Will sail out the window. Oh, he was going to be so upset—and she wouldn't blame him. However, what was done was done.

Taking a deep breath, she tried to sound more composed than she felt. "Since your family has booked the entire inn, setting up the living room is no problem. What time is best for you?"

"No, dear. You don't understand." Looking at her intently, Donna added, "I wasn't asking you to plan a party or set it up. We're going to get the paper plates and drinks and things. I just wanted to see if you minded if we take over the main room. You don't need to be there supervising us, if you're okay with that."

Vivian was flummoxed. In the past, whenever she hadn't been able to be available for her guests, she had asked either her friend Sammie or one of her neighbors to help out. She'd never left guests completely alone at the inn.

Mimi, Donna's daughter, joined them just as Will scampered back with a bright smile on his face.

"Everything good, Mom?" Mimi asked Donna.

"I'm hoping so. It turns out our impromptu party is messing up a special date night." She tilted her head in Will's direction.

Mimi frowned. "Oh. Well, I suppose we could see if the restaurant will let us stay longer…"

Vivian took a deep breath. Though duty was telling her to put that chicken casserole in the oven and remind Will that the guests' needs had to come first…she couldn't. She just couldn't.

"There's no need to do that, Mimi. Will and I won't be gone long. Make yourselves at home, and you have my cell phone if there are any problems."

"Good choice, dear," Donna said. "Take it

from me, date nights with young men like your boy don't come around all the time."

Donna's words had merit, she couldn't deny that. But...what if something backfired? What if they were only saying the words but ultimately would hold her night out against her and decided to leave a bunch of horrible, one-star reviews? She'd heard horror stories from other innkeepers who'd lost clients just because of one carefully crafted terrible review.

"Mommy?"

She reached out and ruffled Will's hair. "Sorry, honey. I, um, I guess I was just thinking about something."

"Well, can we go?" He pulled at his red T-shirt. "See? My shirt is outside out. I'm ready."

Vivian met Donna's eyes before smiling back at her son. "If you're ready, I guess I'd better get ready, too. We'll be on our way as soon as I grab my purse and put on a coat."

"I'm gonna eat two tacos."

"Good for you, Will," said Donna.

"Thanks for the pep talk, Donna," she said.

"Anytime. Please don't worry, dear. Believe me, I've been where you are."

Wondering if that was really true, Vivian decided it didn't matter. What mattered was that for once she wasn't going to put her wants and needs to the side.

"Grab your coat, Will, I'll go warm up the car."

The women chuckled at her boy's enthusiasm, leaving Vivian feeling warmer than ever as she pulled on her coat, said a brief prayer that she wasn't making a huge mistake and finally walked out of her house. She wondered if one mother-son evening out had ever caused so much worry and drama.

CHAPTER FIFTEEN

"It's about time you joined us, Hopkins," Shane said as he parked his Bronco outside Acapulco Joe's. "All the guys were starting to wonder if you were ever going to take us up on our invites."

"Now you won't have to wonder anymore." Graham was used to their ribbing, especially since they had a point about him spending all his time either working or hanging out by himself. More than once, he'd been reminded that no one was going to treat him any differently if they saw he went out and had a good time every now and then.

Opening the door, he had to pause for a moment to acclimate himself. "Whoa."

"I know. It's great, right?"

Great wasn't exactly the word he'd use to describe the place. The Mexican restaurant in the heart of the Broadmoor area of Colorado Springs was an institution. He'd never been. Not only was he not one for going out, he'd also never acquired the love for Mexican food his Yank buddies seemed to be born with. As the blare of canned mariachi music assaulted his ears, he took in the pale stucco walls, red leather booths trimmed with green, the brightly colored Christmas lights draped over cacti and the huge mural of Acapulco Bay on one wall, complete with the famous cliff divers.

All in all, Graham thought the restaurant had the feel of a ride at Disney World. "Are you sure the food's good here?"

"We go here all the time, Sarge. Don't let the decorations fool you. The food's great." Shane's grin brightened. "Plus, there's Skee-Ball in the back."

Skeet ball? Now he was sure he'd ventured into a kids' version of a fine dining establishment. "Let me guess, you guys end up playing skeet ball, too."

"Well, yeah." Shane looked about to add something when the other guys called out to them.

"Sarge! You came!"

"Way to go!" another of his buddies said.

Feeling half the restaurant's clientele staring at him, Graham shrugged. "I told you I would."

"You said you'd try."

"And I did." Five other guys, one of whom

was a second lieutenant, were already seated at the table drinking beer. Of the seven of them, he and Shane were the highest-ranked members, though they'd all long ago elected to ignore rankings whenever they were out together. Graham was glad about that. He'd learned that good friendships mattered a whole lot more than a person's rank when it came down to it.

Just as he was about to take a seat, he caught sight of a familiar face. He froze, sure his mind was playing tricks on him.

But it wasn't. There, sitting in another booth across the room, was Vivian. He'd recognize that auburn hair and those warm brown eyes anywhere. He couldn't see who was sitting across from her, but he had a pretty good idea whom it might be.

"I'll be right back," he muttered to the guys.

"Sarge, what are you doing?"

"I see someone I know." He walked away, realizing belatedly that all his buddies were no doubt watching to see where he was headed. Oh, well. He supposed they'd now realize not only that he went out from time to time, but that he also knew people outside the base.

All that seemed to matter was that Vivian's expression had gone from surprise to wariness to happiness as he approached.

"Graham, I can't believe you're here," she said as she stood up to greet him.

"I was just thinking the same thing about you." Vivian was wearing a loose-fitting green sweater, jeans and suede boots. Gold hoops were in her ears, and she had on some kind of raspberry-tinted lipstick. She looked pretty. Realizing that she was dressed up for her date with her little boy, he smiled at Will. "Hey, buddy."

"Sarge! You're here, too!" Will's shocked expression was almost comical. The fierce hug he gave Graham was anything but that. It absolutely melted his heart.

Leaning down in front of the booth, he met Will's eyes. "It's good to see you, buddy."

"Did you know we were coming here?"

"Nope." Graham pointed to the six guys at his table. "Some guys from the base decided to get out tonight. I don't usually go out much, but it sounded like fun."

"We don't ever go out to dinner, but Mommy made an exit, even though the Vandersome-things are here."

Graham raised his eyebrows at Vivian. "An exit?"

Vivian smiled. "Allow me to translate. I made an *exception*, even though the Vanderhaven family booked the entire inn and are currently having a birthday party in the living room without any supervision."

He couldn't help but chuckle. "You're talking about them like they're some unruly teenagers."

"They might as well be." Still looking aggrieved, she added, "I could tell you stories about the things guests do. Even the nicest people have peculiar notions at times." She lowered her voice. "I really hope nobody sets my house on fire."

She sounded so serious, he found it difficult not to laugh. "I really hope that doesn't happen, too."

Looking chagrined, she said, "I know you think I'm overreacting, but I'm kind of not."

"I'm getting that impression."

Will scrambled back into his booth seat. "Mommy almost decided to stay home, but she'd promised me that we could go out."

When Graham met her eyes, she covered her face with one hand. "It's true, I did."

They looked so happy to be doing something so simple that Graham couldn't resist smiling back. "I'm glad you didn't cancel your night out."

"Me, too, 'cause we're seeing you," Will said. "Are you gonna sit with us? You can if you want, you know. I can scoot over."

"Thanks, but I can't, buddy. I can't abandon the guys I came with. Which means that I've got to go."

Will's face fell. "Oh."

"We understand," Vivian said quickly. "Thanks for saying hello."

Everything inside him was shouting to turn around and walk back to his friends. To remember that there was no future with her, so it was best to simply cut things off.

But he couldn't. For reasons he wasn't sure he even wanted to investigate, he couldn't simply walk away and pretend that he'd be okay with that.

So, he followed his gut and did what he should've done before he left the inn. "Can I have your phone number?"

"I'm sorry?"

"I only have the inn's number. You do have a private line, true?"

"Yes, of course."

"Then, could I have it, please?"

"Why?"

Vivian genuinely looked perplexed, which said a lot about how innocent she was—and how terrible his dating skills were. Obviously nonexistent. Aware that Will was listening to every word, Graham stepped a little closer, then went ahead and crouched in front of her.

"Because I want to be able to talk to you on the phone. And because I also want to see you again."

She worried her bottom lip. "Do you think that's wise? I mean, you're going to move."

"I think it absolutely is wise. Even though I'm going to move…we still can be friends, right?"

"Yes, I guess we can," she said slowly.

"Hopkins, order up!" Shane called out.

"I've really got to go. Give me your number, Vivian."

"Fine." She recited the numbers, and he punched them in. Right away, he called her. "Now you have my phone number, too," he said as he got to his feet.

"I guess I do." Vivian's smile was so sweet, he knew he'd made the right decision. He wouldn't have traded that gift for the world.

CHAPTER SIXTEEN

THEIR DINNER OUT had been fun but also kind of stressful, since Will seemed determined to peek at Graham and his air force buddies as often as possible. Graham had his back to them, but a few of the other airmen had definitely noticed her son's attention. A couple of them even waved.

Will's fixation on Graham was probably typical for a little boy. Graham and his buddies were all physically fit, exuded confidence and were talking and laughing loudly. Of course Will would want to watch them.

Unfortunately, Vivian had noticed everything about those guys because she'd been having a hard time looking away, too. At first she was embarrassed, but by the time she was halfway through her tacos, Vivian had reminded herself that her actions were normal, as well. After all, hadn't she used to do the same things when she'd been dating Emerson? There was nothing wrong with noticing an attractive man.

Vivian also noticed that the guys were good-heartedly teasing Graham about his tiny admirer. Probably about her, too, though she wasn't going to allow herself to go there. Her emotions were too raw where he was concerned.

After reminding Will that they had ice cream at home and so wouldn't need to go to the store and purchase a gallon, she drove them home—and couldn't help but breathe a sigh of relief when she saw that her house was still in one piece.

"Whew. No one burned the house down," she said.

"Mommy, you're silly sometimes."

"I think you're right. Sometimes I'm way too silly for my own good!" That was true when it came to both her worries about the Vanderhavens destroying her house…and with all things that had to do with Graham Hopkins.

Sure enough, when they entered the living room, the whole family was enjoying themselves. A couple of bottles of champagne had been opened, and a giant three-tiered cake was on the table, along with a bowl of ice and the remains of a gallon of vanilla ice cream floating on the top.

Everyone turned when they entered.

"Don't mind us," Vivian said. "We're just passing through."

"Will you stop long enough to have a piece of cake?" one of the women said. "We have plenty."

"More than plenty," one of the men added.

It was impossible to miss her son's look of longing. "What do you say, Will?" Vivian asked. "Do you have room for some ice cream and cake?"

"Uh-huh." When Vivian raised her eyebrows, he turned to the woman who'd offered dessert. "Please?"

"Come help me cut you a piece of cake," the man said. Will didn't hesitate.

"Vivian?" Donna asked as she picked up the knife. "Will you have some, too?"

It would have been awkward if she'd said no, so Vivian wouldn't have refused their kindness no matter what. However, the cake looked amazing, and spending a few minutes with the fun, happy family would be a good way to get her mind off one Canadian airman.

"Thanks. I'd love a slice." Turning to Will, who was watching Mimi put ice cream on his slice, she said, "Sit down on the floor in front of the coffee table, okay?"

A couple of the kids were already sitting there, and they immediately made way for him.

"Come join us over here, Vivian," Donna said.

She sat on the couch next to Donna and rested her plate on her lap. "So, who's the party for?"

"Me," Donna said. "It's my birthday."

"Really? I wish I would have known. Happy birthday."

The other woman's eyes were sparkling. "Thank you. I've always loved birthdays, but this one has been particularly good, since it's the first one in a while that all my family has been with me."

"We're all here," a high school–aged boy said in a dry tone. "The whole clan."

Donna laughed. "Brenden, it wouldn't be the same without every one of you."

As Brenden walked over to some of the other teens, Vivian took a bite of the cake. "Oh my gosh, is this good."

Donna grinned. "Feel free to moan in appreciation, if you'd like. I did."

"I'm tempted to do that, for sure. What kind is it?"

"White chocolate cake with a buttercream frosting and lemon cream filling. It's probably a thousand calories per slice, but it's worth every bite. At least to me." She winked. "It's my favorite."

"I can see why." She looked around the room. "Who made it?"

"We bought it at the Cake Place down the road. Do you know it?"

"I do, though I've never ordered a cake from there. They're really popular. Now I know why."

As the rest of the family broke off into groups and two more kids sat down next to Will, Donna said, "As you can see, we haven't been too rowdy."

Vivian could feel her cheeks heat with embarrassment. "I'm sorry I was so worried. Old habits die hard, I guess."

"No apologies necessary. I would probably be the same way." She crossed her legs. "Did you two have a good time at dinner?"

Glancing over at Will, who had started playing cards with some of the kids, she nodded. "We did." She opened her mouth, about to mention seeing Graham, but hesitated.

Donna raised her eyebrows.

"But we happened to see a man there I know. Will is very fond of him."

"Is he the man you're dating?"

"No. He was a guest here last week." Realizing that explanation didn't make much sense, she added, "He's Canadian, but he's stationed up at the air force base on Cheyenne Mountain. He…well, we hit it off."

"It sounds like he's the best of both worlds. An interesting Canadian who lives locally?" She sighed dramatically. "I bet he's handsome."

"He is. Very."

Donna lowered her voice. "So what's the problem? Didn't you just say that Will likes him?"

"Will likes him a lot. It's almost surprising how much. I've never seen him react like that to any man. Of course, I haven't really dated since his father passed away three years ago."

"That's promising, don't you think?"

She nodded slowly. "It would be, except for the fact that Graham could break his heart." Feeling even more torn, she added, "Donna, Graham has asked for a transfer. He wants to go back to Canada. And who can blame him? Colorado is far away from his family."

"I can blame him!" Donna teased. "You and Will are here…plus, it's not like Colorado Springs is a terrible place to be. It's gorgeous here. He can always fly home, right?"

"There's no sense wishing for him to change his mind. The paperwork has already been filed, and the move has been put into motion. It's going to happen."

"I'm so sorry. That's so hard."

"I don't know why I'm so upset. Or why I'm still thinking about him." Vivian took another bite of the cake. It still tasted just as luscious, but she'd lost her appetite. "Tonight, Graham asked for my cell phone number, and I gave it to him." She grimaced. "For a moment, it was just like I was back in high school and the cutest guy I knew was asking me out. I don't know what I was thinking."

"Probably that you want to talk to him again? Nothing wrong with that, right?"

Staring at Donna, she shook her head. "I'm overthinking everything, aren't I?"

"I didn't say that...but maybe." Looking around the room, Donna added, "I've been married a long time, and I've had the privilege of watching all of my children fall in love. Now, my oldest grandson has a serious girlfriend. If I've learned anything, it's that one doesn't go looking for love all that often. Most of the time love finds us."

"You're right."

"I know I am," Donna said with a chuckle.

As tempting as it was to stay a little longer, it was getting late. Will needed to get to bed, and her day would start before six like always.

She had a big breakfast to prepare for the Vanderhavens before they headed out.

Standing up, Vivian picked up her plate. "How may I help you all clean up?"

"Would you mind if we put the leftover cake in your refrigerator? If we could do that, it would help a lot."

"Of course. I'll go make sure there's room."

"That's it, then. We've already got it taken care of."

"Thanks for sharing dessert with Will and me. Thanks for the advice, too. I think I needed to hear some words of wisdom."

"Anytime, dear. I hope things work out."

Vivian simply smiled as she walked to the kitchen to shift a couple of items in the refrigerator. She wasn't sure if things were going to work out between her and Graham or not.

However, he had been completely right. There was nothing wrong with them being friends. Everyone could always use more of those.

All she needed to try to do was stay calm and not overthink everything. More than anything, she didn't want to be so hesitant around Graham that she regretted her behavior when he was gone.

After all, she already wished she had done a few things differently with Emerson.

She didn't want to be filled with regrets all over again.

CHAPTER SEVENTEEN

IT WAS AFTER TEN, and another day was almost done. Will was sound asleep, the Vanderhavens were essentially out of the living room and Vivian had taken a hot shower. She'd been half-heartedly reading a book on her e-reader when the phone rang.

"Graham?" she asked after a quick glance at the screen.

"It's me," he replied, his voice warm. "You sound surprised. Did you not think I'd call?"

"I don't know." She was tempted to admit all her doubts and insecurities, but sharing so much just seemed wrong.

After a pause, he said, "I didn't even think about the time. I know you get up early. Were you already asleep?"

"Oh, no. I was sitting in bed reading." Remembering all his friends at the restaurant, she said, "I'm surprised you're calling tonight. I thought you guys would be out for a while."

"Some of them are, but I called it a night."

He sounded a little annoyed with himself. "Did something happen?"

"Not at all. I just—well, I've always been kind of a loner. When everyone decided to go to some of the bars down on Tejon, I got an Uber home. I wasn't up for that."

"I guess we have that in common," she said. "I use the inn and Will as excuses to stay home, but I'm not one for going out to bars. I'm glad you called."

"I was going to wait to call until morning, but unless you want a call at oh dark hundred, I knew I'd have to wait until I had a free minute…which could either be at eight or noon or five o'clock tomorrow night."

Vivian smiled at the description. "Such is the life of an RCAF sergeant."

"Yep. I love my job, but not necessarily every single part of it. Anyway, I called for selfish reasons."

"Which are?"

"I wanted to make sure you weren't holed up in a Red Cross shelter because your inn burned down."

She giggled. "I guess I deserved that. I was a bit of a drama queen about leaving the inn with guests on the property. Everything is fine, though. The inn is intact, and I'm snug in my bed."

"I take it those crazy Vanderhavens didn't throw too wild of a party?"

Enjoying his light teasing, she chuckled again. "They'd settled down by the time I arrived. Actually, they were sipping champagne and eating the most amazing cake and ice cream. They offered Will and me some, which was so nice."

"Did you accept?"

"Yes to the cake, no to the champagne." Thinking about being in the room with that huge family, she added, "They really are the nicest group I've hosted in a while. Some of the kids even sat with Will while he ate his dessert. I hope I get to see at least some of them again."

"I'm starting to realize you must meet a lot of great people doing what you do."

"I do. But most are simply good clients, and I appreciate them because they aren't too loud or leave a big mess in their rooms. It's rare that I have guests who I wish would stay longer, or who I would enjoy sharing a meal with." *Like you, Graham*, she silently added.

"What's your tomorrow like?" he asked.

She ran a hand through her hair. "Busy. The group has to leave by eleven. By noon, the cleaning service will have arrived. They'll help me with the heavy stuff and all the laundry. I'm going to have to get some groceries delivered, too. While all that happens, I'll be cooking and finishing up the rooms. Then I have two more clients coming in tomorrow night."

"And it begins again."

She could hear the smile in his voice. "It's the nature of the job. What about you? Do you have a big week? Or is every day and week super busy?"

"Sunday isn't too bad. I'll be doing some PT, then mostly paperwork. Monday and Tuesday will be long, though. We've got some people visiting from Washington."

"That sounds not fun."

"That's because it isn't," he said with a note of humor in his voice.

"Well, I'll be thinking of you."

"I was hoping I could see you and Will sometime. Can I stop by on Wednesday afternoon? Will you guys be free?"

His questions were so sweet. Though she did have a flash of doubt, worrying about Will's heart, she couldn't say no. "We can be free. Would you like to come over here and go for a walk or something?"

"Actually, I thought we could go to the park. Will might like that. The weather is supposed to be nice until the weekend."

"There are a couple of nice parks nearby. That sounds perfect."

"I'll let you go, then. 'Night, Vivian. I'll see you then."

His words were nothing out of the ordinary. However, it was his warm, caring tone that sent a tremor down her spine. "Yes. Good night, Graham."

She could have sworn she heard him smile before he hung up. Which was ludicrous, of course.

But still, she held that feeling tight. It had been so long since a man had whispered goodnight in her ear. She wanted—no, needed—a moment to savor it.

However, minutes later, she forced herself to remember that no matter how much she liked him, Graham wasn't going to be around much longer. She couldn't get too attached—and she really couldn't allow Will to become too attached. She needed to shield him from further heartbreak, didn't she?

But was that even possible? Will might be a little boy, but he was his own person.

Frustrated with her ruminations, Vivian turned off her bedside light. Her shades were only partly drawn, letting in the moonlight and casting her bedroom in a soft glow. Comforted, she looked around the small room. For two months after Emerson had died, she'd slept in one of the guest rooms. Being in their bedroom alone had been too hard.

Eventually she'd gotten used to having a small space. When she remodeled, she'd helped the architect redesign a wing for herself and Will. Now they each had a small bedroom and shared one bath. A hallway led toward the kitchen. Vivian found it to be cozy.

Time had moved on. Soon, memories of Emerson's habit of leaving clothes all over the floor faded. Now, whenever she thought of her husband's messy habits, it only brought a smile to her face. Being able to remember without feeling the pinch of loss had been a big turning point.

She wondered if this new friendship with Graham was another one. Maybe her life was ready to be shaken up again.

She'd never really believed that everything happened for a reason. But maybe in this case, it was true. Graham Hopkins had entered her life at just the right moment. Even though he would one day drift out of her life again, he was giving her the opportunity to realistically consider being in a relationship again. No, that was putting it too plainly.

Graham was pushing her to one day fall in love again.

It still felt a little scary, but it made her excited, too. She'd love to one day have a second chance at love. She'd love that for Will, too. Memories were sweet, but they were a poor substitute for companionship.

Now all she had to do was wonder if she'd be able to go on dates with other men after Graham left.

She pushed back the nagging voice in her head that said Graham wasn't just anyone to her. He wasn't easily replaceable—not for her or for Will.

That might be true, but she'd long given up on counting on anything in her life to turn out the way she wished. Wishes and dreams were for children, not responsible single mothers.

She might not have learned a lot of things over the years, but she'd certainly learned that. In spades.

"I'M SO EXCITED for you to come home soon, Graham," his mother said over their FaceTime call.

"Me, too, Mom." He smiled at her, liking the way her short blond hair was a little wind-blown and Blue, their regal-looking older Weimaraner, was passed out on the couch next to her.

Dogs and his mother and his assorted siblings, aunts and uncles were *home*. Home was a happy place for him. It always had been, even when everything wasn't always happy.

They'd sure been through their fair share of rough patches, too. His father had passed away many years before, back when he and his sisters had been teenagers. So, that had been a rough time, but a few years after, his mother had found love again.

She'd eventually married Luke, an army vet turned salesman. They'd been married fifteen years before he'd gotten sick and died two years ago.

So now Mom was alone again, but his mother had such a positive way about her that Graham never thought of her as being lonely.

"Are you doing okay, Mom? Is Doug coming by?"

"He is, and so are Eileen and Kevin And so are my neighbors. You know I'm surrounded by people who care. You are the one we all worry about."

"No need for that, Mom. No one is even hinting about me getting deployed again. I'm perfectly safe in Colorado Springs."

"I'm not talking about work, Graham. You're so levelheaded and have so much experience, I know you're fine. I'm talking about your personal life."

Oh, brother. "It's fine."

"Don't brush me off. You know what I mean. I worry about you always being so alone. I don't want you to one day wake up with regrets."

"I hear what you're saying." When he'd been younger, he'd been shy and awkward. It had taken him months to get the nerve to speak to Kinsey, whom he'd eventually taken to prom. Now, although there were a lot of women in both the RCAF and the USAF, his relationships with them were strictly work-related.

He'd honestly started to wonder if he just wasn't cut out for relationships. Though he hadn't thought that his two deployments to Afghanistan had done him any harm, maybe they had and he'd just been unaware of it.

But now he realized he just hadn't met the right person. He'd been attracted to Vivian from practically the first moment he saw her. And Will? Well, he was great. Everything he'd imagined a little boy could be. There was just something about the two of them that tugged at his heartstrings. He found himself thinking about them all the time.

Even when he was leaving her side the night before, he'd been wondering when he could see her again.

"You know, my neighbor Jill has a friend with a divorced daughter about your age. Maybe we could plan something since you'll be back here soon."

Getting set up by his mother and her neighbor sounded rough. No, dating anyone but Vivian sounded rough.

"That's not necessary, Mom."

She continued on. "I know you think you don't have time for dating, but believe me, relationships are a good thing." Her voice brightened. "Kinsey's around, too, and she's apparently single. Maybe you two could catch up after all this time."

He mentally rolled his eyes. "All this time" was almost twenty years. He was a completely different person now. His deployments and various duties in the air force had changed him. He wasn't just older—he saw life through a different lens. There was no way he wanted to go back in time—even if it was possible.

When his mother began to speak about coffee dates, Graham knew it was time to interrupt, fast.

"I just started seeing someone here."

"You have?"

"I have."

"Really?"

It was embarrassing to see how amazed his

mother looked—even on his phone's small screen. "Yes, really. Her name is Vivian. She's the woman who owns the inn I went to on Christmas Day. She's a widow and has a six-year-old boy who's adorable."

His mom blinked. "My goodness. Well, how did you start dating her?"

Thinking about Will, he grinned. "It's a long story, but a good one. I'll share it with you when I see you in January."

"Are you sure you should be dating someone right now? Don't forget that you'll be moving back here soon."

"I didn't forget, Mom. But Vivian's special."

Some of the enthusiasm faded from her eyes. "Oh. Well, of course. Well, I'll look forward to hearing all about it."

Glancing at the clock, he said, "I've got to go. Love seeing you on FaceTime, Mom. You look great."

"I could say the same thing about you." She tilted her head to one side. "Come to think of it, I don't think I've seen you smile so much in some time."

After they disconnected, Graham looked in the mirror at his reflection and wondered if he did look different.

Of course, he thought he looked the same, but he couldn't deny that he felt different. Almost as if everything in his life had shifted into the right place.

At long last.

CHAPTER EIGHTEEN

AFTER THEIR LOVELY DINNER, Clay had flown home and Maisie had returned to her usual routine. She took Ziggy for walks, worked on her book, went out to dinner with a couple of her girlfriends and visited with Audrey when their schedules coincided.

All in all, it was her usual well-run, rather stress-free life. It was everything she'd ever wanted back when she and Jared were so unhappy together.

But now it was obvious that her regimented, very calm regimen was far from perfect. Actually, it was kind of boring.

She was stewing on that when she saw Vivian and Will out in the front yard. When Vivian greeted her with a wave and a smile, she and Ziggy walked over to join them.

"Hi, Maisie!" Will said. "No one's inside. Can I take Ziggy into the house for a little bit?"

She knew Will would likely pet the beagle in front of the fireplace. "Of course."

When Will knelt down beside Ziggy, she smiled at Vivian. "I can't wait until Will gets older. I'll have to hire him to pet sit for me whenever I go out of town."

"Audrey doesn't like taking care of him?"

"She does fine, but Ziggy prefers Will." Ziggy was currently gazing up at Will like he was his favorite person in the world. Will was scratching him behind his ears.

"I can see why. He's crazy about that dog of yours. What's new? Are you still working on the same book?"

"I am. It's going slow, but I have time to figure things out. Especially since Clay is out of town."

Vivian shook her head in wonder. "I can't believe you two have hit it off so well so fast."

"Even though we weren't exactly strangers, it's caught me off guard, too, but I'm not going to complain. If I've learned anything over the years, it's that wonderful things don't come along all the time. I don't take it for granted."

"I wish I was more like you. I find myself getting scared about losing control sometimes."

Vivian's phrasing caught her by surprise. "You mean in relationships?"

"Maybe. Or maybe just in life." She bit her bottom lip, then continued. "Emerson lived life the opposite way I do. I guess I'm afraid that if I take more risks, I could get hurt."

Thinking of all the years she'd wasted with Jared, telling herself that she didn't deserve to expect anything better, Maisie sighed. "For what it's worth, I've discovered that it's just as easy to get hurt when one is cautious."

"I never thought of things that way." After glancing at Will again, she added, "You're right."

"I don't think you've given yourself enough credit, dear. Look at your successful inn. That was a risk, and you're doing a good job with it."

Vivian studied Maisie for a long moment, then blurted, "I'm starting to really like Graham. He's going to move away, though. He's going to work at a base up in Canada."

Maisie was surprised, but not shocked. "I suppose that's inevitable. I read in the paper that most airmen are only stationed here for a few years at a time. What are you going to do?"

"What do you mean?"

"Well, you know…are you going to follow him?"

"Of course not."

"You sound so sure."

"I am." She waved a hand. "I mean, my inn

is here. And so is Will's school. And…and a lot of other things."

"Ah."

"You don't sound like you agree."

"It's not my place to agree or disagree. It's just that, well… I've learned that good things don't come along all the time." She grinned. "And good men really don't. If you decide that Graham is one of those good men, you might want to think about what will make you happiest in life."

"I don't think I can choose. Not yet, anyway."

"I have a feeling that when it is time to make a choice, you'll know what to do." Feeling like she'd probably dispensed more than enough free advice, Maisie said, "Now, I think I better get back to work. Ziggy looks sufficiently worn-out."

"Will does, too." Vivian smiled. "Hey, Maisie?"

"Yes, dear?"

"Thanks for the free advice."

"Anytime, dear. Actually, I think our chat helped me, too."

Later, as she was sitting on the couch with her laptop, Maisie realized that all the things she'd said to Vivian had been in her heart. She did need to take some chances.

She was going to start thinking about shaking up her life a bit. It was time.

GRAHAM HAD BEEN able to reschedule his shift so he could get off at two instead of four. When he'd called the night before, he'd asked if they could leave a little earlier.

After reaching out to Maisie to see if she could check on the guests once or twice, Vivian told him that they could definitely do that.

Since she'd also warned Graham that Will wasn't big enough to do a real hike in Cheyenne Canyon or in the state park nearby, they'd elected to go to a small neighborhood park for their first activity.

In truth, her six-year-old probably could have handed most trails at the state park, but Vivian wanted to protect both Will and Graham's efforts. She'd learned that everything could be going just fine, but all it took was one slip or blister and their good time disintegrated into tears. She would've hated it if Graham went to so much trouble just to think he'd done everything wrong.

Things were going better than she'd anticipated, though. It turned out that Graham loved dogs and liked to point out the different breeds to Will, and Will was soaking up both the attention and the information like a sponge.

"There's another beagle, Graham!" Will announced as he led Graham and Vivian on the trail around Quail Lake.

"He's a cute one," Graham said. "And there's a French bulldog, too."

"We're seeing lots of dogs. More than ever before," Will said.

Vivian shared a smile with Graham. Thanks to Graham, her little boy had suddenly become interested in all things dog. It was cute. Adorable, really. Except that Vivian didn't want a dog, and she was pretty sure that was what was going to come next. She was going to disappoint Will—and he was going to take Graham's leaving even harder.

"You're learning lots of different breeds. I'm proud of you."

Her boy puffed up his chest. "Thanks. Tell me again about your dog, Blue."

"Blue is a Weimaraner. She's grayish blue and has blue eyes."

"And a stubby tail."

"That's right. You've got a good memory."

"Mom says I'm good about remembering some stuff, but I forget about other things." Will looked back at her. "Right, Mom?"

"Right. You're good at remembering all kinds of information about dogs but not as good at remembering to give me your papers from school to get signed." Keeping her voice light, she teased, "I don't know why that is."

"It's because thinking about papers isn't fun."

"But still important." Seeing that Will was about to argue just to keep Graham's attention, Vivian pointed to Graham's backpack. "How about we take a break? Poor Graham has been carrying that heavy backpack for almost an hour."

"Are you tired of walking, Graham? Is it really heavy?"

"I'm good, but your mom is right. It's time to take a break."

Looking up ahead, Will brightened. "Guess what? The park is right here. We could stop here if you wanted. You could even sit down."

"That's a perfect spot. Lead the way, buddy," Graham said.

As Will hurried ahead, Graham waited for her to catch up. "He's a lot of fun, Vivian."

"I had no idea that he liked dogs so much. I'm sorry if he drove you crazy with all the questions."

"Questions don't bother me none. Besides, I think all boys like dogs."

"Only boys?"

He laughed. "You're right. I'm sure all kids do."

"And maybe certain sergeants, as well," she teased.

"I can't deny that. A dog slept on the end of my bed every night until I entered the air force. When they give me a desk job, the first thing I'm gonna do is go to the shelter and get another dog."

"You really do miss having one around, don't you?"

"Yeah. Dogs make a home. At least for me, they do." He searched her face. "What about you?"

"I like pets."

"What kind? Cats, maybe?"

She laughed at how stilted his voice had become. "I can tell right there that if I said I was a cat person, our friendship might be over."

"It might be in jeopardy," he joked. "But seriously, it's okay if pets aren't your thing. I get it."

"No, they are. My family had a dog when I was little. He was a black Labrador named Cooper. He was terrific."

Thinking about all the years since, she added, "My husband liked animals but didn't want a pet. He was the type of person who could go and go from six in the morning until ten at night. He wasn't one for staying at home much."

"Which would've made owning a pet hard."

She nodded, glad he understood. "After we had Will, Emerson was home more, but…" Vivian paused, trying to be honest without sounding bitter or selfish. "I realized that having a pet was going to be just one more thing to take care of." She was proud of herself for leaving off *by myself.*

"For you, huh?"

Graham had obviously read between the lines. That had been exactly how things with her and Emerson had been. He'd been all about fun and entertainment and making plans. She'd stayed behind the scenes and kept everything running.

She swallowed. "Anyway, after Emerson was gone and I got back on my feet, I started doing research about what it would take to own an inn or B&B. I soon realized that having a dog was going to be a tough sell. A lot of people don't want a dog around for various reasons."

"They're allergic."

"Exactly. Or they're afraid of dogs. Or don't want pet hair on their things. I can't blame them for that. One day I'd like to have a pet, though."

"One day sounds like the right time."

Graham looked at her with such a warm expression, Vivian felt another burst of longing flow through her. He was so perfect. He liked to hang out at home. He didn't frequent bars all the time. He liked dogs and her son. She could totally imagine the three of them with their "one day" dog going on lots of walks in parks. He would be doing it because he wanted to, as well. Not because she'd nagged or out of guilt because he hadn't been around, but because that was where his interests were. With his family.

"Mom, you're supposed to let Graham sit down, remember?"

Startled, she looked down at Will, who was staring at her like she'd made a huge mistake. "Of course. Graham, where would you like to sit?"

He pointed to a spot a few yards away. "How about one of those picnic benches? I have something inside my pack to show you both."

Will's eyes got big. "What?"

"Come with me and find out."

When they got reached the table, Graham easily shrugged off his backpack. When it landed with a *thunk*, Vivian realized that it was a lot heavier than she'd imagined. She totally should have encouraged him to take it off earlier. "What's inside that thing? Rocks?"

"Nope." As Will crawled up on his knees on

the table's attached bench, Graham unzipped a couple of compartments.

To her surprise, he pulled out a small soft-sided container from the biggest compartment, a thermos and three paper cups. "I stopped by the kitchen this morning and got some oatmeal cookies from Cook. I put together some hot chocolate, too."

Will stared at everything like he'd just pulled out a handful of Christmas presents. "You've been carrying all that this whole time and I didn't even know it?"

Graham grinned at him. "That's because this was a surprise. Are you surprised?"

"Uh-huh."

"Good. Are you two ready to have some?"

"I am," Vivian said. "I was just wishing that I had something warm to drink. It feels chilly when we're not walking."

He held her gaze for a moment. "I know. You don't have on a very thick coat, either. I was getting a little worried about you."

There it was again: his easy, casual reference to her needs. And yet again, she was reveling in the attention. She really needed to get ahold of herself.

Feeling her cheeks heat, Vivian busied herself with the thermos. She unscrewed the top, smiled at the steam that rose from the open container and then filled all three cups.

Just as Will was about to take a sip, Graham rested his hand on the boy's back. "Wait. We're not done."

"There's more stuff in your pack?"

"There is. Because hot chocolate isn't too good without these," he said as he opened up a Ziploc bag with miniature marshmallows. "Do either of you want some?"

"Can I, Mom?"

"Of course."

Gingerly, Will plucked out six and put them in his cup. Unable to pass up the treat, she placed a couple in her cup, too. "You thought of everything. This is wonderful, Graham."

He looked pleased by her words but shook them off. "It's nothing. Just cookies and hot cocoa."

"Still, it's very sweet. Thanks for going to so much trouble for us. It's really nice of you. Right, Will?"

"Uh-huh." Will grinned.

"Thanks for coming to the park with me." Graham looked away. It was obvious that he was uncomfortable with the attention. Just as he did, a scruffy-looking tan-and-white dog trotted over. "Hey, buddy. Who do you belong to?"

The dog just stared up at him and wagged its tail.

"Look, Mom. This dog wants to be our friend."

She nodded. "Or he wants our cookies."

"Butch, here!" A woman who looked about ten years older than Vivian hurried over. "I'm sorry. Every time I take off Butch's leash, he runs off."

"Can I pet him?" Will asked.

"Of course, dear. Butch loves to make new friends."

Will tentatively petted the fluffy dog on the head, then when Butch stretched his neck for a better rub, giggled and petted him some more.

"He likes you, dear."

"I think so, too."

Graham motioned to a pair of German shepherds heading their way. "There's a lot of other dogs around, ma'am. Might want to be careful about that."

"I agree," she said as she clipped back on the leash. "Sorry for the interruption. I guess Butch here thought your family's picnic looked too good to pass up."

"Oh, we're not a family," Will said, his attention still on Butch. "My mom and I are on a date with Graham."

The woman's eyes widened as she smiled. "I'd say it's going well."

As embarrassed as she was, Vivian couldn't help but chuckle. "I'd like to think so."

After the woman wandered away, Butch in her arms, Will grabbed a cookie. "Can we come to the park again, Graham?"

"It's up to your mom."

As much as she wanted to agree instantly, Vivian forced herself to think of the future. "I'm sure you're really busy, Graham."

"I'm not too busy to hang out at the park."

Practically feeling Will's hope, she gave in. It was what she wanted, anyway. "Then, it's a yes for me, too. This has been a lot of fun." She took a bite of cookie so she wouldn't say anything more, but she couldn't deny that it sure felt like a perfect date.

Will gave a little whoop. "I'm gonna go look at those rocks over there, Mom. I think I just saw a chipmunk."

"All right. Stay close, though."

As Will ran off, Vivian glanced at Graham. He was sipping his drink and looked completely relaxed. He didn't look as if he'd been offended by the woman's presumptuous comment about their date going well, either. Actually, it looked as if he was pleased about the whole afternoon.

She wasn't sure if it made the afternoon better or just more bittersweet.

CHAPTER NINETEEN

IT WAS ALMOST three in the afternoon, and Maisie was sure she'd been staring at the same paragraph for a whole hour. Usually, she would have given up and stopped writing for the day, but she'd promised herself that she would finish the chapter she was working on before she took Ziggy for a walk in the park.

Unfortunately, even that bit of a bribe hadn't made much difference in her productivity. She was still stuck, Ziggy was still gazing out the window wistfully and her detective was still bumbling around instead of being smart, devious and charming.

After deleting the last sentence she'd written, she glared at the lone paragraph on the page. "What has gotten into you, Lawson?" she demanded. "You've got two dead bodies, five suspects and a dinner date with Priscilla at seven. She's going to be ticked if you stand her up again. Figure out what to do next!"

Unfortunately, nothing came to mind. She

could practically feel her usually gallant detective glaring at her in annoyance. "Argh!"

Audrey poked her head in the office. "Maisie, what in the world?"

"Sorry. I can't seem to finish this stupid paragraph."

"That's why you're yelling at the computer?"

"I was yelling at Lawson."

Audrey walked closer. "You were yelling at your made-up detective."

"Yes."

Glancing at the mostly blank screen, she chuckled. "I don't think that's helping much."

"You're right. It isn't. Not a bit."

"Maybe you should call Uncle Clay."

Feeling her cheeks heat, Maisie stood up. "I don't know why you think calling him would help."

"Because he's been gone for almost a week and you miss him."

"Audrey, he and I aren't like that."

"Of course you are," she replied. "You smile more when he's around, you see him every night and you practically wake up singing, you're so happy."

Now she was thoroughly embarrassed. "I haven't been acting that silly."

"Who says it's silly? I think it's really sweet," Audrey said. "You two really like each other."

"You think he feels the same way as I do?"

"I know he does. Uncle Clay and I are close, but he isn't coming over all the time because he wants to see his niece, Maisie."

"I guess you're right." Maisie paused. She didn't want to make things awkward for Audrey, but she needed some advice. "Everything with Clay has been so good, I keep waiting for the other shoe to drop."

"Do you think he's not being honest or something?"

"It's not that. It's more like I remember how good things were between Jared and me before it all fell apart."

"But Jared cheated on you."

"Yes."

"You don't really think that's something my uncle would do, do you?"

"Of course not. I just can't help but think that something is going to go wrong." She forced herself to admit her worst fears. "I'm worried he's suddenly going to think that I'm not worth his time."

"Oh, Maisie. You were sure hurt bad, weren't you?"

Not wanting to admit it, she said, "I'm better now."

"If you don't want to call my uncle right now, I think you should do the next best thing. Go take Ziggy for a walk."

"You're right." After clicking a few buttons on her computer, she said, "I've got to get out of this room. We're headed to the park. Want to come?"

"I would, except I have to get ready. I have a date tonight." She beamed.

"Anyone I've met?"

"Nope. It's another first date."

"You are the queen of first dates."

"They're the best kind! Everything is shiny and new."

"I always considered them to be awkward and stressful."

Audrey gave her a quick hug before walking out of the room. "That, Maisie, is why it's good you have Uncle Clay."

Those words were still ringing in her ears when she was walking Ziggy around the park fifteen minutes later. Ziggy's tail was up, his beagle nose close to the ground, and he was close to quivering, he was so happy to be outside on the sunny day.

Maisie realized her mood had lifted, too, especially when she spotted Vivian, her son and that handsome dark-haired man her neighbor had been spending time with.

It looked like Vivian was taking some chances, too.

"Hi, Maisie! Hi, Ziggy!" Will called out.

She waved and let Ziggy pull her toward the trio. "It looks like I'm not the only person out enjoying today's sunshine," she said as she approached.

"We've been looking at dogs and eating cookies and drinking hot chocolate," Will said importantly. "Graham, this is Ziggy."

Graham crouched down next to Will to pet the beagle. Ziggy, of course, wagged his tail and looked delighted by the attention.

Maisie smiled at Vivian. "It's good to see you out and about, dear," she whispered.

"Thank you," Vivian mouthed back. After glancing at the males to make sure they were still focused on the dog, she added, "I'm not sure what's going to happen in the future, but I'm going to try to stop worrying so much."

"That is a good plan. I'm proud of you."

After lingering for another few minutes, Maisie said goodbye. As she and Ziggy started walking, she thought about Vivian's words... and realized her fictional detective would have said the same thing.

"That's it, Lawson," she muttered to herself. "You need to start taking some chances, zero in on some suspects—beginning with that fishy guy you spied in the corner of the library." She could practically see Lawson tip his hat in her direction as she and Ziggy turned the corner and headed home.

It appeared she was going to be able to get that chapter done today after all.

CHAPTER TWENTY

VIVIAN WAS STILL thinking about that when
Graham stopped by again the next day. When
the front door opened, she'd been sure it was
one of her guests. But then, there he was, gorgeous in his uniform.

Two women in their twenties who'd been
lingering in the sitting room did a double take.
Vivian didn't blame them. Graham really was
that handsome.

She loved that he didn't spare those women
a second glance. His focus was entirely on her.
She could practically feel the warmth from his
gaze on her skin.

"Hi," she said inanely after he strode to her
side.

"Hi, Vivian." He smiled again.

She was tempted to reach for him. If not a
hug, then at least to curve her hand around his
forearm. Just for a second, just to touch him.

Instead of doing that, she smiled a little ner-
vously. "What's going on?"

"I had an early shift this morning." He

rolled his eyes. "Most of the time my team is terrific and we work seamlessly. This morning that wasn't the case. When I realized I was about to freak out on practically every person in the room, I knew I needed a break." Looking pleased with himself, he added, "I told my lieutenant that I was taking an hour."

"He let you?" She didn't know anything about military life, but she hadn't thought Graham could go off base whenever he felt like it.

He chuckled. "I'm a master sergeant. He knows better than to tell me no for something like that. Besides, I think he was going to do the same. Sometimes, you've just gotta take five."

"Well, I'm happy you came by. Would you like something to eat?"

"Nah, I just wanted to talk to you. And to tell you that I happened to see your neighbor Maisie this morning when I was out running. We were both over at Meadows Park."

"Oh? She didn't tell me that."

"That's probably because she knew that I wanted to be the one to tell you that I asked her to babysit Will tonight."

She gaped at him. "You did what?"

"Don't be upset. All I want to do is take you out to dinner. We'll be gone for two hours.

Three, tops." He folded his hands behind his back. "What do you think?"

She was feeling flattered but caught off guard, too. "I might have been out of the dating game for a while, but I'm pretty sure you're supposed to ask me to dinner and then wait for me to accept before discussing childcare options."

Some of the light in his eyes faded. "It seems I made a crucial error in judgment."

She might have further explained that it was up to her to determine who watched Will, but she couldn't fault his logic. Maisie was close to Will and completely responsible.

Plus, it wasn't like she didn't want to go out with Graham. She absolutely did. "I wouldn't go quite that far, Sergeant, but I would've liked to have been asked first."

"You're right. Dates are supposed to happen in that order. All I can say is that I just wanted to take some of the worry away for you."

"You also took the option of saying no away," she pointed out.

"No, I didn't. You always have a choice, Vivian. Is that what you want to do? Tell me no?"

She didn't. Honestly, the idea of going out with him alone sounded romantic and fun. She'd love to simply be a girl on a date with a handsome, sweet guy for a few hours. "Graham, did you really just happen to run into Maisie? You, um, didn't happen to stop by her house and knock on her door, did you?"

"I promise. I was out for a run and actually recognized Ziggy before her. We got to talking, and one thing led to another." He sighed. "Vivian, in my defense, navigating around problems is what I do. Sometimes I feel like half my job is trying to smooth as many obstacles out of my superior officers' schedules as I can in order for them to get things done. When I had the opportunity to remove a childcare worry for you, I took it."

Vivian went back to washing dishes, but she couldn't deny that Graham had made a good point. She definitely would have jumped on the fact that she didn't have a babysitter in order to say no.

But now she did…and it was only for a couple of hours…and she knew that Will not only liked being around Maisie, Audrey and Ziggy, but he really liked Graham. He would probably be very happy that his mom was spending more time with him. Though she was still dreading Will's eventual broken heart, she was starting to realize that it might not be right to put that first every single time. Besides, there was every possibility that she and Graham might discover that they weren't as compatible as they'd originally thought they were—and it would be best to find that out sooner than later.

All she had to do was make sure that Graham knew what he was getting into.

"Graham, I feel like you should know something. I want to be completely honest with you."

His smile vanished. "All right."

"I haven't gone on a date since Emerson died. Not a real one, anyway. I'll probably be awkward." Thinking that was already the case, she added, "I mean even more awkward."

"Good. I'll probably be awkward, too, since that seems to be my normal way."

"What time do you have Maisie booked for?"

"Six thirty." His voice softened. "Does that mean you're thinking about it?"

She could say she was just thinking about it, but that wasn't fair. She didn't want to play games with him. "No, it means that I am saying yes."

A slow smile lit his face. "Thank you."

"No, thank you. I'm sorry that the first thing I did was act offended that you tried to make sure my child was taken care of."

"What kind of food do you feel like? Steak? Seafood? Italian? Mexican?"

"I feel like anything that I don't have to make or clean up."

"I'll surprise you, then. I'll pick you up at six thirty. I know it's kind of early, but I'm usually starving by then."

"It's perfect. I'll touch base with Maisie. I'm looking forward to it, Graham."

"Same." Looking pleased, he bent down and lightly brushed his lips on her cheek. "See you tomorrow."

AT SIX FIFTEEN that evening, Vivian was sure that agreeing to a date with Graham had been the worst idea in the world. It turned out that she had no cute date clothes, whatever those were. All she knew was that they weren't her jeans and sweaters, and they weren't exactly the wool slacks and sensible shoes she wore as the owner of a B&B, either.

"I have nothing that's sexy," she said out loud.

Will, who had been lying on her floor, playing a game on her iPad, glanced up at her. "What did you say, Mom?"

Oh, for heaven's sakes. "Nothing, Will. I was just mumbling to myself."

"Are you ready yet? Maisie said Graham is gonna be here soon."

"I still need a couple of minutes."

Her son walked into her bathroom, saw her in just a T-shirt and underwear, and wrinkled his nose. "Mom, you've gotta get dressed."

"I realize that." She motioned with her hands. "That's why you need to get out of here. Maisie said she was going to order a pizza. Go see if it's on the way."

When he darted off, she sent up silent thanks for pizza—and the fact that having it was still a special occasion for Will—and finally made a decision. She had some nice jeans that she could wear with her chunky-heeled black leather boots, she could keep her T-shirt on and add a black wool blazer.

She was staring at her silver jewelry and trying to decide how much was too much when Maisie knocked on her open door.

"I've been sent in to see if you were dressed yet," she joked.

Vivian chuckled. "I'm guessing he told you about my underwear–and–T-shirt outfit?"

"I'm afraid so, dear." Looking her over, Maisie smiled. "You sure clean up good, though. You look fantastic."

"Thanks." Looking at herself in the mirror, she gathered her hair into a ponytail and held it in one hand. "What do you think? A ponytail or down?"

"Down. You have gorgeous hair. Might as well show it off."

She shook it out and popped on a long, chunky necklace and a cuff bracelet. "I think I'm finally ready."

"I'd say so, too…if you take a deep breath and try to relax."

Vivian breathed in and out. "Trying. Thanks again for watching Will, Maisie."

"Of course, dear. Now try and have fun."

"Mom, Graham's here!"

She hurried out before Will told Graham all about how she'd been standing around in her underwear.

"I'm here," she said, coming down the stairs.

Graham turned, quickly scanned her outfit and smiled. "Yes, you are."

Every bit of her kind of buzzed—he was looking at her so intently. It made her feel even more self-conscious. "I hope I didn't keep you waiting. Am I late?"

"No. But I wouldn't have cared if you were." She smiled at him, then realized she was probably acting like a fool. With a witness, too! Feeling her cheeks heat yet again, she met Maisie's eyes.

Maisie grinned and gave her a thumbs-up.

"Are you ready?" Graham asked.

"Yes. I just need to find my purse."

"It's here, Mom." Will lugged it over. "Now go, 'cause pizza's on the way."

"Be good." She bent down and kissed him on the forehead.

"I will. 'Bye!"

Straightening, she said, "Maisie, I have my cell phone if you need anything. And I put the hospital's number on the counter, too."

"Good to know. Thanks."

It was obvious that her neighbor was trying hard not to laugh at her. "I guess I'm ready, Graham."

"I'll have her home before nine, Maisie. 'Night, Will."

Finally, they were out the door. She saw he drove a tan, older-model Jeep Cherokee. He opened the door for her, and she climbed in.

When he closed it and walked around to the other side, she realized that the inside of the vehicle smelled like him. Taking advantage of the time of year—since it was already dark at half past six—she inhaled and closed her eyes, simply enjoying the rarity of being surrounded by his scent.

He climbed inside. "I have to say, Vivian, your boy cracks me up."

"Oh?"

"Nothing's off-limits. He was so cute, the

way he told me all about you standing in your bathroom, trying to figure out what to wear."

She felt her cheeks flush. "He told you about that?"

He winced. "Uh-oh. I guess I shouldn't have brought that up?"

"It's embarrassing, but it is the truth."

"It was flattering for me. It also made me feel a lot better. I realized that I have gym clothes and uniforms. Not a lot of date clothes. I need to step up my game."

And with that, she completely relaxed. "I thought the same thing."

"To be honest, you could have worn anything, and I would still think you look great." He grinned again. "All I see is you."

And...there went her heart. Fluttering like a hummingbird in her chest.

CHAPTER TWENTY-ONE

IT WASN'T FAIR. Just minutes before he exited his truck, Graham had reminded himself that he and Vivian should only be friends. He was moving, she was not, and there was nothing either of them could do about that.

In addition, if he wasn't careful, three hearts were going to get hurt: his, Vivian's and Will's. He needed to make sure that he kept that little boy's vulnerability in mind at all times. The little guy had been through too much for Graham to give him false hope or send him mixed signals.

He'd felt pretty good about his decision to not push for anything more with Vivian. He'd felt good about all his reasons behind it as well. They made a lot of sense.

And then he'd shown up at her place, she'd come down the stairs and his heart had practically stopped.

Vivian had looked absolutely beautiful. Even more gorgeous than usual. And there was something about knowing that she'd gone to so much trouble for him that made him want to pull Vivian into his arms and kiss her until they couldn't see straight.

He was always the steady one. The middle child. He'd been the kid who did his best to get along with everyone. Growing up, he hadn't been all that good-looking. A bit on the skinny side and a little late on his growth spurt, too. He'd never been the kid the other guys picked on, but he hadn't been the one who was sought after, either—not by the coaches at his high school, and not by the girls.

All that had changed when he'd gone into basic training. He'd developed some muscles, then worked out and got even more. He'd grown into his voice, and his steady, somewhat sedate personality suddenly became a plus. Now he was a popular master sergeant because he rarely got flustered.

But he wasn't flashy.

All that explained why discovering that Vivian had tried so hard to make a good impression meant the world to him. It wasn't something that he was used to.

Now, as he sat across from her at the restaurant, watching her savor every bite of her cranberry–white chocolate tart, Graham was starting to wonder if he'd ever be able to go back to keeping her firmly in the friend zone.

"What?" she asked, then placed a hand over her mouth. "Oh, no, do I have something in my teeth?"

"Not at all." When she still looked unsure, he said, "I…well, I was just thinking about how nice this evening was." He mentally groaned. *Nice* was not anywhere close to how she looked. "I mean, I don't go out to nice dinners like this very often." As in never.

"I don't, either." She laughed. "Did you hear that lie? You already know that I don't go out without Will *at all*."

"Maybe that means it's time we did something about that."

"Maybe…"

Graham knew he was playing with fire, but he couldn't seem to help himself. His brain felt mixed up, like he wasn't sure what he wanted.

Or maybe it was that he suddenly wanted too much.

"I can't eat another bite." She looked down at her tart with a guilty expression. "Are you sure you don't want to try a bite of this?"

"I'm sure. But I bet you can take it home if you'd like."

She shook her head slowly. "I have a feeling this is the kind of thing that is meant to be savored in the right situation. Back home, when it's encased in a Styrofoam container?

It's just going to be one more thing laden with too many calories that I should avoid."

"I'll get the check, then."

When they were walking to his Jeep, he noticed that the ground had a light layer of frost on it. He reached for her elbow. "Do you mind if I help you? You're in those fancy boots."

"Oh. Thank you."

It felt only natural to move his hand from her elbow to around her waist while his other hand took her arm. It might have been his imagination, but he was pretty sure Vivian leaned closer to him and even relaxed a bit.

He hoped that was the truth, because that was how he was feeling. He wanted to be closer to her, because she made him feel comfortable in his own skin. With Vivian, he wasn't trying to be someone he wasn't. She seemed to be perfectly fine with the man he was.

After he helped her into the truck, he let himself in his side and warmed up the engine. "I'll pull out in a minute or two, Vivian. I've learned the hard way that it's easier to let this old girl take a minute in the cold."

"I don't mind. I was just looking at the stars."

He peered through the windshield. "Not as many as usual."

"Since you're up on Cheyenne Mountain, I bet you're used to seeing even more."

"There's some precipitation in the air, so it's not nearly as clear as usual. But the sky is pretty. It always is here."

"Did you grow up with gorgeous, clear skies in Windsor?"

"We were on the northern edge of Lake Erie. I grew up with a healthy appreciation for humidity in the summer and lake-effect snow."

She chuckled. "I never thought about that."

They were silent as he drove the short distance to her house. All too soon, he was parked in her driveway. He turned off the engine.

"You didn't need to do that. I can get out on my own."

"No, you can't. I'm going to end this the right way and walk you to your front door."

"Just like it was a real date."

She'd said those words so quietly, Graham wondered if she even realized that she'd uttered them out loud. "Don't get mad, but it felt exactly like a real date to me," he said.

"I think so, too." She smiled slightly. "Though, I guess if this had been real, I'd have spent the last ten minutes wondering if you were going to kiss me good-night."

He laughed. "Is that right?"

"Oh, yeah. It's a concern, you know," she said, her voice filled with mischief. "A girl has to be ready for anything."

"Just for the record, what are your opinions on that, Miss Parnell? Do you kiss on the first date?"

"As a general rule, no." Obviously still playing, she flipped her hair over one shoulder. "But I have made exceptions in certain situations."

Unable to help himself, he leaned in and gently brushed his lips against hers. When she didn't pull away, he kissed her again, with far more intent. He still kept it gentle but didn't try to hide his feelings.

It was everything he'd imagined it would be. Vivian's lips were soft and pliant, and the way her upper body leaned closer had been so sweet.

When he pulled away at last, Graham already felt her absence. "Ah, Vivian," he murmured.

Her eyes were wide and her lips slightly parted. After another second passed, she swallowed. "I… I don't know what just happened."

"I do," he said. "I finally did what I'd been wanting to do for the last two hours."

"Even if we're just friends?"

"Vivian, I know keeping things between

us platonic and easy is the smart thing to do, since I'm going to be moving eventually. But where you're concerned? I can't seem to help myself. All that ever seems to matter is that you're next to me, and I am so glad about that."

She was, too. Man, she was so glad…but it scared her. She was no young girl, but was she ready to become emotionally invested…just to lose someone she was in love with again?

In love?

The air between them seemed to crackle with emotion. And maybe tension. Or regrets from her.

She opened the door and stumbled out. "I need to go," she said as she shoved the door closed.

Graham jumped out and raced to her side. "I'm sorry," he said as caught up to her on the walkway to the inn. "That kiss was my fault. No, everything was my fault. I knew better. I *know* better. Please don't leave mad. Let me apologize."

She placed her hand on the front door handle. "There's nothing to apologize for. There are two of us here, Graham. I knew what I was doing." Averting her eyes, she whispered, "I wanted you to kiss me, and I'm not going to shame us both by pretending that I didn't love every second of it. But just because I wanted that, it doesn't mean that things should change between us."

"I know you need to go, but we could talk about it some more. I could call you later." He knew he sounded desperate, but he didn't care. What mattered most was how Vivian was feeling. He would hate it if she pulled away from him because she didn't think he could keep his distance.

"Not tonight. Good night, Graham. Thank you for dinner."

She opened the door and stepped inside. Shut the door right behind her.

Through the window, he could see her talking to Maisie in shadow. He heard feminine laughter.

Before they realized he was still standing on her front porch, Graham walked back to the truck. Turned the ignition, put his truck in Reverse and backed out. As he drove down her street just a little too fast, the Jeep's engine made a low screech of protest before it settled into third and then fourth gear.

"Sorry," he told the truck. Or maybe he was apologizing to Vivian.

Shoot. Maybe he was even apologizing to himself for ruining his plans. He really wasn't sure anymore.

CHAPTER TWENTY-TWO

"HONEY, I'M HEARING what you're saying, but don't you think you might be overreacting a bit?" Maisie asked. "I mean, it was just a kiss, right?"

Sitting across from her in the living room, Vivian bit her lip. When she'd first come inside after the date, she had intended to simply smile, say she had a good time and thank Maisie for babysitting.

But her whole body had felt like it was wound up. Too wound up to counsel herself. The things that had been tumbling around in her head were dangerous.

So she'd told Maisie everything. All about the dinner and their flirty conversation and her stupid confession about first-date kisses.

And then Vivian had described the way Graham had kissed her, which had drawn the above response from her friend.

Realizing that Maisie was still waiting for a reply, she said, "Well, yes, it was just a kiss, but it felt like more than that."

"More, how?"

And that was the real question, wasn't it? Digging deep, she made herself admit what was really on her mind. "It felt like I was making a big first step away from Emerson."

"Which was scary."

"It was so scary, Maisie."

Maisie leaned forward. "Maybe you should think about things another way. Maybe it wasn't you pulling away from Emerson but taking a big first step toward something new." She kicked her legs out and rested her toes on the ottoman. "Like a first step toward a new way of living. Like a new, happier Vivian."

Vivian tried that on for size. "I don't know about that." After reflecting another second, she added, "Maybe that's my problem. I'm not even sure about what I want to do five years from now. Or who I want to be."

Maisie raised an eyebrow. "Who says that you need to know all the answers now?"

"Well, you kind of are."

Maisie chuckled. "If I'm making you feel that way, I'm sorry. Vivian, you know my story, right? When Jared and I got divorced, it was the culmination of a lot of hard feelings and a lot of pain and bitterness. Then, when lawyers got involved, the divorce proceedings went on for months. Eventually, even our kids got involved."

"They were teenagers, right?"

"Yes." She blew out a breath of air. "Next thing I knew, it wasn't just me and Jared trying to unravel twenty years of marriage—it was Jared, me, Allison and Jenna, too.

"So…things got even worse. The twins were hurt and felt torn between us. Jared and I tried to put them first, but we didn't always succeed." She shook her head. "I'd give a lot to be able to go back and handle things differently."

Vivian was stunned. She'd known that Maisie had been divorced, and she'd also known that her husband had had an affair. But there was still so much pain in her voice. After all this time, it seemed Maisie was still healing. "You still see the kids, though, right?"

Maisie nodded slowly. "I do now, but there were a few months when I doubted either of them would want to spend time with me." She lowered her voice. "It was the darkest time of my life."

"I'm so sorry."

She sniffed. "Thank you, but the reason I brought that up wasn't for sympathy. It was to remind you that I had no idea if I was ever going to be able to get a good night's sleep again, let alone figure out my future."

"What happened? Time?"

"Yes, which is something we both know you can relate to. But I also gave myself permission to be open to things I hadn't planned on. Such as quitting my job at the bank."

"And starting to write mysteries."

Maisie nodded. "And now I'm getting reacquainted with Clayton, who was my first crush."

"I don't know if Graham and I are going to have the kind of happy future that you and Clayton seem to be destined for."

"Of course you don't. But you're never going to know if you don't give him a chance, right?" She shrugged. "And if it doesn't work out, you might find someone else who is every bit as amazing and kisses even better than Graham."

Vivian chuckled. "I see where this is going. You're saying I need to stop worrying so much."

"Bingo! Vivian, I love you, and I know you have a lot on your plate and you've already been through so much. But it would be really good if you didn't take every little thing in your life so seriously."

"Thanks, Maisie. Your support means the world."

"You are very welcome," Maisie said as she got to her feet. "That's what friends are for, right?"

"Absolutely." Vivian walked her to the door. "Thanks again for watching Will."

"He's a doll. I loved every minute of it." After giving Vivian a quick hug, she pulled her coat more tightly around her shoulders. "See you soon. Sweet dreams."

"You, too."

Vivian stood at the door, watching Maisie walk to her house under the glow of the street-lights. Then, after checking on Will and making sure the house was secure, she took a hot shower and then crawled into bed. When she saw her phone light up, she smiled.

Thanks for tonight, V. Best night I've had in months.

She felt the same way. She just wished those feelings didn't also fill her with a sense of panic.

THE NEXT MORNING, she woke up feeling even more confused than before. Vivian hardly had time to gather her thoughts, though, because her phone was ringing off the hook. An hour later, she wanted to pull her hair out. How could she have been so stupid?

It was a holiday weekend and the inn was now fully booked. Every room was going to be occupied—even the tiny attic space she usually only ever reserved for extended families.

Worse, it sounded as if most of the people knew each other and had called her inn as a last resort. There was nothing wrong with that, but she had a feeling that they were going to be very different from her usual type of older guest who went to bed before eleven.

At the very least, she was sure they would all be coming into the inn after midnight. At worst, they were going to bring the party there.

By the time Will woke up and she'd said goodbye to her one guest from the night before—an older woman who had come into town to visit her grandson at the Air Force Academy—Vivian was running around the big house like a whirling dervish. Will sat on the floor with a new box of Legos and glared at her.

"You said you weren't gonna have to work all day."

"I know, but I can't help that we had a lot of guests book rooms this morning."

"We didn't have anyone on Thanksgiving."

"I know. But that was special."

His expression turned mutinous. "I'm not special?"

Well, he had her there. How was it possible that a six-year-old could twist her words around so easily? Worse, why did it seem like he was right and she was the one who was so wrong? Still trying to gain control of the conversation, she said, "You know you are special, but this is our life. We live in a bed-and-breakfast. This is how I pay our bills."

"It's still not fair that we always have to be here. We can't do anything, Mommy."

The knife in her heart twisted just a little bit more. "I know it's frustrating when we want to go have fun and we can't, but it's not all horrible, either."

"I know."

Somehow, those words, combined with a look of pained resolution on his face, made her feel even worse. "Don't forget, I'm home every day when you come home from school. And when you're off on holidays. Some of your other friends have to go to camps and babysitters."

"Dean is on a skiing trip this week."

Well, there it was. She couldn't compete with Dean and the ski trip, just like she couldn't compete with all the little boys whose dads took them out to play baseball or to go fishing. Since she couldn't think of anything to say to that, she turned around and went back to the kitchen.

Eight hours later, after Will had had a six-year-old meltdown followed by a nap, after which the two of them had watched *Transformers*, Vivian had a meltdown of her own.

It had turned out that her booked guests did all know each other and were determined to party all the way till dawn. Though they weren't disrespectful or rude, they were determined to enjoy themselves. After a short dinner out, they'd brought their food, booze and music to her living room.

She supposed she couldn't blame them.

But her patience with their party thinned by one in the morning. As the group continued laughing, dancing and singing to some of the worst karaoke music Vivian had ever heard, the small hand on the clock headed toward two. Then three.

That was when she shut the party down.

Her guests apologized, cleaned up their mess…and then continued to celebrate in one of the rooms. It was at that point that Vivian had felt like crying.

By 4:00 a.m., she was sure that she was not

only the worst mother in the world, but the worst B&B proprietor as well. She was exhausted. And lonely. And so tired of juggling all her responsibilities while leaving herself and her needs at the very bottom.

"Will was right," she told herself. "You could've said you were closed for the night. The money you're making isn't worth this. Not when you count all the hours you spent cooking and cleaning for the guests. Or babysitting the party."

It wasn't like the group was terrible, either. She'd had worse guests.

The problem was that she didn't want Will's memories to only be of her working. Or of him playing by himself and staying out of the way of the guests.

"You need to do something different," she told herself. "It's time to stop worrying about the consequences and start making some changes."

CHAPTER TWENTY-THREE

A FEW DAYS LATER, she was gaping at Graham in the kitchen. "You can't be serious." And that was the nicest way of phrasing what she thought about Graham's suggestion. "I can't go to Canada with you."

"I am serious."

"It's not that easy."

"I also don't think it's that hard," he countered. "Come on, Vivian. Think about how much fun it will be. I'll take you and Will to a hockey game. The Red Wings have a home game coming up."

As incentives went, that one wasn't all that great. After all, didn't hockey games involve fighting and blood? "I don't know. A professional hockey game might be a little violent for a six-year-old."

"Viv, do you really think I'd do anything to hurt Will?"

"Well, no."

"I wouldn't. Not ever." His voice turned even more cajoling. "I promise, Will's going to love watching hockey. You will, too. But there are plenty of other things we can do. We can go tobogganing. And sip hot chocolate at Navy Yard Park, or walk along the river, or go to Willistead Manor. It's an old manor house, and they decorate it to the hilt for Christmas. We can tour it and see all the decked-out trees. I know you'd like that."

He sounded so convincing. "I probably would."

He smiled. "And, when I'm not running you all around Windsor, we can relax at my parents' house. It's a big old farmhouse. There are three fireplaces and even a big library. My family loves to just hang out and play cards."

She couldn't remember the last time she'd done that. "It's tempting."

"I promise, my mother isn't difficult at all. Her favorite thing to do is watch British baking shows and knit. The rest of my family is the same way. No one is going to set up any parties or fancy dinners or worry about little boys being little boys. You can relax for once and not worry about a bunch of guests and cleaning up after their messes."

Just the thought of doing nothing but relaxing sounded like heaven. And she'd always wanted to watch that British baking show. "You don't think it will be awkward? I mean, your family is going to assume there's something going on between us." Which would be correct, but that was beside the point.

"If they do think that, they won't be wrong," Graham said. "I like you, Vivian. I like Will, too."

"We like you," she replied, feeling a little silly. "But what about us being careful about Will's heart? What if he gets attached to you?"

What if she got even more attached to Graham than she already was? She closed her eyes. That was what she was really worried about. Against all her better judgment, Vivian was falling in love with Graham. It scared her half to death.

Graham gazed at her intently. Seeming to make a decision, he took a sip of his coffee. "I'm pretty certain that all of us have already become close. As much as I would like to say that you and I can be in charge of our feelings, I don't know if that's true. And I'm okay with that. I like being friends."

"You're purposely misunderstanding me."

"I think you might be purposely making everything harder than it has to be. This is just a visit, Vivian. It's not a marriage proposal."

She knew what he meant. She also realized that he was saying exactly what she should be thinking. And that she should be relieved.

But why did that comment kind of sting, then?

Pushing all those thoughts away, she focused on keeping things simple. The chance to take a trip, making Will her focus instead of the inn and her guests, and create a fun memory for them both. Put that way, there was nothing wrong with it. Nothing at all.

And hadn't Maisie just reminded her about how important it was to live a little bit instead of always being so cautious?

Before she lost her nerve, she nodded. "Okay."

Graham had been taking another sip of coffee. He set his cup down so quickly some of the brew sloshed over the brim and onto the table. "Did you just say okay?"

She nodded again. Summoning her courage, she said, "Graham, you're right. You are absolutely right. There is nothing wrong with me and Will taking a vacation just like everyone else in the world."

"There really isn't." His lips twitched, like he was trying not to smile.

"I would also love to meet your mom and the rest of your family. I can't wait to see the place where you grew up."

"I can't wait to show it to you, Vivian." Reaching for her hand, he linked his fingers with hers. "I also can't wait for my mother to meet you and Will. I know she's going to think as highly of you as I do."

"I hope so."

"I can't wait for you to tell Will. The three of us are going to have the best time." He pressed his lips to her brow, then stood up, grinning from ear to ear. "Okay, you just relax about everything. I'll make all the arrangements and then call you to double-check that it all works. Okay?"

She laughed. "Okay."

"It's so great to see you so happy. I'm going to do my best to keep you smiling, Vivian. I promise, you're going to be so glad you said yes."

Minutes after he left, she sat back down and tried to tell herself that she was being impetuous and foolish. Reminded herself that nothing really serious could happen between them, because Graham was going to move and she had her business in Colorado.

But, to her surprise, none of those warnings seemed to make the slightest bit of difference in how she felt. She wanted to spend more time with Graham, she wanted to give Will a fun vacation and she wanted some sweet memories to savor long after Graham was gone.

Surely there was nothing wrong with that.

CHAPTER TWENTY-FOUR

A WEEK LATER, they'd flown to Detroit, then driven over the Ambassador Bridge into Windsor, Ontario. Knowing they were just minutes away from home, Graham felt his spirits lift even more. After almost eight months, he was home again. He could hardly believe it.

Suddenly, even the most aggravating things about the trip home didn't seem so bad. Vivian had been shocked by the long lines of cars and trucks waiting to go through customs at the border.

She'd looked even more worried when he'd shared that people sometimes had to wait for hours to get through.

Their journey across the border had been relatively quick, however. Both Graham's Canadian citizenship and his position in the RCAF had allowed them to sail through without any trouble.

"Not too much longer now, Will," Graham said from the driver's seat of the SUV he'd rented for the week. "We'll be at my mother's house within fifteen minutes."

"Are you excited?" Vivian asked.

"Kind of."

"Only kind of?" She turned around to see what Will meant.

"I thought it would be different here, but everything looks just like it does in Colorado."

Graham chuckled. "You sound disappointed."

"We're in a whole different country. I thought there would be snow everywhere. And maybe some moose."

"That's on you, Graham," she teased.

"I can't deny that." Unable to help himself, Graham had gone a little overboard, regaling Will with stories about his childhood. He'd laid it all on so thick, even he was tempted to believe that half the country constantly went ice fishing, hunted for elk and had to detour around moose crossing the street.

He frowned. "I guess I did make it sound like my hometown was a little rustic." More loudly he said, "A lot of things are just like in your hometown, but not everything. We have some different favorite restaurants, like Tim Hortons and Swiss Chalet. A lot of people in Canada speak French, too. That's different."

"I haven't heard anyone speak French yet."

"You will." But Graham figured the kid had a point. Maybe he shouldn't have talked quite so much about the many wonderful things they were going to do up North. He realized now that he'd made Windsor and the surrounding area sound like a combination of the Matterhorn at Disneyland and the Swiss Alps.

Vivian chuckled. "Try not to be too disappointed, Graham. Believe me, even first graders can be a hard sell at times. They're not all that easily impressed."

"I'm beginning to think you're right."

"How much longer until we get to your mom's?"

"Not long. Less than ten minutes."

Beside him, Vivian reached for her purse and started digging through it.

When he noticed her frown, he reached out and rubbed her arm. "Viv, are you all right?"

"I guess so."

That wasn't exactly the answer he'd been looking for. "What are you searching for in your purse? Did you forget something?"

"No. I just need to put on some lipstick and brush my hair."

"Why?"

"Uh, because I'm meeting your whole family?"

He couldn't believe she was worried about

that. "First of all, you look beautiful. You always do. Second of all, no one is going to care how you look."

She groaned. "Graham, sometimes you are such a man. Of course they're going to care. I care. Don't you?"

Answering that one seemed like a bad idea. Seeing as how Vivian appeared so determined to create a good first impression, Graham kept his thoughts to himself. When he turned onto a narrow, windy street, he smiled. "We're almost home."

Will had his nose pressed to the window. Beside him, Vivian zipped up her purse and looked around with interest.

Graham tried to see the familiar street from her point of view. He supposed it didn't look all that impressive. His parents had bought an acre lot back in the '80s and had slowly remodeled and added things over the years. The backyard had always been his favorite part. There were a number of gravel walkways weaving through his father's gardens. About the time when his brother was in high school, their mom had built a stamped concrete patio and set up a fire pit. The first night it was done, all of them had gathered together. Mom had passed around straightened coat hangers, announcing that they were going to have s'mores.

He'd gone from planning to get out of the house as fast as he could to sitting around the fire with everyone for hours, relishing the company of his family.

Now that he'd spent so much time away, Graham was so glad that he had memories like that to hold close.

"This is it," Graham announced as he pulled into the long driveway. The moment he parked, the front door of the house opened.

He barely had time to open his door before his mom rushed forward.

"Graham!"

A lump formed in his throat as he quickly got out, then held his mother close. As usual, she was wearing jeans and a soft sweater. She also had on the same perfume she'd worn for as long as he could remember. "Hey, Mom," he said. She felt a little frailer. Maybe a little smaller?

"It's been too long." She reached up and kissed him on the cheek. "It's so good to see you."

"I feel the same way." When he stepped away, he motioned to Vivian and Will, who'd gotten out on their own and were quietly watching his reunion. "Mom, please meet

Vivian and Will Parnell. Vivian and Will, this is my mom, Gwen Evans."

Vivian reached out her hand. "It's so nice to meet you. Thank you for having us."

"It's my pleasure. I'd be lying if I said I hadn't been as excited to meet you two as I was to see my son." Leaning forward slightly, she added, "Will, I picked up some toys for you."

"Really?"

"Really," she replied with a smile. "Hopefully, I didn't do too bad of a job. It's been quite a while since I went shopping for a six-year-old."

"That's so sweet of you, but you didn't have to do that," Vivian said.

"Of course I did," his mother said. "It might have been a while since I've entertained a first grader, but I do remember that sitting around while adults catch up can get pretty boring."

Will's eyes got big but he didn't say anything, just scooted closer to his mom.

"We've been traveling for a while, Ma. Let's get inside."

"Of course. It's chilly out here, too." Grabbing ahold of Vivian's roller bag, she led the way to the front door. Vivian followed with her carry-on bag on her shoulder.

Graham picked up his duffel bag with one

hand and Will's small roller bag with the other. "What do you think, buddy?" he asked.

"Your mom is really nice."

"I'm glad you think so. I told you she was, though. I wouldn't have lied about that."

When they got inside, Blue was lying on the floor in the entryway. She raised her head, seemed to recognize his scent, then scrambled over to him. Her whole body was wiggling. He knelt down and ran his palm along her muzzle. "Hey, girl. You remember me?"

She sidled closer, obviously enjoying every rub and pet.

"Will, this is my mom's dog, Blue. Would you like to get to know her?"

"Uh-huh." After Graham helped Will hold out his hand in front of Blue's nose, the little boy looked in love. "She's a really nice dog, Graham."

"She is. She's the best." Sensing that the boy would enjoy petting the dog for a few minutes instead of sitting in the kitchen with his mom, Graham said, "I'm going to be over there, okay?"

"Uh-huh." It was obvious that any worries the boy had about being in Graham's mother's house had disappeared.

When Graham found Vivian and his mom in the kitchen, his mother was making a pot of coffee and Vivian was standing awkwardly in the doorway.

"Sorry about that. Will wanted to meet Blue."

His mother's voice turned a little more wistful. "I swear, I think that dog knew you all were coming today. She spent most of the morning staring out the front window."

"I really missed her."

"I think she missed you, too." Still smiling, his mom turned to Vivian. "Do you have a dog, dear?"

"No, I don't."

His mother frowned. "You don't? Well now, that's a shame. All kids need a dog. Especially a little boy who lost his father, I think."

Graham felt a bit of his happiness fade as he noticed his mother wasn't exactly acting like her normal easygoing self. And he couldn't believe she'd brought up Vivian's husband already. "Mom, what in the world?"

Vivian pressed her palm on his arm, relaying that she was okay. "Will has always wanted a dog, but since I run a bed-and-breakfast, that isn't possible."

"I guess not. I'm sure you keep very busy with all those strangers in your house." She poured two cups of coffee into mugs. "Do you want a cup, too, Graham?"

"Thanks, Ma."

"Sit down, Vivian. Make yourself at home."

Vivian looked a little wary but sat down. She seemed a little gun-shy and he didn't blame her. They'd been at his mother's house for less than fifteen minutes, and she'd already needled Vivian twice.

Worried, he sat down next to Vivian and leaned close. "Sorry about that. I… I bet my mom is just nervous."

Vivian raised her eyebrows but said nothing.

"Uh, do you need anything?" he asked.

"I'm fine."

That meant, of course, that she wasn't. "Would you like to go to your room and rest for a minute?"

"Oh, for Pete's sake. She's fine, Graham. Stop hovering." His mother laughed, but it sounded a little forced. "Vivian is probably having a difficult time not being the host, right?" When Vivian just smiled weakly, she added, "Dear, please stop worrying and relax. After all, this is my kitchen, not yours."

The comment was the truth, but her words had a definite edge to them. Graham was perplexed. His mother was usually one of the most giving people he'd ever known. She was also usually a whole lot more tactful.

"That's probably true," Vivian said. "I am used to taking care of other people."

Graham was pretty sure something more was going on, but he hoped whatever was in the air would dissipate soon.

"See, son? Nothing to worry about. I'm sure we'll all get along just fine for this one week. Now, tell me all about how your flights were. Did you have any trouble?"

Graham answered his mother, but he kept darting glances at Vivian. She didn't look all that happy, and his mother was still acting pretty strange.

This week that he'd been looking forward to for days was off to a pretty rocky start.

CHAPTER TWENTY-FIVE

So, THINGS BETWEEN her and Gwen were odd. That was the only way Vivian could describe it. The woman was pleasant and helpful, but there was also a certain edge to everything she said to Vivian.

At least, it felt that way to her.

She could tell that Graham thought something was off, too. She'd caught him staring at his mother in confusion more than once. Most recently, five minutes ago, when Gwen had announced that she'd like to be the one to show Vivian her room for the week.

"You can take her bags up in a minute, Graham. I want to show her some things first."

"What about Will?"

"I figured he could choose between Eileen's and Doug's old rooms. Both are made up and ready. He can figure that out later."

"I can bring him up with us, Gwen. That way we can get him settled at the same time," Vivian suggested.

"Oh, we'll have time to do that later. Come now, dear. I want to show you something."

Vivian met Graham's gaze as she turned to follow his mother up the wide staircase. "Tell Will I'll be back down in a minute."

"Don't worry. I've got him."

"Okay." She felt a little foolish, but it did seem odd that his mother was determined that she come up all alone.

When they stood on the upstairs landing, Gwen said, "I've never seen Graham like this. You two must have gotten really close."

"We have."

"Hmm."

Walking down the hall, she pointed to the open doorway. "That's the bathroom for the three rooms here. Towels and such are in baskets on the metal rack in the corner. Meredith, Kinsey and I tried to think of everything you might need, but we might have overlooked some things."

"Thank you. I'm sure I'll be fine." Belatedly she realized that Meredith was Graham's sister, but Kinsey's name didn't ring a bell. "Who is Kinsey? Is she a neighbor?"

"She's a close friend of the family. A very close friend of Graham's."

It was difficult for Vivian not to gape. Was Graham's mother really throwing another woman in her face? Though it was tempting to let the comment slide, Vivian had been around long enough to know that Gwen had brought up her name for a reason. "What do you mean by that?"

"Oh, nothing, dear. I mean, it's nothing for you to worry about."

She was here on a short vacation. That much was true. Though it was tempting to push Gwen a little bit, Vivian refrained. "I'm sorry, which bedroom is mine?"

"This one here. It's Meredith's old room."

Vivian peeked in, noticing a double bed, light teal paint and a worn wicker dresser and desk. "This will be perfect. Thank you."

"It's no trouble."

"May I see the rooms for Will to choose between?"

"Of course." She walked to the room next door and turned on a light before doing the same thing to the room on the other side of Meredith's.

Both looked much like Meredith's. Each was a little bare but comfortable enough. "I have a feeling he's going to want to be in Graham's brother's room."

"Do you think so?"

Since the other room was pink, she was fairly sure. "Where is Graham's room?"

"Why?"

"No reason. I'm just curious."

"His room is on the other side of the house. I doubt you'll have a reason to see it."

"Yes, ma'am." Vivian was tempted to start laughing. Gwen was acting as if she was a frisky teenager instead of a thirty-year-old widow.

Gwen folded her arms over her chest. "Dear, you are as lovely as can be, and your boy is adorable, too. Graham seems to think very highly of you. But I think you're setting yourself up for heartbreak. He's moving back here. You two will be far apart."

The sad thing was that Vivian was sure Gwen was right. It was nice to pretend that things between them could be different, but they both had responsibilities that had to come before a new relationship.

Vivian knew that, and she had almost come to terms with it. But Gwen's dangling another woman in her face didn't seem right. Nothing in Graham's personality had given her reason to believe that he had another woman in his sights. "Are you trying to tell me that he has a current relationship with Kinsey?"

"All I'm trying to tell you is that Kinsey lives here and you never will. Take it from a woman who has been in your shoes, dear. A long-distance relationship rarely works. Add a child into the mix, and it's close to impossible."

"Mom? Why are you talking about Kinsey?" Graham asked as he walked up the stairs carrying two suitcases, Will trailing behind him.

His mother froze before laughing softly. "I'm not saying anything that you need to worry about, dear. That's what you get for eavesdropping. Vivian and I were just talking about how good it will be for you to get back to your old life."

Graham looked genuinely perplexed. "What old life? I joined the air force when I was eighteen."

"All I meant was that soon you'll be back here for good, and your time in Colorado will just be a memory."

Vivian inhaled sharply. Will was standing right there. "This is hardly the time or the place for this conversation." Looking over at Will, she softened her voice. "Would you like to choose your room?"

Will didn't move. Staring at Graham, he said, "You're going to leave us for good, Graham?"

"No." He pulled Will into his arms, raising his head and frowning fiercely at his mother.

"Even when I get transferred here, we'll still see each other a lot. I promise."

His mother's confident expression crumpled. "Graham, I didn't mean—"

"I have no idea what you meant, but you can be sure we'll talk about this later, Mom. For now, I think it would be best if you gave us some space."

Vivian didn't think Gwen was going to move, but then she turned and walked downstairs. When she was out of sight, she said to Will, "Want to see the two bedrooms? They're on either side of mine, just like at home."

Will ignored her. "Where is your room, Graham? I want to be near you."

"I'm downstairs off the kitchen, but there's no bedroom next to me."

"Oh."

"Come look at my brother's room. He has airplane posters all over his walls."

"Like the ones you fly?"

"I don't fly planes, just help people decide where they fly to. You're going to like this room, though." He held out his hand.

Watching as Will followed Graham into his brother's old room, Vivian took a fortifying breath. She wasn't sure what was going on with his mother, but the dynamics had sure taken her by surprise. She hoped Graham had some ideas of what to do next, because she sure didn't—and they had another six days to spend in Gwen's house.

CHAPTER TWENTY-SIX

THEIR FIRST EVENING in Windsor had turned into something of a disaster. After the confrontation with his mother, Graham had done his best to soothe Will's spirits and whisper to Vivian that he would speak to his mother as soon as possible.

Vivian had gazed at him with trust in her eyes, which was such a relief. He'd hugged her close and pressed his lips to her forehead. "I promise I'll make this right."

"I know you will."

He'd eventually showed Vivian and Will the rest of the sprawling farmhouse, and they'd gone for a short walk down the street with Blue.

When they returned, Meredith was there, and they had lasagna for dinner. Meredith and Vivian had seemed to get along well, much to Graham's relief. It was also obvious that his sister sensed something was going on with him and their mother, but she held her tongue.

After the late meal, Will was tired, and Vivian announced that she was going to put him to bed and go to sleep as well. As tempting as it was to ask Vivian to come back to his side after she put Will to bed, he held off. Vivian was giving him plenty of signs that she needed some space, and he supposed he didn't blame her.

Meredith smiled at him as soon as they were out of sight. "Wow, Graham. She's amazing."

"I think so, too. She's not only as kind as can be, but she's so strong. She's such a good mother, too. And I wish you could see the way she runs her inn. She's so organized and focused on every detail. Honestly, Vivian could put some of my commanders to shame."

"I can't wait to get to know her better."

"Thanks, Mer." Graham paused, half waiting for their mother to either apologize or add her praises. Instead, she remained silent.

"Mom, what is going on?"

"I'm not sure what you're talking about."

He absolutely did not want to play this game. He was tired and wanted nothing more than to sit in front of the fireplace and catch up and reflect on how nice it was to finally be home. "I'm talking about how you brought up Kinsey—and how you've been far less than welcoming toward Vivian."

His mother stiffened and then leaned back

in her chair with a sigh. "I think you're making a mistake with Vivian and Will, Graham," she said at last. "You told me on the phone that you and Vivian were simply friends."

"We are friends."

"I think there's something a whole lot more there." When he tried to interrupt, she said, "I saw the way that both Vivian and her son looked at you, son. There are practically stars in their eyes! If they aren't in love yet, they're well on their way."

"What is wrong with them falling in love?" Meredith asked.

"What is wrong is that you've told me that you're heading to one of the air force bases near here. You're going to break their hearts, and they've already had their hearts broken before."

"Is this about Dad dying?" Meredith asked.

Their mother winced. "I suppose, in a way, yes." She lowered her voice. "Don't forget, I know what it's like to lose a spouse at a young age. Vivian and I are a lot alike, except I didn't just have one child at home, I had four. She's got a lot on her plate, and walking into a relationship that has no future is a surefire way to get hurt. Then, there's Kinsey, who's so excited for you to come back to Windsor. I'm sure once you two connect, you'll realize that she's a much better fit for you than Vivian is. Graham, you should've kept your distance."

Graham was floored. In some sort of convoluted way, his mother was trying to push Vivian away so she wouldn't get hurt in the future.

"Mom, life doesn't work like that," he said at last. "You can't sabotage people's happiness because you want to try to save them from getting hurt in the future."

"That's not what I'm doing."

"I'm sorry, but I think it is. What's worse is that your plan isn't going to work anyway. Kinsey and I were a couple in high school, but that was a long time ago. She and I never even wrote each other when I entered the air force."

After pausing to collect his thoughts, he added, "In addition, during all this time, I've hardly dated at all. I had even started to think that maybe love and marriage weren't going to ever happen for me—and then I met Vivian. Now I realize that I was simply waiting for the right person."

Meredith reached out and squeezed their mother's hand. "You've got to respect Graham, Mom. He's happy with Vivian and Will. They're obviously happy to be with him. What happens next isn't our business."

"You're right. You're both right." She ran

a hand through her hair. "I'm sorry, and I'll apologize to Vivian in the morning."

"Thank you. I'd appreciate that," Graham said.

"I was so excited that you're going to be stationed closer, I didn't want you to regret your move."

"Or maybe ask not to return to Canada?" Meredith murmured.

"That did cross my mind. I... I don't know what is wrong with me."

"It took a lot of convincing to get Vivian to come visit, Mom. I not only talked up my hometown but my family, too. Please don't make me regret introducing them to you."

Looking even more aggrieved, Gwen stood up. "I promise I'll be better tomorrow. And now, I think it's definitely time to go to bed. See you in the morning."

When they were alone, Graham smiled at his sister. "Thanks for your support."

She chuckled. "No problem. I didn't see this coming, but I guess I should have. Mom has asked me more than once what I thought about you getting attached to a woman that you were going to be moving away from."

"What did you tell her?"

"That sometimes a person's heart overrules their brain. It might make sense to keep Vivian at a distance, but it's obvious that your heart has other plans in mind."

"It sure does," he murmured.

GRAHAM WAS GRATEFUL that his mother stayed true to her word. The next morning, she made pancakes for everyone, fixed Will some hot chocolate and politely apologized to Vivian.

Vivian accepted her apology gracefully, which Graham was also very thankful for.

Glad that the drama appeared to be over, Graham asked his mom to help him find some snow pants in Will's size, along with mittens and a hat. She dug out a bin that she kept for the grandchildren and pulled out a black bib, green mittens and a gray hat. When Graham handed them to Will, the boy asked what he needed them for.

"Tobogganing."

"Really?"

"Oh, yeah. I'm taking you to the biggest hill around. You're going to love it."

"Mom! Did you hear what Graham said?"

Vivian laughed. "You two are going to have a lot of fun."

"What she means," Graham replied, "is the *three* of us are going to have a good time."

Vivian frowned. "I'm not so sure that's a good idea."

"It is. You're going to love it, Viv."

An hour later, the three of them were at the top of the chute, positioned together like a trio of dominoes. Will was in the front, outfitted in his borrowed bib and gear. In the middle was Vivian, wearing a fleece, a pair of Meredith's ski pants and an adorable bright red hat. She had her arms wrapped around Will. Graham was in the back, holding on to Vivian securely.

"What do you think? Are you ready?" Graham asked.

"Yes!" Will cried.

The gate opened, the attendant gave them a good push and down they sailed. Bits of snow and ice flew in their faces as they raced down the track. Graham did his best to keep his weight balanced firmly in the center of the sled so they wouldn't fall over to one side.

It was almost impossible, though—they really were going fast.

"Oh my gosh, oh my gosh, oh my gosh!" Vivian chanted while Will squealed and laughed.

Graham didn't want to do anything but hold on to them both forever. He felt exhilarated and free. Like they'd all finally let go of the constraints that had been holding them back and were at last sailing forward.

Far too soon, the track leveled and their toboggan came to a stop.

"What did you think?" he asked.

"It scared the life out of me, but it was so fun," Vivian exclaimed. "I'm so glad you encouraged me to go."

"Will, what about you?"

"I want to go again." He turned his neck to look back at Graham. "Please, Graham? Can we do it again?"

When Vivian met his eyes and nodded, Graham smiled. "Of course, buddy. You're exactly right. Once is never enough."

CHAPTER TWENTY-SEVEN

AFTER THE SOMEWHAT rocky start, Vivian's trip to Windsor had been absolutely wonderful. Each day they did at least one activity centered around Will. After tobogganing, they'd ice-skated the next day, and attended a Windsor Spitfires junior hockey game the following evening.

By the second period, Vivian had forgotten that she was supposed to be worried about Will seeing a hockey fight and was on her feet rooting for the Spitfires at the top of her lungs. Meredith, her husband, Tom and their high school–aged son, Clint, had gone with them. All of them had gotten a big kick out of her turning into such a rabid fan.

The rest of the days had been filled with walks along the river, a day at the movies and even an afternoon doing a puzzle together when the wind had picked up and the temperatures had dropped. To Vivian's amusement, she'd even gotten the opportunity to meet the infamous Kinsey, who was very pretty, very sweet and very uninterested in Graham. Even Gwen had seemed embarrassed by her failed attempt at meddling.

This evening, to her surprise, Will had asked to stay home with Gwen. The two of them were going to make pizzas, eat ice cream, and watch Avengers movies.

Will had hardly looked their way when they'd walked out the door.

Vivian had been excited to have a real night out. She'd enjoyed spending so much time with Will, but she couldn't deny how nice it was to put on something a little fancier, curl her hair and be with Graham alone.

He'd taken her to Jackson Park, which was a fifty-nine-acre park just south of downtown Windsor. They walked its gorgeously lit walkways and admired the decorated memorials and tall Christmas trees entirely made out of lights.

Graham was very proud of the park and kept spouting off trivia and facts as they strolled. "Not only are there both World War II and Korean War memorials here, there are over ten thousand plants to view in the warmer months."

As much as she loved his enthusiasm, she couldn't resist teasing him a bit. "Ten thousand plants? My goodness."

"I'll take you some time. Everyone loves the flowers."

"I'm sure I will, as well."

Graham's smile faltered. "Wait, are you teasing me?"

"Maybe just a little. I think it's cute that you know so much about this place, though I never pictured you to be a botanical garden type of guy."

He stopped and looked at her in obvious surprise. "Do you not like Jackson Park?"

"Of course I do. I love it." How could she not? The lights, together with the snow, the music from various local choirs and orchestras, the containers of poinsettias, and the cups of delicious hot chocolate in their hands, created a magical atmosphere.

He still looked concerned. "I thought about taking you along the river, or even to Caesars concert hall. But this has always been one of my favorite spots."

"Oh, Graham. You picked the perfect place. It's very romantic," she added, then realized that she might have been assuming too much. "I mean, festive."

He chuckled as he reached for her hand. "I like romantic better." Leaning close, he said, "I know I still have a lot to learn in the romance department, but I'm trying."

"I don't think you have anything to learn. I'm having a great time."

"Our dinner reservations are in thirty minutes. We better head to the car."

She held his hand as they walked toward the exit, Graham walking slow so she could continue to ooh and aah over all the light displays. Walking with him, with only the multicolored lights illuminating the space, Vivian felt her heart hitch.

For so long, she'd wondered if she'd ever fall in love again. Most of the time, she'd convinced herself that it could never happen. She realized now that she had kept herself closed off from even considering another marriage. It all had sounded too scary.

However, she was starting to understand that none of the men she'd met had been Graham. He had been worth waiting for. He was worth overcoming all the doubt and fear in her heart.

"I thought a lot about places to take you, Vivian," he said as they got in the rental car. "I thought about taking you to Chimney Park Bistro, but that can get a little stuffy, so we're going out to a little Italian place near the lake. I hope that's okay."

"It sounds great."

When he parked on the street, she was

immediately charmed. The restaurant was small, and twinkling white lights festooned the grounds. Jazz music sounded from the speakers. The music, the lights and the heavenly aroma of Italian food combined to make the perfect atmosphere.

"Right this way," the host said after Graham gave him his name. The gentleman seated them in a back corner next to the fireplace.

Touching the white tablecloth and looking around at the walls adorned with hundreds of black-and-white photographs, Vivian couldn't imagine a more charming place to spend their last evening in Windsor.

"You've outdone yourself tonight. Everything is just perfect," she said after they'd ordered their food and drinks.

"I'm glad you like it." Looking a little shy, he added, "I know this was a huge step for you, Vivian. Not only did you have to trust me, but you had to trust Maisie to take care of the inn for you. I wanted you to know that I don't take that trust for granted."

He was right. She'd taken a big step out of her comfort zone to come on this trip, but it had been so worth it. "This wasn't easy for you, either. Will and I are a lot to take on."

"Not so much."

"You know what I mean." She smiled. "Graham, when Will and I say goodbye to you at the airport tomorrow, I'm not going to have a single regret. Even if we ultimately decide to only stay friends, I'll always have these memories. Not only has every day been so special, but it's reminded me that there's more to life than work. I need memories to hold on to and experiences to remember—and maybe even laugh about."

"Like the time you yelled at the goalie at the hockey game?"

"Yep. And the way I squealed like a little girl when we flew through the air in that toboggan." She sipped her wine. "Even just working on the puzzle with your mom was great, because I was savoring the moment instead of doing what I usually do—wonder when I can get up and get another four things done."

He reached for her hand. "I'm going to have a lot of amazing memories, too, Vivian. Maybe most especially this moment."

"Why?"

"It's just us, you look beautiful, your smile is so sweet and I know it's not going to be the last time I take you out."

Her smile faded as his words sank in.

"You mean that, don't you?"

He nodded. "Every. Single. Word."

"Your salads," the waiter said as he approached. "Which one of you ordered the Caesar?"

"I did," Vivian said with a weak smile.

The moment had faded, but she knew Graham's words wouldn't fade from her memory for a very long time. They were too special, too heartfelt, too everything.

She just hoped he was right and that this was just the beginning of something for both of them, not the end.

CHAPTER TWENTY-EIGHT

IT HAD BEEN a long day of traveling. After hugging Gwen goodbye, Graham had driven Vivian and Will back to the airport. Vivian hadn't been surprised to see that her son found the journey back to Detroit to be never-ending.

Vivian had felt the same way. Not only was she fighting off tears, but the morning traffic had been bad through customs, over the bridge and on the interstate toward Detroit. By the time they arrived at the airport, Vivian was ready for a break.

Unfortunately, they'd still had to go through security and make a connection in Chicago before they landed in Colorado Springs at five.

She'd clung to Graham when they'd said goodbye, hating that she was acting so silly when she'd see him again in a week. However, she couldn't help but wonder what the future held for them. She knew Graham was going to be heading to his new assignment for several days. He was anxious to get some answers about his duties; she was anxious to discover when he would be leaving Colorado Springs for good.

By the time they'd retrieved their bags and walked outside, all Vivian wanted to do was take a hot bath and have a mini pity party.

"Mom, there's Maisie!" Will said as they approached a long line of cars. "Hi, Maisie!"

Maisie walked around her car and hugged him tight. "Will, you're back! I've missed you!"

"I missed you, too."

"Did you have fun?" she asked as they loaded their suitcases in her trunk.

"Uh-huh. Mommy cried when we left."

Maisie raised her eyebrows but didn't comment, which Vivian was very thankful for. "Anyone hungry?"

"I am," Will said.

"Let's get you something to eat, then."

While Maisie drove, she kept up a steady stream of conversation, filling them in about the latest snowfall, Ziggy's antics and the new restaurant that had opened downtown.

After they picked up some chicken at a drive-through, they were back home in no time.

"Thanks so much for picking us up and for taking care of the inn," Vivian said when

Maisie parked. "I bet you can't wait to sleep in your own bed tonight."

"I am looking forward to that, but I'm even more anxious to hear about your trip. Mind if I stay awhile?"

"I'd love it if you did." She needed to talk through everything that had happened.

"Get settled and I'll meet you in the sitting room in the back of the house."

"I'll be back in five."

Maisie chuckled. "You can even take ten if you need to."

After taking the time to change, wash and pull her hair back, Vivian joined her. Maisie had gotten them two cups of hot tea and a small plate of cookies. "You're amazing, Maisie."

She laughed. "You better watch out. I started to really get into running this little place. Audrey said she's afraid I'm going to start leaving out trays of cookies and snacks on the kitchen island every afternoon."

Vivian smiled, liking the image. "Thanks for doing such a great job. I know we talked often, but did you have any trouble you didn't tell me about?"

"Nope. There are a couple of things you need to know, but it's nothing urgent. I wrote you notes. Now, enough about me. How was Canada? What's his family like?"

"Well, Graham's sister Meredith, her husband and her teenaged kids are all supernice. And his brother, Doug, came over for a few hours one afternoon, too, with his wife, Susan, and their kids. Will played with them the whole time and had a ball."

"And…"

"And Graham was wonderful. He was attentive and fun and romantic. He was amazing."

"I want to hear all the amazing stuff…but I'm getting the feeling that there's something you're not telling me."

"Well, I don't think his mother was all that fond of me."

Her eyes widened. "Really?"

"We got off to a rocky start. She made some pretty snide remarks, and she let me know that Graham's ex-girlfriend was in town."

"No way."

Vivian shook her head. "It all ended up being a big misunderstanding or something. The ex is from high school, and she is sweet but not at all interested in Graham." Weighing her words carefully, Vivian added, "Gwen apologized, saying how she just didn't want me to get my heart broken because Graham will be moving away."

"That's awfully presumptuous."

Vivian nodded. "I thought the same thing." She shifted, tucking one of her legs under her. "So, things did get better, but I never knew quite what to say to her."

"I bet that was hard."

"It was, and it was kind of sad, too. I would've liked to have the chance to really get to know her instead of constantly feeling like I was on my guard."

"What did Graham have to say about it?"

"After his mom apologized? Not too much. But what could he do? We were staying in her house—and Gwen wasn't exactly wrong. Our future is up in the air."

"Take it from me, doll—everyone's future is up in the air. None of us know what's going to happen next week, next month or next year. She shouldn't have been preparing for your breakup when you haven't even become a couple, officially."

"I think you have a good point."

"If I had to guess, I bet Graham's mother was also feeling a little threatened."

"Really? I don't see why. In just a short time, Graham will be living near her, and I'll be here."

"That's true, but if you're the first woman he's brought home, then she hasn't had to share him before. My brother's mother-in-law was like that. She'd always say things like she couldn't wait to see Carli but never Bill."

"Are you serious?"

"Oh, yeah."

"Well, did she get better?"

"Nope. Carli was so used to dealing with her parents and their demanding ways, she didn't even try to make things better." Maisie sighed. "Which is probably why Carli and Bill's marriage didn't last too long."

Maisie's story didn't make her feel any more hopeful. "Apart from that, we had a great time. I enjoyed the hockey game, and Will loved everything—from tobogganing to hanging out with Graham's family and playing with Blue, his mom's dog. He was all smiles the whole time."

"Was Gwen nice to him?"

"More than nice. It was just me that she had a problem with."

"When does Graham get back?"

"In a week. He had to report to his new commander and meet with the team for a few days."

"Hopefully he'll have some good news for you."

Vivian shrugged. "I don't know, Maisie. Even if Graham wasn't going to transfer right away, he would eventually. And I've worked really hard on this inn. How can I just throw it all away? What would I even do in a new city, let alone a different country? As much as I want there to be, I don't see how we can have a future together."

Later that night Vivian worked on her reservation schedule, answered emails and got groceries delivered. When she tucked Will into bed, he hugged her tight.

"Glad to be home?"

"Uh-huh. Canada was nice, but I like it here, too."

His simple statement was music to her ears.

Maisie had been right. No one knew what the future had in store for them. All that mattered was the present.

And, at present, she had a sweet little boy who was happy to be home. That was enough for her.

CHAPTER TWENTY-NINE

AFTER SEEING VIVIAN and Will off, Graham spent most of the next day with his brother and Susan. It had started to snow again, with the weather reports indicating that they would get at least six inches overnight. Susan had been prepared for the weather and had made a thick chicken-vegetable soup and a loaf of sourdough bread to go with it for dinner.

Afterward, they sat around the fireplace in the living room and gazed out the picture window that faced the woods, watching the snow fall. The scene and the food were so familiar. He couldn't count the number of times he'd eaten a soup dinner next to his siblings on a cold winter's night when he'd been a kid.

Now he was coming back. Well, kind of. He'd be stationed in Kingston, which was where Canada's tactical aviation base was located. Kingston was about a six-hour drive from Windsor. A good distance from home, but still a whole lot closer than he'd been since he enlisted at eighteen.

He'd have the privilege of seeing his family more often. But, boy, would he be far from Vivian and Will. How would he ever be able to fill the gap they'd leave behind if they were no longer in his life?

"So, how was Mom?" Doug asked.

He wasn't sure how to answer that. "You see her all the time. I guess she was the same."

That's when he noticed Susan and Doug exchange glances. "What are you two not telling me?"

"Nothing," Susan said quickly.

"Uh-huh. What?"

After Susan and Doug exchanged glances yet again, his brother cleared his throat. "How did she get along with Vivian and Will?"

"Fine." That was certainly true—when it came to Will, anyway.

"Really?"

"Doug, you're driving me crazy. What are you trying to say—or not saying?"

"Only that Mom had a lot to say about you bringing them home."

"Well, at first she was pretty rude to Vivian. But when I called her out on it, she settled down. She even apologized to Vivian." Thinking back to the week, he added, "You both saw her when we had lunch together. Mom was fine then, right?"

Doug nodded. "Right."

Graham felt like they were leading him into a conversation he didn't want to have but went with it. "To be honest, Mom was trying to discourage Vivian because she was worried that someone would get hurt if we started something between us. Even though she's not exactly wrong to worry—things are going to suck if I move here and we can't figure out how to continue to see each other—I told Mom that it was my business and not hers. She didn't seem really happy about that, but I think she came to terms with it."

Susan snorted. "If she did, then you and Vivian should count your lucky stars."

Finally, it was all coming together. "Wait, this isn't just about Mom trying to prevent Vivian and me from having a long-distance relationship, is it?"

Doug shook his head.

"Oh, man. I'm sorry, Susan."

"It's certainly not your fault! Besides, we're all right now. Gwen used to be a lot worse until I told her that I wasn't going anywhere."

Doug took her hand. "I had to talk to Mom, too. I told her that she was going to lose us both if she didn't get over herself."

Graham raised his eyebrows. "What did she say then?"

"About what you'd imagine. She pretended she didn't know what I was talking about, grumbled and then apologized."

"I thought things had been fine with her and Vivian, but maybe they weren't." Starting to worry, he said, "If Mom was still being difficult, I wish Vivian would've confided in me. I definitely would have either talked to Mom again or taken Vivian and Will someplace else."

"You would've done that?" Doug asked.

"Absolutely. They were here as my guests."

"They really do mean a lot to you, don't they?" Susan asked.

"They do." He turned to his brother. "Doug, you know how shy I was growing up. Even back in high school, it took me weeks to work up the nerve to ask Kinsey on our first date."

Doug smiled. "Believe me, that was agonizing for all of us."

Not offended, Graham chuckled. "I just assumed that I was always going to be alone. Like, I don't know, that I'd be married to the military or something. But after being around Vivian, I think I've just been waiting for the right person. She's special to me. Will is, too."

"If she's the one, then the best thing to do is stop worrying about what Mom thinks and concentrate on Vivian," Doug said.

"That's great advice," he said.

Doug smirked. "That's because I'm older and wiser than you."

Graham rolled his eyes. His brother was still the same as he'd been when they were kids: kind, protective and a little full of himself. But he wouldn't want it any other way.

Deciding to spend the night at Doug's, Graham hung out with him and Susan for a while longer, watching the game and catching up. He called Vivian a little later that evening. They were two hours behind, so it wasn't that late for her and Will.

"Graham, hey," she said as soon as she answered. "It's good to hear from you."

"How was your first day back?"

"Long." She laughed. "Will and I have been trying to get back into the swing of things."

"Do you have guests already?"

"No. Not until Thursday."

"Is that Graham?" Will called out.

"There's someone else here who wants to talk to you," Vivian said. "Here he is."

"Hi, Graham!"

"Hey, buddy. What's going on?"

"A lot! Guess what?"

He couldn't stop smiling. "What?"

"Mom and I are looking on the computer at ice-skating lessons."

"Are you now?"

"Uh-huh. You can't play hockey unless you can skate, you know."

The boy's earnest voice was adorable. "I reckon that's true."

"You're really good at skating, Graham. You skated really fast the day we went."

"I can skate well, but I don't know too many kids in Canada who can't. We excel at winter sports around here."

"When I get pretty good, would you go skating with me again?"

This kid. He practically owned his heart. "Of course. I'll even skate with you when you aren't that good."

"Really?"

"Really. I'm sure we'll get to go at least a couple of times when I get back." Before he moved.

"When are you coming home?"

Home. The boy's innocent question made Graham's heart clench. It was the sweetest thing—and reminded him once again that it wasn't so much about where he was as much as who was there waiting for him. At this moment, home was absolutely Colorado Springs. "In a week."

"I wish it was sooner."

"I do, too, but I have work and you're going back to school, right?"

"Yeah."

"See? We have things to do. The time will fly by. Now let me talk to your mom, okay?"

"'Kay. 'Bye."

He heard Vivian murmur something to Will as she moved to another room. "Hi, again," she said. "Did I really just learn that you are going to be my son's new skating partner?"

He smiled. "Well, I told Will I could take him a couple of times when I get back, if it's okay with his mother…and if he likes skating lessons. He might not."

"It's okay with me…and I'm pretty sure he's going to like his lessons. Even if he doesn't, he likes you, so he'll still want you to take him."

"Well, there are worse things," he teased.

"I'm just giving you fair warning that he'll likely be begging you to skate every time he sees you. Get ready to rent a bunch of skates."

"Oh, Vivian. Like any true Canadian, I have my own pair."

"Do you really?"

"I didn't get them out when we went to the rink because they haven't been used in years. But I'll bring them back and get the blades sharpened. Then Will and I will be set."

"How are things going?" Her voice was freer, less tentative.

Which brought him to the second reason for his call. "Frankly, not as well now that you two aren't here. But I do have news. I got an email from my new commanding officer. He's going to be out until Thursday, so he sent over my orders today."

"And?"

"I'm scheduled to report to Kingston on March first." It had been hard not to share the news with Doug, but he'd wanted Vivian to be the first to know.

"So we have six weeks."

"Yes. More or less." It was hard to keep his voice upbeat. By the time he got back to Cheyenne Mountain, it would be closer to five. He knew, too, what those five weeks would entail. Paperwork, entrance and exit interviews, meetings with officers. It was going to be tough to squeeze in as much time with Vivian and Will as he wanted. But he would do whatever it took.

"Viv, I know this is hard, but we'll find some way to work this out. You're important to me. You're both important to me."

"Graham, let's not talk about this right now. Not over the phone, okay?"

Her voice was quivering. "All right, if that's

what you want. So, what else is going on with you?"

"Would you mind if we just talked tomorrow? I've, uh, got scones in the oven. I should probably make sure they don't burn."

She was upset, he could tell. "I understand." Though it was tempting to ask her to stay on the line to discuss their future there and then, he knew he couldn't force her to. "You get some rest, okay?"

"I will."

"Tell Will good-night and that I'm bringing my skates."

Her laugh was adorable. "Will do. 'Bye, Graham," she added softly.

"'Bye," he replied before he hung up. Two days felt like an eternity. Far, far too long to go without seeing her smile.

CHAPTER THIRTY

THE FOLLOWING MORNING dawned bright and sunny. The sky was a robin's egg blue and the air was crisp and cold—a true Colorado winter day. After getting up early to put a vegetable strata and blueberry muffins in the oven, Vivian pulled on a thick sweater, made a cappuccino and sneaked outside to spend a few minutes alone on her front porch.

She was glad that it was going to be a relatively light day. Will was heading back to school, and her next set of guests weren't scheduled to arrive until the day after. She was going to use the extra time to put away the rest of the Christmas decorations, try out a few new recipes and do some thorough cleaning.

And figure out what she was going to do about Graham.

Thinking about their phone call the night before, she didn't know whether to smile at the thought of Graham bringing home his skates, or cry.

was the problem, of course. After Emerson died, she had done her best to stay numb. She'd learned that if she didn't feel anything too deeply, she wouldn't be in danger of falling apart. Of course, she also hadn't been genuinely happy in a lot of ways.

Graham's appearance in her life had forced her to move on. It had been a little rocky, but freeing, too.

But now that she had moved on? Well, she felt thwarted. It was like God had given her a chance to have a family again, just to pull it away from her. She couldn't believe Graham was only going to be in town for six more weeks.

Boy, that news had hurt. Feeling glum, she sipped her drink.

"Uh-oh. Are you thinking about all the things I did wrong while you were gone?" Maisie called out as she approached. Beside her, Ziggy looked especially jaunty with a bright red bandanna tied around his neck.

Her neighbor had on black-and-gray leggings, a long-sleeved gray top, and a black vest, knit cap and gloves. Her shoulder-length bob peeked out from under the cap in a smooth wave, and her face glowed, despite the fact that she had next to no makeup on. All in all, Maisie looked like a model for one of the high-end athletic-wear stores. "How is it possible that you always look so cute?" Vivian blurted.

Maisie's smile dimmed. "Um, what?"

"Sorry. I was just sitting here thinking, and that was the first thing that came to mind when I saw you. I'm jealous of your put-together look."

"If I'm looking put-together, it's all an illusion, dear. And I promise, this fancy workout set has nothing on you." Smiling at her dog, she added, "Though I have to say that Ziggy might be outshining us both in his new bandanna."

Vivian smiled as she petted the dog. "I was about to say that, too."

Taking a seat on the stoop next to Vivian, Maisie frowned. "What's wrong, Vivian? Is Will all right?"

"He's fine. Since he heads back to school tomorrow, he's having a lazy day. I left him sprawled out on the living room floor. He's watching TV and playing with his Legos." After debating about whether to say more, she added, "Graham is going to be assigned to his new base in about six weeks."

"Oh, my. I knew he was going to move, but I guess I didn't think it would be so soon."

"I didn't think so, either. Even Graham

seemed a little surprised that everything was moving so fast."

"I suppose he can't tell them never mind?"

Vivian chuckled. "No. Besides, I wouldn't want him to. Graham is not only missing his family, he's missing his home country. I completely understand. I really do. Except…"

"Except that you're going to miss him."

She swallowed the lump that had just formed in her throat. "I am. I really am, and it doesn't even make sense. I mean, we've only known each other a few weeks. Maisie, I dated Emerson for years before we got engaged. Didn't you date your husband for a long time, too, before things got serious?"

"We did." She winced. "I wouldn't exactly say that all that time helped us much, however. Jared and I didn't have a very happy marriage."

"I'm sorry," Vivian replied. "I wish you'd been happier." Looking back now, she wasn't sure if she and Emerson would've lasted a lifetime together. They were very different and not always in the most complementary ways. Would she have simply gotten used to her husband's need for adventure? Would he have gotten tired of her always refusing to join him? She didn't know.

Reaching down to stroke Ziggy's back,

Maisie said, "Oh, I've long since come to terms with that. I'm not proud of what happened, and I do wish things had been different, but the past has brought me to where I am today, and I'm grateful for that."

Vivian noticed that Maisie was smiling. "Are you smiling because you're content, or is there something else going on?"

"You could say that. Clay and I have now seen each other several times!"

"I'm so happy for you."

"I can't believe how amazing it's been. I never expected to feel this way about another man—it's really taken me by surprise. Everything inside me has been trying to point out ways that the two of us can't work."

"But your heart is saying something else, isn't it?"

Maisie nodded. "More importantly, I'm realizing that I want to see where this relationship is going to go. I think Clay feels the same way. He recently told me that he might be moving here permanently."

"Maisie, that's amazing."

"It is. He's amazing, too." Looking flustered, she added, "I'm excited, but nervous, too."

"Because..."

"Because when it comes to love and relationships, I don't think I'm any braver than any fresh-faced teenager."

"If that's the case, you're in good company. I don't think I'm any braver, either."

Maisie leaned back on her hands. "How about this? Even if we don't resolve everything right away, our lives have sure taught us that nothing has to be fixed or solved in a day, right? You and Graham can talk things out. Plus, he's in the air force. That young man can always fly here to see you, right?"

"Right." Smiling at her friend, Vivian added, "Where there's a will, there's a way, you know? I have to try and think positively."

"Good girl." After giving her a brief hug, Maisie got back on her feet. Ziggy barked happily, obviously ready to continue their walk. "At the very least, we'll help each other get through the next month, right?"

"Right." As Maisie and Ziggy walked off down the street, Vivian finished her drink and headed inside. It was time to begin her day—this time with a bounce in her step.

Two days later, Vivian received the nicest surprise in the mail. Mrs. Vanderhaven had sent her a handwritten thank-you note, conveying the whole family's appreciation for their stay at the Snowdrop Inn. She had enclosed a gift certificate to be used at the mall, relaying that the whole family thought Vivian should take herself out shopping and enjoy a treat.

It was a generous gift, and the sentiment was nice. However, as much as she might enjoy getting a new date outfit or a new pair of shoes, Vivian realized that what she really wanted to do was take Will to the sporting goods store to get a pair of skates. Everything she'd read about ice-skating said that properly fitted skates, even inexpensive ones, were better than rented ones.

It was a splurge, but she wanted Will to enjoy his skating lessons as well as his time on the ice with Graham. She knew he wouldn't do either if his feet were hurting the entire time.

Sitting on a bench at the ginormous sports store, Vivian eyed the clerk who was helping Will. "Are you sure these will work? They're a half size smaller than his regular shoe size."

Kneeling in front of him, the woman felt for Will's toes. "Yes, ma'am. Hockey skate sizes are a bit different than tennis shoes." Smiling at Will, she said, "Remember what we talked about when you first sat down?"

"Yep. It's all about my heels."

"Good job. So, how does your heel feel? Is it snug?"

"I think so."

She moved a finger around the top of his foot. "How do your toes feel? Can you wiggle them around?"

Will frowned. "Not too much. It's pretty tight."

After examining each foot carefully, she said, "I think we're set."

Bracing herself, Vivian said, "I guess we'll get the skates, then. How much are they?"

"They're on sale." She pointed to a brightly printed sign as she helped Will get out of each skate. "Plus, since he's a new customer and skater, we run an additional discount."

The price was amazing. Much better than she'd anticipated. On a whim, Vivian decided to use her credit card to pay for the skates instead of the gift card.

When they left the store and entered the mall, Vivian looked down at Will. "What do you think? Do you like your new skates?"

"Yep. I think Graham is gonna like them."

"I bet he will. When I told him that you were going to start lessons soon, he was excited. Of course, he can't wait to help you, too."

Will nodded.

Vivian waited for him to say something else, but he didn't.

She knew her little boy, and this wasn't normal behavior for him. Seeing an empty seating area, she led him over and sat down.

Will sat down in the chair next to her. Remaining quiet, he looked at all the shoppers and kicked his feet back and forth.

Something was really bothering him.

Knowing she needed to choose her words with care, Vivian took a second. Will liked to please her, so she didn't want to lead him in a conversation where he would say whatever he thought she wanted to hear. "Tell me what you're thinking about, honey."

He met her gaze, then turned away quickly. "It's nothing."

"I think we both know you're thinking about something. Won't you please tell me?"

He pursed his lips. "I don't think I want to skate anymore."

"What? This morning you couldn't wait to go to the store to try on ice skates. What happened? Do the skates hurt your feet after all?"

He shook his head.

"Will, please talk to me. I can't read your mind, and I don't want to keep guessing."

"What if Graham doesn't come back?"

"He will."

"No, Mommy. I mean when he goes up to live with his real family. He's not going to want to see us anymore." His bottom lip trembled. "He'll forget about me."

She was about to remind him how easy flying to Detroit and driving to Windsor had been, but then she realized Will wasn't worried about plane flights or logistics.

At last, everything clicked into place. "You're going to miss him."

He nodded. "I don't want him to leave us."

Vivian sighed. They were in the middle of the mall, festive music was still playing around them and she had a box of ice skates on her lap. All in all, it felt like a bad place to share a heart-to-heart, but she supposed it didn't matter.

"I'm going to miss Graham, too," she said. "I wish he wasn't going to live so far away."

"Can't you tell him to stay here?"

"You know I can't do that."

His forehead wrinkled a bit as he thought hard. "Couldn't you at least try? We could learn to make his favorite foods."

He looked so optimistic, the conversation was breaking her heart. "Will, you're a big boy now. You and I both know that Graham isn't moving to eat tourtière or poutine. He's moving to Canada for a couple of reasons. He has an important job with the RCAF, remember?" After Will nodded, she added. "He also wants to be closer to his family, which I'm sure you can understand. They were really nice, right?"

He nodded. "They were really nice. I wish we could be his family, too."

Oh dear Lord, that hurt. Vivian wracked her brain, trying to think of something meaningful to say that would make him feel better. Unfortunately, she was drawing a blank.

Probably because she was trying her best not to say what she was really thinking—that she wished the same thing.

Desperate to cheer them both up, she got to her feet. "You know, I think we need to go to the food court and eat some chicken nuggets. But first, I want to stop in at my favorite store and get a new outfit."

Will groaned. "Nooooooo."

"I know. It's going to take a lot of patience, but I think you can do it," she teased.

"Last time we went in there you took forever."

"How about this? I promise to try to be quick if you promise not to complain more than two times while I'm trying on clothes." Ruffling his hair, she added, "If you can do that, I'll buy you a shake to go with your chicken."

"Promise?"

"Yep. Ready?"

He was still dragging his feet. "You're not gonna make me get clothes, too, are you?"

"Nope."

"Fine."

When they started walking, she noticed there was a new spring in his step. He might still be sad and worried, but at least he'd shared what he had been feeling. Things weren't perfect, but they didn't have to be.

All they needed, at least for now, was each other.

CHAPTER THIRTY-ONE

GRAHAM HAD HOPED to zip down to Detroit, catch a midmorning flight to Chicago, then get on a connecting flight to Colorado Springs by midafternoon. He soon learned that everything about that optimistic plan had been a bad idea. Customs had taken almost an hour longer than usual.

Then there had been a wreck on I-75, which led him to miss his flight out of Detroit. He pulled some connections and was able to get another flight out, but it was delayed because of weather.

When he finally landed in Colorado Springs, it was seven hours later than he'd anticipated. Worse, he'd had to text Vivian that he was going to miss Will's second skating lesson.

Of course, she'd texted him back, assuring him that he shouldn't worry about it, but Graham still did. Vivian had told him about her conversation with Will. Though it was obvious she was trying her best not to make him feel guilty, he still did. He'd promised the boy that he'd do something, and he'd messed up.

After retrieving his duffel bag at the baggage claim, he walked outside. It was snowing. Not anything unusual for January, but the crummy weather felt like the icing on his ruined cake. Just as he was about to get on his phone to call an Uber, Brad, his Santa Tracker friend, called out to him.

"Graham! Long time no see," he said, reaching out to shake his hand.

"Absolutely. How are you?"

"Freezing. My girl and I just got back from an all-inclusive in the Dominican Republic."

"Wow. You have a good time?"

"The best. Kim is my fiancée now."

"Hey, man, that's great. Congratulations!"

"Thanks. Kim's in the bathroom, but as soon as she comes out, I'll introduce you."

"Can't wait to meet her. Did you pop the question on your trip?"

"I did." Looking almost bashful, Brad added, "You wouldn't believe how nervous I was. I think Kim knew something was up, too. I mean, why else would I have ordered a bottle of champagne at the table? But she still acted surprised and said yes."

"I bet she thought it was perfect."

"We've only been dating six months, but it

feels like forever, you know? When we were in the Miami airport, she got a *Brides* magazine, and it didn't even bother me that she was already thinking about locations and bridesmaids and honeymoons. I'd marry her tomorrow if I could."

Graham was impressed. "I guess you knew she was the one from the start?"

"From practically the first moment I met her. She's the best." Looking over Graham's shoulder, Brad's eyes lit up. "Hey, here she is." He raised his voice. "Kimmy, come over here. I want you to meet someone."

A pretty gal with long dark hair and a sparkly ring on her hand approached. "Hello."

"This is Sergeant Graham Hopkins. Remember I told you about him? He's the Canadian guy I met on Christmas Eve."

"It's nice to meet you," Graham said. "Congratulations."

"Thank you." Kim gazed at Brad like he was her whole world. "I'm so excited!"

When she shivered, Brad frowned. "Sorry, babe. Here it's snowing, and you only have on jeans and a sweatshirt. We gotta go, Graham."

"Good to see you."

Brad turned around after they took a few steps. "Hey, are you going to the base? I can give you a ride?"

Normally Graham would've jumped at the offer, but he didn't think he was up for being around the happy couple. "Thanks, but I'm good."

"You sure?"

"Yep. Take care now."

"Nice to meet you," Kim called out as she took hold of her wheelie bag with one hand and Brad's hand with her other.

Unable to help himself, Graham watched the two walk toward the parking lot. Neither seemed to be aware of the snow swirling around them as they laughed and smiled at each other. It really was sweet to see.

And then a shot of envy hit him hard. He'd been on his own for all his adult life. Until Christmas Day, it hadn't even bothered him. He'd almost taken it for granted that he was never going to find a special woman to share his life with.

But then he'd met Vivian and Will. Almost instantly, they'd grabbed hold of his heart and made him think about a future that could be different. He wanted nothing more than to make plans with them for the future. To simply sit around her house and watch it snow or play Legos with Will or go sledding.

Boy, it was going to hurt when he said goodbye and moved to Kingston.

He had his orders, though, and even though he'd requested the transfer, it wasn't like he could ask to come back. And as much as he wanted to be with them, he didn't know if he could miss out on even more birthdays, weddings, and gatherings—even for her.

It wasn't like he could ask her to give up her bed-and-breakfast and move to another country with him, either.

Besides, they'd only known each other a month. It was too soon to even suggest such a thing.

"Sergeant Hopkins, is that you?"

He turned to find his lieutenant-colonel striding toward him. Gathering himself together, he stepped forward. "Yes, sir."

"I heard you've been up north. Have a good trip?"

"Yes, sir."

"Need a ride to the base? I'd be happy to give you a lift."

"Actually, I do."

"I'm glad I found you, then. Ah, here we are," he said as a black Suburban approached, driven by a very young-looking airman. "I swear, they look younger every year."

"I was just thinking the same thing."

"Well, let's hope this one is from Nebraska and not Florida. Those Southerners can't drive in snow worth beans."

"Yes, sir."

When the kid drew to a stop and then hopped out of the driver's seat, he stood at attention. "Quinn, sir."

"At ease, Quinn. Thanks for giving us a ride. This is Sergeant Hopkins."

Quinn nodded. "Good to meet you, sir."

"Just Sergeant, Airman. I'm not an officer, remember?"

"Ah, yes, Sergeant."

"Where you from, son?" the lieutenant-colonel asked.

"Alabama."

He scowled. "Of course you are. Well, come on, then."

Graham grinned to himself as he got in the back seat of the vehicle while the lieutenant-colonel got in the passenger seat next to the visibly rattled private. Poor kid.

It was going to be a long ride to the base.

CHAPTER THIRTY-TWO

GRAHAM HAD CALLED a little after six the night before. He'd been full of apologies for missing Will's skating lesson and had even offered to swing by that evening.

Vivian hadn't wanted to refuse his offer, but she hadn't been up for the emotional toll his visit would take, so she'd admitted that it wasn't a good time. There had been an accident near the ice rink, making the trip home in bad weather even more difficult. Will had also been upset about Graham missing his lesson.

Even though she'd reminded him that there was nothing Graham could do about traffic and late flights, Will was only six. The only thing he wanted to focus on was that Graham had said he was going to be there and he wasn't.

Vivian knew part of the problem was that her son was hungry and tired. She hadn't wanted to make Graham feel worse by coming face-to-face with Will's little-boy tears.

So, she'd told Graham that she still had to

do some prep work for the next morning's breakfast service.

He'd sounded disappointed.

She was, too—especially because she'd started imagining the two of them trying to make a relationship work after Graham moved. Life was full of unexpected moments and changes in plans. It was going to be hard enough for her when planned phone calls got canceled.

But what about her son? How was he going to handle it?

When he'd asked to take her out as soon as she could find a babysitter, Vivian suggested he come over while Will was at school instead. He'd told her that his next few days at work were going to be relatively uneventful. For a moment, she'd thought Graham was going to refuse, but he'd ultimately said he could be over around eleven.

That was a good time for her. By eleven, breakfast had been served and put away, and her guests had either checked out or were out exploring Colorado Springs. The cleaning service would arrive just after noon to help her prepare for the next round of visitors.

So, all in all, Vivian knew she should be relaxed and ready for Graham's arrival.

Unfortunately, she felt anything but.

Yesterday's snowfall had been significant.

Although it was no longer snowing and blue skies were peeking through the clouds, it was still bitter cold. She had on flannel-lined khakis and an ancient raspberry-colored fisherman's sweater. Usually she stayed far away from anything red or pink, but for some reason she never thought this particular shade of raspberry clashed with her auburn hair.

Knowing how much Graham liked his sweets, she'd also made a fresh cinnamon-apple coffee cake. The kitchen smelled heavenly. She knew he would enjoy that, too.

So, she looked okay and had made sure he would be comfortable. But as for what they were going to be talking about? That was going to be tough.

Graham was wearing his uniform when he arrived. It was camouflage, something called his OCP, which stood for operational camouflage pattern. He looked as handsome as ever when she greeted him on her front stoop.

"Hello, Sergeant." She walked into his open arms and hugged him close.

He wrapped his arms around her. "Boy, it's good to see you, Vivian." He bent down and kissed her lips lightly.

She responded, resting her hands on his chest. His scent surrounded her, almost bringing tears to her eyes. She was starting to hate how much her body responded to his, knowing how hard it was going to be when he left.

"Come on in. I made a coffee cake."

Right away, he unlaced his boots and placed them by the door.

"You don't have to do that, you know."

"Will it save you a few minutes of mopping?"

"Probably."

"Then I need to do it," he said simply as he followed her to the back of the house. When they entered the kitchen, he stopped and took a deep breath. "You know, I was disappointed to not be taking you out. But this room smells so good, I think it was the right decision."

She smiled at his joke. "I'll cut you a slice of cake. Coffee, too?"

"Of course." When he saw the packet of coffee on the counter, he picked it up. "What's this?"

"Exactly what it looks like. I found this package of Tim Hortons coffee when I was at the grocery store the other day. I can't get you an official double double, but this might be close."

"You didn't have to do that."

"Maybe I wanted to," she said as she placed a thick slice of cake and his coffee in front of him.

Graham didn't touch either until she sat

next to him. "Thank you for going to so much trouble, Vivian."

"It's the least I could do. You were such a good host when we were in Canada." Feeling a lump form in her throat, she forced herself to smile. "I bet it was hard to come back."

"Want to know the truth?"

"Of course."

"I thought it might be hard, but I couldn't wait to come back to the Springs. I thought about you all the time, Vivian. Well, you and Will."

His words were sweet, but it was the look of longing on his face that made her heart jump. "I thought about you all the time, too," she admitted softly.

He took her hand. "At least I'm here now."

Graham was being so loving. Meeting his eyes, her pulse spiked. Maybe he had some good news for her. Maybe he'd decided to stay after all. "When do you go back?"

He kissed her knuckles before releasing her hand. "The same date. March first."

"Right." She swallowed her disappointment. Why did she do this to herself? Why did she keep dreaming about things that were never going to happen? Graham was going to move. He was going to move to Canada, and that was that. Sure, they could try to see each other from time to time, but to what end?

"Graham, I've been thinking a lot about us."

His brown eyes warmed. "I've been thinking about us, too."

"I…well, I wonder if we need to start cooling things off between us."

"Where did this come from? I thought you bought Will some skates and he and I were going to go skating together."

"I did say that. And I did plan for it. But he's gotten really attached to you already. I'm afraid that he's not going to understand how little we'll be able to see you after you move."

"I can call him, Vivian. We can FaceTime."

"It's not the same, though."

"It's not the same, but we can make it work." When she hesitated, his voice deepened. "Don't you want him to see that I can still be his friend even when I live someplace else?"

"Of course. But you know that's not what I mean."

"I'm pretty sure it is." He leaned a little closer. "I know it's going to be hard, but we can make this long-distance thing work."

"As much as I want it, too, I don't see how that's possible. Especially not long term." Practically feeling the disappointment wafting off him, Vivian looked down at her plate. "I'm not trying to be difficult, just realistic."

"Vivian, what's realistic is that planes still fly back and forth. You don't even have to fly to Ottawa or anything, either. Just fly to Detroit."

"I thought your base was farther away. It's a six- or seven-hour drive, right?"

"Yes, but you can take a Porter over."

She knew he was referring to a regional Canadian airline. It was a good idea, but at the moment, it sounded like just one more hoop to jump through. "How long would we do that for?"

"As long as we feel like it."

She wondered if Graham was being obtuse on purpose. Holding up a hand, she said, "Will is only in first grade. We can't have a long-distance relationship for eleven more years."

"Then move."

She gaped at him. "What?"

He smiled. "That's what I wanted to talk to you about. How about you and Will just move to Canada with me?"

He sounded so cavalier. As if he didn't realize that moving for her not only meant moving to a different country but also leaving the Snowdrop Inn. "I'm not ready to do that."

"There's not much of a choice. I can't stay.

Even if I told my superiors that I'd like to stay here, it wouldn't be possible. I need to go to the base where I'm sent, when I'm sent."

"I know. I'm just really sorry."

"Vivian, what are you saying?"

"I'm saying that I don't think our relationship can go anywhere," she added at last, feeling as if she was about to be sick. "I want to be with someone who is actually going to be with me. You know, like in the same city."

"That's it? You're just going to break us up before we've even had a chance to start something?"

"I'm really not trying to be difficult. I just don't want Will to get any more emotionally involved if we don't have long-term goals."

"My long-term goal is to make a life with someone who thinks that a few sacrifices are worth it."

"'A few sacrifices' sounds noble when you just shoot it off in a sentence like that. But the reality is hard—and is filled with a lot of uncertainty."

"I'm in the air force, Vivian. I've been deployed. I realize that."

Hurt that Graham was acting as if she was giving up on them without a second thought, she added, "Try to see things from my perspective, Graham. I had a marriage and a life, and it was all pulled out from under me. It took a while, but I finally got back on my feet. Now I have security. I can't just walk away from it without a second thought."

"We've only known each other a little over a month. Can't we see where this goes before you say it's not possible?"

"If it was just me, then I would agree with you a hundred percent. But Will is involved. I can't risk hurting him."

He shook his head. "This isn't about Will. If I don't ever see him again, then he's going to be upset, but he'll also be fine. The same thing goes for you if you date me and then a year from now we break up."

"This is different."

"Is it? Everything in life is uncertain. Accidents happen, planes get delayed and not every relationship is destined to end with a happily-ever-after." He took a deep breath. "Vivian, you're pushing me away because you're worried about your heart. You're scared to try again. You'd rather push me and a good future away instead of trying to make something work."

She gasped as his words sank in. Both because he had hit such a raw nerve and because he was right—she *was* afraid of getting hurt again and losing everything.

But what was wrong with that?

"You're right. I am afraid, and I don't want to get hurt again. But don't act like the things you're asking me to do are insignificant. Selling my business and moving to a new place is huge. It's a lot."

"I know that."

"Do you? Because you aren't acting like it. You're acting like I'm being petty and selfish. Honestly, Graham, I feel like you aren't even listening to me."

"I'm listening, I just don't agree."

"Just because you don't agree with me doesn't mean that I'm wrong."

"Giving yourself a second chance is huge, too, Vivian. The risk is great, but the payoff is, too. If you were willing to take a chance on us, then you'd be making us a family. A second-chance family."

His dark eyes met hers. She stared back, feeling devastated. "I'm sorry," she said at last.

"I am, too." Without looking at her again, he got up and walked away. Out of her life. Out of her dreams.

CHAPTER THIRTY-THREE

MAISIE WAS SURE her eyes looked like a raccoon's. Thirty minutes ago, she'd been staring at her computer screen in the back corner of her favorite coffee shop. Next thing she knew, Allison was saying hello. Then Jenna had appeared!

And then she'd started crying and hugging her daughters tight. It had been the best moment.

Now they were sipping lattes across from her, just like they used to do when they'd come home from college.

"I simply can't believe you two are here," Maisie told Jenna and Allison. "And yes, I realize I've already said that five or six times."

"You can say it as much as you want!" Allison teased.

Jenna grinned. "We've had fun planning this surprise. I'm so glad Audrey didn't give you any hints."

"I didn't know she was so good at keeping secrets. I think I've been underestimating her," Maisie said with a laugh.

"When I first texted her about our plans, she was all in."

"So, are you girls going to tell me why you're here, or is that a secret, too?" When she saw them exchange glances, she added, "I love seeing you both, but I wasn't expecting you to take time off work and fly to Colorado."

Always the leader, Jenna spoke. "You know we felt bad about not spending Valentine's Day with you this year."

"I think you knew that I understood."

Ever since the divorce, her girls had always spent the day with her. When they were still in high school, the three of them would order pizza, eat ice cream and watch *Sleepless in Seattle*. Once they started college, at least one of them would drive home, acting the whole time like there was nothing important going on at school. Now that they both had jobs, she hadn't expected them to get away.

To her surprise, she'd hardly thought about their tradition this year. Clay had spoiled her, coming over with both Chinese takeout and a dozen red roses.

The girls exchanged glances again. "We also knew you had plans, Mom," Allison said with a smile.

"Are you two here to meet Clay?"

"Of course! You didn't think you could hide him from us, did you?"

Maisie supposed she should've guessed that was the reason for their visit. "It's lucky that he's in town. He divides his time between here and Texas."

"We know," Jenna said. "He told us all about it."

Allison grinned. "He's supercute, too, Mom."

"Wait. What?"

"Audrey gave us his phone number, so we texted him," Allison continued. "Then he set up a Zoom call with both of us."

"He's really nice. We approve," Jenna added.

"I guess Audrey isn't the only one who can keep a secret, hmm?"

"Nope. He said to tell you he's not normally this sneaky, though, so you don't need to worry."

Maisie laughed. "So are we all getting together this weekend?"

"Yep. Tomorrow night," Jenna said. "We wanted to have you to ourselves first. Plus, there's something else you ought to know."

All traces of her girls' pretty smiles disappeared, putting her on alert. "Can you tell me here or should we go back to the house?"

"We might as well get it over with," Allison said. "Dad's getting another divorce."

"Ah." Maisie leaned back and tried to figure out how she felt about that. At the moment, all she felt was ambivalence. At long last, Jared was firmly in her past. Starting over in Colorado Springs, being housemates with Audrey and launching her new career as a writer had helped propel her forward. Clay's attentiveness and care had also helped. She would never miss her relationship with Jared again.

Realizing that her girls were staring at her, waiting for a response, Maisie asked, "How is he doing?"

"Not too good," Allison replied. "Dad said that Erin was the one who asked for the divorce. She found someone else, supposedly."

So Jared had gotten a taste of his own medicine. If she had been talking to anyone else, she would've made a snarky comment. But these were his daughters, and they loved him. "That's too bad."

Jenna furrowed her brow. "That's all you're gonna say?"

"Yep. Unless you want to talk to me about how you're feeling."

"I feel sorry for Dad, but I'm glad I won't have to deal with Erin anymore."

"I thought she'd gotten better."

"No," said Allison. "She was awful to the end."

Thinking back to the times she'd had to talk to Erin to coordinate the girls' birthdays and holidays, Maisie completely agreed. "Well, you know I wasn't a big fan of hers, either." She stood up and started packing away her computer. "Should we go? We need to get some snacks for tonight."

"Sounds good. I can't wait to see Ziggy!"

"He's going to be thrilled to see both of you," Maisie said as they walked out the door. "Almost as happy as I am."

CHAPTER THIRTY-FOUR

IT WAS IRONIC—instead of feeling better about her decision to end things with Graham, Vivian felt even worse. Over and over she replayed their conversation. Maybe her heart had been in the right place, but she kept second-guessing herself.

Especially when she remembered how hurt Graham had looked.

Then there was Will. Vivian had been trying to prevent Will from getting hurt, but pushing Graham away seemed to hurt him worse.

The only thing that prevented her from calling Graham back and apologizing was that March first was just around the corner. She didn't know if her heart could bear to patch things up just to tell him goodbye again.

So, Vivian tried to think of other things and keep busy. She'd begun deep cleaning some of the rooms. And she decided to try out some new recipes, which was the reason she was currently in the kitchen.

She'd also been booked solid for the last few weeks. The Vanderhaven clan had enjoyed themselves so much, they'd left amazing reviews on several sites. They'd praised the Snowdrop Inn so much that she now had reservations leading into March. She was on track to have her most successful year yet and was finally going to be able to make some of the improvements she'd been dreaming about for a long time.

After a rocky number of days, Will had bounced back. He was still taking skating lessons and said he wanted to be a hockey player when he grew up.

So, all in all, she should have been doing great. But all she could think about was how empty she felt inside. Graham had listened to her worries and helped remind her that every little problem at the inn wasn't actually a matter of life and death.

He'd helped her so much, and now he was just days from moving away.

More than once, she'd been tempted to text him, just to wish him well. But she was pretty sure he wouldn't appreciate the gesture. Who could blame him, anyway? All he'd asked was that she give them a chance, and she had been too worried about her heart to even do that.

Will walked into the kitchen with an irritated look on his face. "They're at it again."

He was talking about the couple in the suite in the attic. They were supposedly celebrating their fifth wedding anniversary, but so far they had acted completely unhappy. They'd bickered when checking in and acted like they didn't even want to be in the same room together.

Vivian put down the spoon she'd been using to stir the soup. "What's going on now?"

"First, the man said the woman was wearing something that looked like a…" He scrunched his nose. "I forget what he said, but I don't think it was very nice."

"Oh, my."

"Then he told her to go change, and she told him to stay out of her business 'cause he doesn't care about her anymore." Will's eyes got big. "And then he told her to shut up!"

"Uh-oh." Wincing, she asked, "How did you hear all this? You weren't spying on them, were you?"

"Mom, everybody heard! Well, everyone but you, 'cause you're in here cooking. Two ladies even came out of their rooms, and they looked upset."

She turned off the burner, wiped her hands

and pulled off her apron. "I guess I'd better go get involved. Are they still in their suite?"

"I don't know. I hope they leave soon."

"Maybe they'll patch things up. That would be good, right?"

When he simply shrugged, she looked at him in concern. "What's that shrug about?"

"I don't care about them, Mom." He looked down at his feet and mumbled, "All these people do is stay in our house, eat what you cook and make a mess. Lots of them don't ever come back, either."

Each word felt like a tiny slap in the face. Will was entitled to his own perspective, but it certainly made her feel as if everything she'd told Graham—about the importance of stability and making sure that Will was happy—was a bunch of baloney.

Time and again, Will had made comments about how he didn't love sharing his home with strangers. She'd either brushed them off or privately blamed them on little-boy immaturity. She should've remembered that her son was used to people coming in and out of his life. He would've missed Graham, but he probably would have coped better with a long-distance relationship than a lot of kids his age.

"I'll go see how Mr. and Mrs. Pushkin are doing," she said.

When Will made a move to follow, she said, "You don't need to come along, honey."

"But I still want to come."

To her dismay, she could hear the Pushkins yelling at each other the moment she opened the kitchen door. They had moved from their attic suite to the entryway. Vivian increased her pace, just imagining what the sweet pair of sisters in the room closest to the front door were thinking. She hoped they were still at the zoo.

They were not; their door was open a crack, and they were watching the escalating argument with concern. The couple vacationing from Germany was there as well. The husband was filming the Pushkins' antics with his cell phone. His wife just looked confused.

Her stomach sank. If this was posted on one of those review sites, all her positive reviews weren't going to mean very much.

When the Pushkins' voices got even louder, Vivian knew she couldn't hesitate another second. "Stay over here, son," she murmured as she strode toward the argumentative pair. Steeling herself, she called out, "Bob? Stephanie? This isn't the place for your conversation."

Both of them ignored her.

"Excuse me," she said again.

"Stay out of this," Bob said.

"I'm afraid I can't, since you are choosing to do this on my property."

"Did you hear that, Bob?" Stephanie yelled at her husband.

"I heard that you can't quit complaining."

When they still didn't stop, Vivian opened the front door and stood on the front stoop, holding it ajar. "If you two won't stop arguing or leave, I'm going to be forced to call the police," she said in a firm voice. She'd never had to do such a thing, but she supposed there was a first time for everything.

Both turned and looked at her in surprise.

Vivian held up her phone. "I'm serious."

"Fine." Bob started toward the door, his wife by his side.

But just as they were about to walk through the entryway, Stephanie said, "This is all your fault."

"If you had just listened to me, we could have gotten it figured out."

"I don't need to listen to you. Just stop!" And with that, Stephanie pushed Bob.

To everyone's shock, Bob pushed Stephanie right back. She stumbled and knocked into Vivian.

And she, who had been standing on the edge of the top step, lost her balance and fell. In a perfect storm of mishaps, her head hit the top step and started bleeding.

It started bleeding a whole lot. Vivian gasped as she held her hand to her head.

"Vivian?" one of the elderly ladies called out.

"Mom!"

"I'm okay," she said…just as her world went black.

CHAPTER THIRTY-FIVE

GRAHAM WOULD LATER wonder what had led him to not put his phone on silent at work. He did so religiously every morning before he exited his vehicle. He'd forgotten to do so that morning.

Another unusual thing had been that he wasn't in meetings that afternoon. Instead, he was spending most of the day filling out paperwork for his impending move. There was an old saying that the air force never used one piece of paper when five would do.

So, Graham had been sitting at his desk, filling out multiple pieces of paperwork, each essentially saying the same thing, when his phone's shrill ring pierced the silence. When he saw it was Vivian, his heart turned over. He'd really missed her. Maybe she'd had a change of heart. "Vivian?"

"Graham, it's me!"

Not Vivian but Will. The boy sounded upset. "What's wrong? Are you okay?"

"Graham, something's wrong with my mom. You've gotta come over."

He was on his feet in an instant. "What happened?"

"Mom fell, and she's bleeding really bad."

"She's bleeding? From where?"

"Her head." He sniffled.

Graham pulled on his jacket as he grabbed his keys. "Did you call 911?"

"She said not to, but I don't know," the boy added, sounding more stricken. "The man and woman who knocked into her said it looks real bad."

He motioned to the airman on duty that he had to leave for an emergency. "Are you at home?" he asked Will as he strode through the main doors toward his Jeep.

"Uh-huh. But no one knows I'm calling. I'm using Mom's phone, 'cause she left it in the kitchen." His voice quickened. "I didn't know what to do, so I called you."

"Are there other adults there?"

"Yeah, but they don't look very happy. One lady said that she wants to check out now. I don't know how to do that, though."

"Listen, I'm in my car. You go back to your mom's side and tell everyone that I'm on my way. You tell them that your mom's boyfriend is driving over from the air force base, okay?" He hoped that would make everyone think twice before saying anything else foolish to an upset little boy.

"Okay. Um, are you sure you're on your way?"

"I just exited the gates," he said as he returned the salute of the guard on duty. "I'll be there in ten minutes."

"Promise?"

He turned left and cruised down Broadmoor Road. "I promise. Now go sit by your mother. Hold her hand, and I'll be there in a few minutes."

"Okay."

Graham exhaled when he heard the phone click off. His head was spinning, imagining every worst-case scenario. What if Vivian was passed out? What if one of the guests was taking advantage of the situation and attempting to leave without paying or was asking Will to do something?

Graham knew he was jumping to conclusions and that it was likely that every single person staying at the inn was currently trying to help Vivian. But there was always that one person who couldn't be counted on.

And it only took one person to seriously hurt Will.

Accelerating, he pulled into the inn's parking lot seven minutes later. When he saw the ambulance's flashing lights, he breathed a sigh of relief. Someone had called 911. He was so glad.

He saw emergency personnel rushing forward as he exited his vehicle. There was a small group of people near the front door. As he approached, he noticed that Vivian was on the ground, and a worried-looking Will was next to her. He was holding her hand. Someone had placed a blanket around Vivian and a coat around Will's shoulders.

Instinctively, Graham wanted to go to Vivian's side, but he knew better. The emergency personnel were moving everyone away and asking her questions. As much as he wanted to help, the best thing he could do for her was to wait to one side and stay out of the paramedics' way.

However, there was someone else who looked like he needed Graham's attention.

"Will!" Graham called out.

Immediately, Will turned his way. With a relieved cry, he jumped to his feet and ran toward him.

Graham knelt down and pulled the little boy into his arms. When he felt Will tremble and start to cry, Graham rubbed his back. "It's okay," he murmured. "The medics are gonna help your mom."

"You got here fast," he said. "You didn't lie."

Will's honesty was humbling. Right then and there, Graham knew he never wanted to disappoint him again. "I wouldn't lie to you," he said as he gently placed a finger under the boy's chin so they could meet eye to eye. His eyes were tear-filled, but he didn't look quite as distraught. "Okay?"

He nodded. "Okay."

"Okay, then. I'm just going to check in on your mom."

He got to his feet just as the EMTs were helping Vivian sit up. She had blood on her face that looked like it had come from a cut on her head. One of the techs was kneeling next to her and holding a cloth against a spot just above her temple.

"Graham," she said, sounding surprised. "How did you get here?"

"Will gave me a call."

"Are you okay, Mommy?" Will stepped closer.

Graham reached for his hand and pulled him back to his side. "Let's let these folks help your mom, okay?"

He nodded but still looked worried.

The paramedic turned to him. "Are you her family?"

Wishing he was, he said, "I'm her boyfriend. Does she need to go to the hospital?"

"We're going to take her in. She needs a CAT on her head and stitches."

"I'm sure I'm fine," Vivian said.

"You need to get checked out, ma'am."

"But—"

"I'll take care of Will," Graham said. "He and I will go to the hospital and wait for you there."

"But my guests…"

As the EMTs loaded Vivian onto a stretcher, Vivian's friend Maisie and a man about her age stepped forward. "We'll take care of everything, Viv."

"Thanks so much."

"What hospital?" Graham asked.

"Penrose."

"Thanks." He released Will's hand to walk to Vivian's side. "I'll be there soon."

"I think there's blood—"

"I'll bring you some fresh clothes, too."

"No, I meant there's some on the sidewalk."

"I've got this. Stop fussing."

After exchanging a few more quick words with the two techs, Graham stepped away so they could carry her to the ambulance. He reached for Will's hand. "If your mom is giving me directions, I think it means she's going to be okay."

"I wish I could ride in the ambulance, too."

"I don't think there's room for you, buddy."

"I know. But it would be neat to see the inside. Do you think they're going to turn on the sirens again?"

"I don't think so, but we're about to find out."

"Yeah."

Will sounded so disappointed, Graham chuckled. It looked like everything was going to be all right after all. If Vivian was coherent and worrying about bloodstains on the sidewalk and Will was wishing he could ride in the ambulance, Graham figured they had gotten through the worst of it.

After the ambulance pulled out, he noticed the inn's guests standing around, two of the people looking really upset. Maisie and her friend seemed to be taking in the scene as well.

"Something's going on, but we'll take care of it, Graham. Don't worry," said Maisie. "You and Will go on to the hospital."

"I need to get a couple of things for Vivian. Oh, and clean up the sidewalk."

"We'll get that."

"Thanks for being here."

"We're happy to do it. Right, Clay?"

"Absolutely." Clay held out his hand. "Clay Stevick."

"Good to meet you. Graham Hopkins." Knowing Will was right next to him, he added, "Do you want me to help you with the guests?"

"Nope. Go get whatever you need and get on out of here."

"Will, come show me where your mom's closet is. She needs a sweatshirt or something to put on."

"Then we'll go to the hospital?"

"Yep."

As Will pulled him into the inn and down the hall, Graham decided that he was going to do whatever it took to make things right with Vivian. They needed each other. Maybe they were already a family and hadn't even realized it.

It was time they caught up.

CHAPTER THIRTY-SIX

FEELING A BIT like a nursery school teacher, Maisie shuttled all the guests back into the inn after Graham took Will to the hospital. Clay stood to one side, but his gaze was sharp, as if he was trying to figure out what had happened. To her relief, the guests didn't scatter. They were standing awkwardly in the entryway, most looking to be as shaken by Vivian's accident as she was.

Figuring it was best to give them some direction, she announced, "Everyone, my name is Maisie, and I help out here from time to time." That was a bit of an overstatement, but she figured Vivian would forgive the fib. "This is Clay. He's my…uh, significant other." She took care to avoid Clay's eyes, certain they were lit with amusement.

"Now, um, you all heard the same thing as I did. Vivian needs to get some tests run and stitches. I'll be here cleaning up, but feel free to let me or Clay know if you need anything or have any concerns."

An older lady shook her hand. "I'm Tabitha, and this is my sister, Violet. If you or the police have any questions, just let us know. We saw everything."

"We're supposed to stay until tomorrow. Is that still okay?" Violet asked.

"Of course."

"Good. We have tickets to see a show downtown."

"We'd better go get ready," Violet said as she ushered her sister into the guest bedroom off the entryway.

A family of four were climbing the stairs to their room. The wife paused briefly to say that they were fine and would continue their stay.

That left only an uncomfortable-looking couple in the entryway.

"What did the owner mean about the police being called?" the man asked Maisie.

"I'm not exactly sure. I don't believe they were called."

"I hope not, because her accident was not our fault."

Clay walked to Maisie's side. "We just got here. What happened?"

"We were arguing," the woman admitted. "About nothing, really."

"Arguing is what we do," the man said. "I mean, it's what we got used to doing."

The woman looked at her husband. "Today put everything into perspective. I think we need to change how we do things."

"I'm still not sure how your argument resulted in Vivian hurting her head," Maisie said.

"We were arguing right here and Vivian told us to take it outside, which I acted like was an inconvenience."

"We both walked out in a huff." The woman's cheeks were flushed. "I'm afraid one of us bumped into her, and she fell."

"So it was an accident," Clay said.

"It was, in the sense that neither of us intended for her to get hurt," the husband said. He rubbed a hand over his face. "But even though it was an accident, I can't say that we aren't responsible. If we hadn't been arguing in the first place, Vivian would've never had to get us out the door."

"We both feel horrible about this," the man's wife added.

As far as Maisie was concerned, their regrets were coming a little too late and were directed to the wrong person. "I'll ask Vivian what she wants to do," Maisie said. "As you know, we weren't here."

The couple exchanged glances. "Vivian has

all of our contact information. We were going to check out, anyway. I'd like to go ahead and do that."

"I'm sure everyone will be pleased to see us on our way."

"That sounds like a plan. May I have your names? I'll look through the registration and make sure everything is in order."

"Sounds good."

A half hour later, the Pushkins were gone, and the small bloodstain on the front stoop was cleaned up.

Realizing that the other guests were gone for a few hours and that they were alone, Maisie sat down at the kitchen table next to Clay. "How crazy was that?"

"It was one of the stranger situations I've witnessed of late."

"Did you and your ex ever fight?"

"No. Pam was more the type to keep things to herself and stew."

"Jared and I argued, but never in public. We tried our best to be civil in front of Jenna and Allison. I'm pretty sure Jared hated what was happening between us as much as I did."

"I hope that couple really wasn't at fault. It didn't seem like it, did it?" Clay asked.

Maisie shook her head. "I think if someone

had hurt Vivian intentionally, Will would have at least told Graham."

"They've gotten close, haven't they?"

"I don't know. Vivian made it sound like they'd broken up because he was moving."

"That's a shame. If I've learned anything, it's that at the end of the day, the people you care about matter more than anything. All the small stuff will work itself out."

She nodded. "If I found someone that I didn't want to be apart from, I'd make that a priority."

"I intend to do that very thing."

He was looking at her intently. "Clay, what are you saying?"

"I'm saying, now that we've found each other again, I don't want to let you go. You're my priority."

Her heart started beating fast. "Clay, really?"

He nodded. "What do you say? Do you want to give the two of us a real, honest-to-goodness try?"

Maybe she should be asking him what he meant. Was he suggesting marriage or just being exclusive? After all these years of being alone, it occurred to her that she was good with either. All she really wanted or needed from him was a commitment.

Which was what he was offering. "Yes," she said at last.

"I was hoping you'd say that," he said as he pulled her onto his lap.

CHAPTER THIRTY-SEVEN

"I'M SCARED TO see Mom in the hospital," Will announced when they were almost at Penrose.

Graham figured the reason likely had to do with his father dying in a car accident. He didn't think Will remembered much about his father's death, but he didn't know for sure. He'd never asked Vivian if Emerson had been dead on arrival or if he'd lived for several days. "Why is that?"

"She doesn't like hospitals. She told me."

His voice was very serious. Graham wasn't sure about the right way to continue the conversation, but he figured it probably didn't matter what he said. What mattered was that Will felt like he was being heard and that his feelings had value.

"If she doesn't like hospitals, then I think it's really good we're going to see her, don't you?"

Will nodded, but he didn't look much more at ease. His hands were curved around the edge of his seat.

"Is there something else you're worried about?" When the boy lifted his shoulder but didn't reply, Graham pushed a bit. He'd had enough experience training new recruits to know that sometimes people needed a little push to speak their mind. "I really am interested, Will."

"I didn't like hearing that man and woman arguing. I don't think it's fair that Mom had to tell them to be nice to each other."

Will had told him the whole story as soon as they'd gotten in his Jeep. "I bet she didn't like it, either. No one likes listening to other people not get along."

He sighed. "I wish that wasn't her job."

"Taking care of guests?"

He nodded. "Having people at our house all the time."

It was sure beginning to feel like he was in the middle of a minefield. There were a lot of things on the boy's mind, each more important to him than the next. Graham wanted to value each concern, but he didn't want to say the wrong thing, either.

"What has your mother said when you told her how you felt?"

"I've said some stuff, but I never told her all of that. Not really."

"Any reason you haven't?"

"Because all she's going to do is get sad. She tells me all the time that the people coming to the house pay the bills."

That just about crushed his heart. "I can see how you might worry about your mother getting sad, but maybe you ought to give her a chance? She might be glad that you're sharing how you feel."

"I don't know."

After parking the car just outside the emergency room, Graham said, "Let's go see your mom. After she gets home, there'll be plenty of time to talk about everything else. I know she likes to hear what you have to say."

"Will you help me talk to her about her job?"

Will was killing him. "I will, as much as I can," he said gently. "But I think we both know that you have to be the one to tell your mom how you're feeling."

He sighed. "Fine."

Graham held Will's hand as they walked into the emergency room. The moment they passed through the sliding glass doors, he was hit with the smell of pine-scented cleaner and damp coats. The waiting room was packed with people: a few kids were whining, a baby was crying and one poor soul looked bedrag-

SHELLEY SHEPARD GRAY 323

gled enough for Graham to surmise that he'd
been living on the streets.

Will gripped his hand tighter.

Graham went directly to the intake desk.
Two men and a woman were behind comput-
ers. When they approached, the woman motioned them over. "May I help you?"

"An ambulance took my mom over here,"
Will said importantly.

The woman's gaze softened. "What's your
mother's name, honey?"

"Her name is Vivian Parnell," Graham sup-
plied. "This young man is obviously her son."

"My name is William Parnell, but everyone
calls me Will."

"I'm pleased to meet you. And who are you,
sir?"

"I'm a family friend. Graham Hopkins."

She moved her mouse, clicked a few buttons and smiled at Will again. "Your mother
is right back over here. All we have to do is
get some information and you can go on back
and see her."

"Is she okay?" Will asked.

"I think so, honey. It looks like the docs
only had to patch her up. I bet she'll be ready
to go home soon."

She asked Graham a few standard questions
and gave them visitor badges. "See the lady

in the llama scrubs?" When Will nodded, she said, "Her name is Elaine. Go on over to her. She'll take you on back to your mother."

"Can Graham go, too?"

"He sure can." She smiled at them both as she motioned the next person in line forward.

When they met Elaine, she pushed a button to open another door and guided them through a maze of cubicles, each with a light blue fabric curtain surrounding it.

"I'm sure your mother is going to be happy to see you," she said.

"Yeah, my mom doesn't like hospitals." He blinked. "Sorry."

"It's okay." Elaine smiled at him. "A lot of people don't care for this place too much."

"Are you sorry you have to work here?"

"Nope. I like making someone's bad day a little bit better. At least I try to." She opened the cubicle's curtain with a snap. "And here's your mom."

Still holding Will's hand, Graham led him inside. He had been ready to caution Will to be careful with his mom, but Vivian was sitting in a chair. She had a nasty-looking bandage on her head, but otherwise she looked like her usual beautiful self. "Will! And Graham, too." Her expression was hesitant, but at least she was smiling. "I'm so glad you're both here."

Will hurried over to her but stopped before touching her. "Are you hurt bad, Mommy?"

"Not too bad. I could sure use a hug, though."

Graham shared a smile with the nurse as Will rushed the last bit of space and hugged his mother tight. "You have a big bandage on your head."

"I know I do." Looking at Graham, she said, "Even our sergeant should be impressed with me. I had to get eight stitches."

"Eight is a lot," he said, finally stepping closer. Unable to stop himself from touching her, he bent down and kissed her cheek. "I probably would've fussed."

"She was very brave," Elaine said. "Especially when we had to give her some shots."

"Those didn't feel good," Vivian said.

"Did you get a CT scan?" Graham asked.

"I did. That's what I'm waiting to hear about."

"I'll go see where the doc is," Elaine said. "You all stay put."

Worried that Vivian might be hurting more than she was admitting to, Graham held out his hands to Will. "Want to hop up on the bed?"

"Okay."

Lifting him onto the table, Graham whispered, "You're doing a great job." When Will smiled, Graham felt like he'd just done something right.

Moments later, a young doctor wearing glasses came in with an electronic tablet in his hands. Elaine followed with a cart.

"How are you feeling, Vivian?" he asked.

"Much better, thank you."

He scanned the tablet before looking her way again. "How's your pain? Do you have a headache?"

"Just a small one. It's not too bad, though."

"We got your scans back. They look good."

"I don't have a concussion?"

"No concussion." He smiled.

"I'm so glad. That's really good news," Vivian said.

"I think so, too. It also means I'm going to send you home. I'm assuming these two guys are going to get you there safely?"

"Yes. This is my son, Will, and my friend Graham."

"Graham is in the Royal Canadian Air Force," Will said importantly.

"That's great. If he's in the military, chances are good that he's used to following instructions," the doctor joked.

Graham chuckled. "Absolutely."

"Will you two make sure Vivian rests the rest of the afternoon and evening?" the doctor asked.

"I'll be happy to do that."

"That means no cooking or running around after guests—or little boys—until tomorrow afternoon." When Vivian opened her mouth to protest, the doctor added, "You don't have a concussion, but you have a good little bump. Give yourself some time to recover. I promise you'll feel better in the long run."

"Okay."

"I'll make sure my mom rests, too," Will said.

"It looks like you're in good hands. You take care, Vivian," the doctor said before walking out of the room.

Elaine stepped forward. "I'll go through how to take care of your stitches, and then we'll get you out of here."

As the nurse continued talking, Graham glanced at Vivian. She was staring back at him, love shining in her eyes. Obviously, something had changed for her. He couldn't wait to find out what that was.

He did know that he'd stepped aside long enough. He was going to fight for her. Fight for them both. What they had was special. Too special to give up.

Too special not to do everything in his power to make it last.

CHAPTER THIRTY-EIGHT

THEY'D HARDLY TALKED on the way home. Will had fallen asleep practically from the moment Graham left the hospital parking lot, which was a good reason to stay quiet. However, the main reason Vivian hadn't said much was that she didn't know how to thank Graham without dissolving into tears.

He'd not only left work the minute Will had called, but he'd gotten her fresh clothes and arranged for Maisie to take over at the inn, all while Will had stayed glued to his side. He'd been so wonderful at the hospital, too. He'd been concerned without being overbearing and helpful without acting autocratic. He'd been everything she'd ever needed—even though she'd pushed him away.

Will kept staring at him with stars in his eyes. Vivian had even spied several nurses smiling at him. Even her nurse, Elaine, had whispered to Vivian that Graham was a keeper.

Vivian knew that was true.

Just as she knew that he was still moving far away and she'd soon be alone again.

When they pulled into her driveway, Graham said, "Stay here. I'm going to carry Will inside and then come back for you."

It would be so easy to continue to let him pamper her, but it was time to get back on her own two feet. "There's no reason for that. All I have is a little cut on my head."

"There's every reason. Wait for me, okay?"

She nodded, because he didn't deserve her arguing with him. But when she caught sight of Graham carrying Will in his arms, Vivian was so glad she'd stayed put. Her son was sprawled like a rag doll against Graham's chest while he navigated the front walkway before disappearing through the front door. Her heart lurched.

That right there was what she'd always wanted for Will. And, yes, for her as well. Someone to stay by her side and help carry her burdens. Someone to treat Will with care and affection. Someone they could both trust.

The only problem was that Graham was asking her to make a sacrifice in order to make their future together work. So far, she'd been unwilling to do that. But what if she'd been thinking about everything all wrong?

What if she'd confused her need for stability with being selfish and stubborn?

When Graham tapped on the passenger door, she jumped.

He was studying her closely. "Are you all right? Is your headache worse?"

"No, nothing like that." She smiled weakly. "I… I guess I drifted off for a moment. Sorry."

"No reason to apologize," he said as he helped her unbuckle. "You ready to get out of here?"

"So ready." She took his proffered hand, realizing that she felt a little fuzzy as she got to her feet. "Gee, I guess I'm a little more worn-out than I realized."

"We'll take it slow."

Each step felt like an effort, but at last she was inside.

Maisie and a handsome older man she assumed was Clay were also there.

"Vivian, no offense, but you look like you've been in a brawl," Maisie teased as she gave Vivian a gentle hug. "You're getting quite a bruise on your face."

"Really? My cheek felt tender, but I was hoping it looked better than it felt."

"Don't worry about it," Clay said. "You'll just look tough."

Liking that idea, Vivian grinned. "Maybe

my battle scar will make future guests think twice before giving me a hard time," she joked. Realizing that it was especially quiet, she said, "Where is everyone?"

"Well, the Pushkins left, and the sisters had tickets for a show. The German couple went out as well, but they're back now, as is the family upstairs. They said they were in for the night. So all is quiet."

"I can't thank you enough."

"We were happy to help," Clay said. "Between us, Maisie and I got everything back in order. All you need to do now is rest."

"I will." She turned to Graham and held out her hands. He clasped them lightly. "Thanks for helping me so much today."

His expression softened as he ran a finger over her knuckles. "I'm so glad Will called me."

Warmth filled her heart, making her yearn for so much more—but it was late, and he'd already done so much. It was time to let him go. "I'll call you tomorrow. Maybe then we can talk?"

"That won't be necessary. I'm going to stay here tonight."

"You don't have to do that."

"I'm afraid I do."

"You heard the doctor. I don't have a concussion, Graham."

"I remember that, but getting a good night's rest isn't going to hurt you. I'll sleep on the couch. If any of your guests or Will needs something, I'll take care of it."

"You are making too big a deal out of this." She cast Maisie a plaintive look.

But all Maisie did was shake her head. "I'm sorry, Viv, but I'm afraid I'm on Graham's side. If we don't insist on helping, you're going to be up at five making muffins or something."

"I'll be fine."

"I know you will, because I'm going to make sure of it," Graham said. When she started to protest again, he raised a hand. "Vivian, relax. I'm not saying I'm going to live here all the next week. It's just for one night." His expression was solemn. "One night. Why argue about it?"

She opened her mouth to fuss, then shut it again. Did her pride really matter more than accepting his help? "You're right. Thank you."

"Thank you," he replied. He pulled out his keys and, turning to Maisie and Clay, he added, "I have to run to the base, check in and get my stuff. It won't take long. I'll be back in less than an hour."

"Sounds good. We'll hold down the fort till you get back," Clay said.

Before Vivian could think of something else to say, Graham pressed his lips to her forehead then walked out the door.

"He's right, you know," Clay said.

Vivian had been in such a fog, she'd forgotten her friends were still in the room. However, Clay sounded so sure of himself, she couldn't help but respond. "About what? Me needing a babysitter?"

He walked closer, a scar on his eyebrow capturing her attention before she could hide it. "He's right about you being worth it."

She didn't know whether she should be offended or just shocked by his comment. "I'm sorry, what?"

He half smiled. "Don't worry. You're not the first person to think that I should mind my own business. It's just that after everything that has happened in my life, I've learned that time is precious. Maisie and I were apart for years, and only by the craziest coincidence did we connect again. But I can't help but wish that I'd taken more chances in the past. Or maybe believed in happiness a little more."

"I thought you two were just kids when you moved away."

Clay inclined his head. "We were. I'm not

saying that everything in my life would have been different if I'd had her by my side, but I can't help but think that my future is going to be a lot worse without her in it."

"You already know that?"

"I knew it in an instant."

"He's moving away soon. And it's not like I can just up and leave. I have a business here." She privately realized that she was just saying words, however. She'd enjoyed running the Snowdrop Inn, but she didn't love it. Not now that she remembered what love really was.

"I'm not asking you to leave or change or even believe a word I'm saying," Clay said quickly. "All I do want you to think about is that you two might not have known each other very long, and you might not want to move to Canada—or even want to move at all. But if he's the type of man to drop everything at a moment's notice, take care of your son and then sleep on your couch—all without you asking him to do any of it? Well, that seems pretty special to me."

Maisie came rushing back in. "Will is in pajamas and sound asleep in his bed. Now, my dear, it is your turn." She looped a hand around Vivian's elbow. "What do you think? Are you ready to call it a day?"

Vivian was barely able to look away from

Clay. Everything he had said resonated with her. He was right: Graham Hopkins was a man in a million. Was she really ready to let him go just to keep herself company with a list of what-could-have-beens?

"Vivian?" Maisie prompted. "Are you dizzy?"

"Hmm? Oh, no. I was just thinking about something that Clay said. I… I think it's time I lay down. Maybe it's past time." She smiled wanly. "First, though, a hot bath."

"I'll help you get set up."

"'Night, Vivian," Clay said. "I hope you feel better."

"I will. And thanks."

"You're welcome, but like I said, it's all up to you."

His words continued to play in her head as she entered the little two-room apartment that she and Will shared in the back of the house.

"I'll start your bath. You get your things together, sweetie," Maisie called out.

Walking to her chest of drawers, Vivian pulled out her favorite set of flannel pajamas and took off her shoes and socks.

When she padded into the bathroom, Maisie had a towel waiting for her and bubbles in the tub. "I can't thank you enough," she said.

"No thanks needed," Maisie said from the

doorway. "You just relax and get some sleep. Take the night off, Vivian."

"You know what? I'm going to happily do that."

She closed the door after Maisie left and walked back to the bathroom. Stared at the bruise on her cheek and the bandage on her temple. Gave thanks that she wasn't more hurt and that Will was fine, too.

It turned out that she didn't need to always be strong; she just needed to allow herself to lean on someone else every once in a while. Or, as the case may be, several someones.

CHAPTER THIRTY-NINE

A FIRE WAS crackling in the hearth, and two candles were burning when Maisie returned to the inn's living room. Clay was sitting on the couch. He'd taken off his pullover and was now just wearing his worn jeans and a faded blue T-shirt. He looked gorgeous. Honestly, the whole setting was so homey and romantic and inviting. It was also completely inappropriate.

"Clay, you can't just go making yourself at home in here."

"Sure I can. We've been here all day."

"But we're going to leave as soon as Graham returns."

"I understand," he said as he got to his feet. "And we will leave as soon as he gets back." He walked closer and looped his arms around her waist. "But until then, we might as well enjoy ourselves."

She was pretty sure she was blushing. "You're crazy, you know that?" Maybe she was, too, since she'd linked her hands around his neck and was in no hurry to push him away.

"Maybe I'm crazy, but I think it's more of a case of me taking advantage of a good opportunity. This is a lovely space, the fireplace can be lit with a flick of a switch and it's the end of a very long and unexpected day."

"But still…"

"If I was taking advantage of the situation, I would've made you dinner in her kitchen and poured you a glass of her wine. Relax."

Unable to fault his reasoning—or make herself wait any longer—she kissed him gently. "Fine."

"Kiss me again."

She complied, happy to be close to him, enjoying the feel of being in his arms and gratified to know that while Graham and Vivian might have a long road ahead of them, she and Clay didn't. She knew without a doubt that she would do just about anything to make a relationship with Clay work.

Of course, she also knew what the alternative was like.

When they returned to the couch, she said, "Vivian seemed like she was in a daze. At first, I thought it all stemmed from her fall, but she said that she was thinking about something you told her."

He looked a little guilty but nodded. "I'm afraid I probably dispensed a little too much free advice. Did she seem upset?"

"No," she said, thinking about it. "It was more like she was puzzled. What did you say?"

"I told her that while I understood that there were a lot of things keeping her and Graham apart and that all of those things were likely valid—" he paused as he propped one of his feet on the edge of the coffee table "—I pointed out that there might be something more important that was worth holding on to."

"Love?"

"Yep."

"That was very sweet."

He smiled. "Maybe, but it's true." After a pause, he added, "I also mentioned that Graham is a great guy who seems to be willing to do whatever it takes to take care of her."

"Clay, you hardly know him!"

"I know. But only a guy can appreciate another guy volunteering to spend the night on this here sofa. This thing is on the short side, Maisie. His back is going to be killing him in the morning."

She chuckled. "I never would have suggested that short-couch sleeping was a sign of love, but you might have a point."

"Just for the record, I'd sleep on this old sofa for you, Maisie." Rubbing his back playfully, he added, "I just might need a couple of ibuprofen in the morning."

"Right back at you."

He took hold of her hand. "What do you say that one day soon we do something really romantic?"

"Since you've spent most of your life doing extreme adventure sports with other military folk, I'm almost afraid to ask what you have in mind."

Looking amused, Clay grinned. "Military folk?"

She pretended to roll her eyes. "You know what I mean. I'm just trying to prepare myself. Does your romantic activity involve hiking, snowmobiling or skiing? If it does, I'm going to need some new outdoor gear."

"It's nice to know that you'll go hiking with me soon. But, uh, I was thinking of something else."

Gazing into his eyes, Maisie felt foolish. He was being serious, and she was giving him a hard time about his job and his interests. "I'm listening."

"I like all three, but I was thinking of something more along the lines of a bottle of wine, a fancy dinner out and jazz."

She'd told him on their first date that those three things were at the top of her romantic-evening list. She'd meant it but had only mentioned them in jest. Jared had never been one for wine, jazz or expensive meals out.

As for other men? Well, she'd rarely given any of the men she'd dated more than two chances to see if they clicked. First and second dates didn't involve evenings like the one he described.

Emotion filled her throat as she struggled to answer. "If we had a night like that, it would be the first one I've ever had."

Clay looked nonplussed. "You mean to tell me you've never been wined and dined like that? Ever? Your ex didn't do those things with you?"

She shook her head. Feeling uneasy and embarrassed, Maisie waited for him to change his mind. Maybe he was thinking that if no other man had thought she was worth so much trouble, then he shouldn't, either.

"Maisie Arnold, are you free on Saturday night?"

"Yes."

"Plan for me to pick you up at six thirty, okay?"

"Okay."

"Good." He leaned over and kissed her lightly just as the front door opened.

"It sounds like Graham has returned."

Getting to his feet, he reached for her hand again. "Let's go see how he's doing. And maybe find him a couple of extra blankets or something. He's going to need them on this couch."

CHAPTER FORTY

IT WAS LATE. He'd hurried to his quarters, grabbed his things and barely stayed long enough to make sure no one needed him for anything urgent.

Graham was thankful his commander had been so understanding about the way he'd taken off with barely a word to anyone. Luckily there hadn't been anything too important going on—if there had, he wouldn't have left his post no matter what. But still, his actions had been irregular both for his department and for himself. Graham didn't remember another time when he'd acted so impulsively.

As he was heading back to his Jeep, Captain Howard called out to him. "Sarge, hold up."

"Sir?" he asked.

His captain shrugged off Graham's salute. "You sure got everyone in a tizzy today. It's not every day that Sergeant Hopkins takes off without a backward glance."

"Yes. I'm sorry, sir. If you—"

Howard interrupted. "No, no. Don't apologize. You know I'm worried about you, Graham. Not protocols. How are you?"

"I'm fine, sir."

"What about your girl?"

It took him a minute to grasp what his captain was asking. Everyone on the base now knew he had someone special in his life. "Vivian is going to be okay. She's home from the hospital. She was in a crazy accident. I'm glad she wasn't hurt any worse." He smiled. "I can't believe you already heard about it. Looks like the gossip mill hasn't had time to revise it yet."

"Give it time," Captain Howard said with a chuckle. "By tomorrow night, either a gun, a dog or an angry mother-in-law will be involved. It seems no story around here can be spared from a few elaborations."

"I can deal with that. It's thinking about Vivian getting more injured than she already was that worries me."

"I'll hope for fresh gossip soon, then," he said with a smile.

"Sir?"

"I mean it in the best way, Graham. We're all glad you found this gal. I look forward to meeting her."

And now everyone was practically planning his engagement! Graham stuffed his hands in his pockets. "This is a new thing for me. I'm not sure how I feel about being the focus of so much talk."

"It's good talk, I promise. Everyone cares about you." Captain Howard raised his eyebrows. "Our mighty, notoriously unflappable Sergeant Hopkins runs out in the middle of duty because of an injured girlfriend? I'd say that was a noteworthy event."

Graham felt even more self-conscious. "I don't know whether to be more embarrassed about the way I left or the fact that everyone is sure I have no life."

"Don't be embarrassed at all. You're human and have someone who cares about you. That's something to be proud of in my book."

"Thanks, Captain. I think I needed to hear that."

He motioned to the canvas backpack Graham was holding. "You heading over to see her?"

"Yes. Vivian has a little boy who's six. Will and I have gotten pretty close. I want to be nearby in case he or his mother needs something."

"Have you already taken leave for tomorrow as well?"

"Yes." To his surprise, he hadn't even thought twice about taking so much personal time so he could be there for Vivian.

"Good. I hope she feels better soon, Graham."

"Thank you, sir."

After he got in his Jeep, he turned the heat on high and pulled out of the parking lot. He'd gone about a block when his truck's screen beeped, signaling an incoming call.

Clicking a button, he said, "Hey, Mom."

"I saw you called earlier. I'm sorry I missed it. What's up?"

"Vivian got hurt today. I'm on my way over to see her and spend the night on her couch."

"Oh my gosh! What happened?"

As succinctly as he could, he relayed the story.

"Oh, the poor thing. I'm sure she's going to be sore in the morning."

"I think she already is."

"So, you're driving over to check on her again?"

She sounded tentative. "Yes, but also to be with Will. He had a pretty hard time seeing his mom taken to the hospital by ambulance. I think it brought back memories of the car accident that took his father's life."

"Ah. Well, yes. I can see that."

Graham was caught off guard by her tone again. "Mom, what is going on?"

"Nothing, Graham."

He realized he was protective of Vivian and Will. "No, something is going on. You're sounding all odd."

"Odd?"

"Okay, hesitant, like you've got more on your mind than you're saying."

"I think you're exaggerating," she said quickly.

Now he was getting annoyed. "Mom, I'd rather you simply tell me what you're thinking instead of making me guess."

"All right, but I hope you won't take it all the wrong way."

"Take what?"

"That I still think you're getting too emotionally involved with her."

"We've already been through this. Besides, what happened to you telling me that I needed to get more emotionally involved in my relationships?"

"I'm glad about that. Of course I'm glad. But the problem is that you are going to move soon. Plus, she has a child. Are you really ready to take on raising another man's son?"

"Since Will's father is dead, I would have to say yes. Mom, I can't believe you're cautioning me about Vivian and Will. Luke took on the lot of us when you and he got married. You two were really happy, too."

"You're right."

"If I'm right, why do you keep warning me about her?"

"I'm sorry. I…well, I can't help but feel dismayed. I mean, after all this time, you finally meet someone, but she can't move and she has a child."

His mother still wasn't listening. "Those aren't obstacles to me."

"That may be true, but they aren't the easiest building blocks on which to start a relationship."

"Everything you are seeing as wrong or as problems, I see as advantages. I don't want or need Vivian to be a different. She wouldn't be the woman I've fallen in love with if she didn't have a son."

"You're in love with her?"

"I am, Mom. Vivian's beautiful and sweet. She's strong and fun and easy to be around. She cares not only about Will and me and her friends, but she cares so much for all the guests in her home. I don't want to change a thing about her." He hoped his mother heard the steel in his tone. "It's time you respected not only her, but my feelings for her."

There was a moment's pause, and then Gwen said, "You're right. If she truly is the woman for you, then I'm happy for you. No, I'm happy for you both."

Graham tensed, waiting for her to add something else. When his mother remained silent, he was stunned. "Wait, that's it?"

She laughed lightly. "You just reminded me why you've always been my sounding board. You are levelheaded and not afraid to point out truths—or when someone is wrong. I'm not going to argue with your good sense."

Sitting alone in the dark parking lot, Graham realized that it was time to take some of his own advice. He needed to stop second-guessing himself and stop worrying about how Vivian might react if he told her he loved her. In short, he needed to get on with it.

He stepped out of the vehicle, pulled out his backpack and clicked his key fob to lock it. "Love you, Mom, but I've gotta go," he said, already heading to the inn's front door.

She chuckled lightly. "I know. I love you, too. Let us know if you need anything."

"Thanks. 'Night."

Walking into the house, Graham realized that the future was still up in the air.

One thing had changed, though. He was now willing to fight for a life with Vivian and Will. Somehow or someway, he was going to make it work.

CHAPTER FORTY-ONE

IT WAS EARLY in the morning. Vivian had woken up sore and bruised but feeling much better than she had the night before. Before she took a shower, she peeked into the living room and spied Graham sleeping on the couch in his jeans and T-shirt.

A blanket covered his midsection, and a pillow was under his head. His bare feet were hanging off the end of the sofa. He appeared to be sound asleep, which she was thankful for, since he looked extremely uncomfortable.

So much had happened between them that it should have been awkward that Graham was sleeping just a few feet away. But she liked having him there.

Vivian didn't feel that she needed him to keep her safe or take care of things at the inn. But she sure did feel happier whenever she knew he was nearby.

That alone should have been the first clue that she'd had a change of heart about her future.

However, it was the way her whole body seemed to be bracing to see him that made Vivian finally face the facts—she had fallen in love with him.

Vivian elected not to take her usual shower. Her head was still sore, and she didn't want to either wash her hair or figure out how to style it without disturbing her stitches. Instead, she elected to tie her hair back carefully and put on an old baseball cap of her father's. After applying a swipe of mascara and a bit of blush, she proceeded to go down to the kitchen.

Knowing her guests would be looking for breakfast in a couple of hours, she started the coffee maker and pulled out the bacon from the refrigerator.

"What are you doing, Vivian?"

She must have jumped a foot in the air before she turned to face him. "Graham, you startled me!"

"You surprised me, too," he said as he approached. "It's barely five in the morning. Don't you think you should be resting?"

"No. I've got guests here. They'll need to eat."

"I thought we already discussed this last night. You were going to take it easy."

"I know, but I'm well enough to do my usual routine."

"I know you're stubborn enough."

She raised an eyebrow. "I don't know if you noticed, but the Snowdrop Inn is a bed-and-breakfast. People expect to get breakfast. It's kind of a thing."

"So you're going to make a fancy meal even though the doctor said to take it easy."

"I did take it easy. Now stop scowling at me. I need to do my job."

"How about you let me do it?" He staved off her protest with a determined look. "And don't start with the fact that I'm not a cook. I can follow directions."

Since she had been planning to simply pull out some frozen items and put bacon in the oven, she decided not to argue. "Thank you. That would be very nice of you."

"What would you like me to do first?"

"Put the bacon on the cookie sheet?"

"I'm on it." He washed his hands. "You look cute in that ball cap, by the way."

"Thank you." She pulled out a sausage casserole and two different kinds of muffins. "It's a little on the frayed side, but it's still my favorite. It was my dad's."

"Was he a Mustang?"

She knew he was probably amused by the somewhat goofy-looking horse on the brim. "He was. He played baseball for years." While

Graham placed the pan in the oven, she poured them each a cup of coffee.

"Did he encourage you to play, too?"

"No." She shrugged her shoulders. "My mom fully embraced my choice to wear tap shoes from the time I realized I could make noise while I walked. I was a dancer."

His eyes lit up. "Is that right?" Stepping close, he said, "Can you still tap-dance, Vivian?"

"A little bit." She could probably do more than that. One didn't practice as much as she did without retaining some muscle memory.

"I can't wait to see."

She giggled. "Oh, no. I never said I was going to tap-dance for you."

He grinned. "Sorry, but you've just given me a brand-new goal where you're concerned."

"A new goal? What was the first one?"

"To get you to love me back."

She blinked. Had he just said what she thought he did? Her mouth went dry. "Graham?"

"Sorry. I didn't mean to spring it on you like that." He averted his eyes. "Looks like this is another instance where it's painfully obvious that I don't have a lot of experience when it comes to relationships."

She pressed her palm to his chest. "Tell me what?"

"That I love you, Vivian. It's a permanent thing,

too. I'm not falling in love or think I'm that way. I'm all in, no holds barred, in love with you."

"Oh, Graham."

"Listen, it's okay if you're still trying to figure us out. I'm not going to rush you. I just want you to know that I'm here and I'm not going away."

"Not going away? What are you saying?" Before she thought better of it, she blurted, "Are you going to stay here after all?"

Every part of him seemed to deflate. "No. I meant it figuratively. I'm still going to Canada, Vivian. What I am trying to say is that I want you to come, too." He held up a hand. "And before you say anything, let me add this. I want to marry you. Maybe not next month, but I'm certain of it. I want you to be my wife. I want Will to be my son. I want to have more kids, if that's what you want, too. But more than anything else, I just want to be with you. Look, I know I'm pushing, and I know it's a lot to ask, but isn't it worth it? Isn't a future together—isn't another chance at happiness—worth it?"

Yes, it was.

She wanted to lean into him and tell him everything he wanted to hear. She wanted to say yes and laugh because he magically pulled out a ring and sealed their fate.

But she wasn't naive, and leaving everything she'd built in Colorado Springs wasn't going to be easy.

"Graham, I love you. And everything you're saying sounds amazing, and I want to say yes."

"But?"

"But I think I need to think about it for at least a little bit. And… I need to sit down with Will. I think I know what he's going to say, but I've learned that he doesn't do real well with surprises. Can I do that?"

"Of course. As long as I know we've got a chance, I can wait as long as you need."

He kissed her then, pulling her into his arms and holding her close, telling her without words how much she meant to him.

Feeling as if she was in a fog, she walked him to the door, said goodbye and softly closed the door behind him.

Then, for a few seconds, she allowed herself to imagine that everything he had said could actually happen.

CHAPTER FORTY-TWO

As LUCK WOULD have it, Vivian had a group of demanding guests settle in for the next two days. They were polite and respectful but thought nothing of asking her for decaf when she brought out coffee, hot tea when she brought out decaf and gluten-free snacks when she'd spent the last hour baking cookies.

They also wanted her help making dinner reservations, finding tickets for the Cog Railway and her assistance in acquiring lavender bubble bath that supposedly was only sold to guests staying at the Broadmoor Hotel.

Her personal life was just as full. Will's teacher had decided that they needed to do some kind of cute St. Patrick's Day project, since March was just around the corner. Between helping Will look for pictures of green things in magazines, driving him back and forth to his skating lessons, and jumping through a bunch of hoops to procure fancy bubble bath, she wasn't left with much time to think.

She'd been so busy she'd even recruited Maisie to help with the guests—warning her that they were needier than most.

Maisie hadn't been the least bit fazed. She helped mollify the guests and even brought over some of Audrey's old magazines for Will to comb through.

Once the St. Patrick's Day project was safely put away in Will's backpack and Vivian's guests had departed for a concert downtown, Maisie poured them each a glass of wine.

"Put your feet up, dear. You look beat."

"I kind of am. It's been a heck of a week."

"Well, it did start with you in the hospital."

Vivian carefully touched the neat row of stitches on her hairline. "Gosh, I wasn't even thinking about that. I've just been trying to keep up with the rigors of first grade!"

"Those school projects always sound so fun until—"

"Until they're not." Vivian chuckled. "When Will first told me about it, I was actually looking forward to sitting at the kitchen table with him and doing nothing but looking for green items in magazines. But then, of course, I forgot about the project and so did Will." After taking another sip of wine, she admitted, "I feel like the worst mom."

"Well, it got done, right?" When she nodded, Maisie held up her glass to toast. "Then you're doing great. Don't beat yourself up about things that don't matter."

"You're right."

"I'm getting the feeling that there's something else going on, besides mom guilt."

"Oh, yeah." After taking another sip of liquid courage, Vivian blurted, "Graham loves me, I love him and he wants to marry me whenever I'm ready." She waved a hand. "And of course this means he wants us to come with him to Canada, because he's heading there really soon."

Maisie chuckled. "That's it? Oh, pshaw. What in the world are you so stressed about?"

"Ha," Vivian replied to her friend's sarcasm.

Maisie's expression turned more serious. "What worries you the most?"

Vivian appreciated that Maisie was just letting her speak, rather than trying to force her views on her. She took a deep breath and really thought about it. "The only thing that I'm not worried about is marrying Graham. Isn't that crazy?"

Maisie shook her head. "Nope. Honestly, I think if you weren't sure that he was the one, then you wouldn't be so stressed out about everything else."

"I hadn't thought about it that way." Her

friend was right. If she wasn't sure if she loved Graham, or that being married to him would make her happy, then none of the other things would matter. She'd simply stay put. "I told Graham that I needed time to speak to Will about this. You know, to make sure that he's ready to have Graham permanently in his life."

"Vivian, anyone with eyes can see that boy adores him and that Graham feels the same way. I'm sorry, but Will's feelings are not what's holding you back."

It was kind of hard to hear that expressed in such a no-nonsense manner, but her friend wasn't wrong. "I've already decided that I love Graham. I know he loves me, and that even though I want to give Will the opportunity to talk things through with me, I'm not really that worried that he won't jump at the chance to have Graham as his stepdad."

Maisie looked at her intently. "So, that leaves you worried about shuttering your business, moving to Canada or…there's something else that's holding you back. Are you afraid to get married again?"

Maisie's question felt intrusive. But then she started thinking about her marriage with Emerson, and that first year of widowhood when she'd alternated between extreme grief and inexplicable anger that he'd left her on her own.

"Wow, Maisie. Way to get right to the point."

She winced. "I'm sorry if I overstepped. I'm trying to help, but I do have a tendency to go a bit too far at times. Just ignore me, please." Appearing even more troubled, she added, "I've been doing a bit of soul-searching myself, you see. I had a rocky marriage with Jared, and it ended even worse because of his affair. So I had to dig deep to ask myself if I was ready to not only love again but to trust again. I don't want to drag Clayton into my world if I'm not ready."

"What did you discover?"

She smiled. "That for me, I'd rather risk getting hurt again than be safe but unfulfilled. A few bumps and bruises are worth it if it means falling in love again."

Vivian thought about her own recent accident. It hadn't been fun, but she'd survived. It had also helped bring Graham back into her life. When she thought about it that way, the accident had been worth it. "I know what you mean."

"I appreciate that. I'm twenty-five years older than you, Vivian. I want to live my life and not just let it go by." She lowered her voice.

"But that doesn't mean I think you should do the same if you're not ready."

"I think I'm ready. I know I can be happy in Canada, and I'm even looking forward to being a military spouse." She laughed softly. "You know what? I think the main thing that's been on my mind is this darn B&B. I'm so attached to the business I've started, and I'm proud of its success. But at the same time, I'm tired of the hours and the stress."

"And the hunt for lavender bubble bath?"

She laughed. "Yes."

"Well, I have a solution for that."

"Which is?"

"Let me buy the inn."

"Maisie, are you serious?"

"Very serious."

"But what about your job?"

Maisie shrugged. "I do have a job I love. I love writing my detective series. But I'm pretty sure I can do both. I've enjoyed my experiences helping here."

"You've really been thinking about this."

"I have. I've even talked it over with Clay. Not that I want to push you out of town or anything, but it's been tempting to dream about the possibility." She took a deep breath. "Vivian, if you decide to go, Clay and I will buy this house and live where I am now. Audrey said she'd move in to help with the day-to-day needs of the guests."

"Audrey's willing to do that?"

"She's tired of working retail." Sounding more excited, Maisie added, "We even talked logistics. If Audrey wanted to go out of town or take a night or two off, Clay and I would come over."

"You'd divide up the chores."

For the first time, Maisie appeared hesitant. "That's the plan, though maybe it wouldn't work in real life. I can cook fairly well, but I'm not as talented as you are. Audrey is a great baker, but she doesn't have your warm and cozy personality. Your regulars might decide that the Snowdrop Inn isn't as wonderful as it used to be. The whole plan might implode."

"But you want to give it a try."

She nodded. "I figure at the end of the day, it's just a bed-and-breakfast. If people come and don't love their stay, they'll probably go someplace else, and that's okay."

"There are plenty of guests who are easy-going and don't expect or want special treatment."

Maisie smiled. "They might be just fine with the changes, then."

"Okay. Now all I've got to do is figure out when and what to tell Will."

"Vivian, I have an idea about that. It's just an idea, of course…"

"So far, your ideas have been great. I want to hear it!"

"Let Graham be the one to talk to Will."

Vivian knew that was the perfect solution. Graham would handle the conversation with the greatest of care, and it would mean so much to both him and Will. In addition, Graham would also realize that she loved and trusted him enough to be in charge of that very important moment.

"You're absolutely right, Maisie. Why didn't I think of that in the first place?"

"It doesn't matter if you decide to go that way or not. It was just an idea."

"And a good one." Vivian's heart was so full. She wasn't sure how she and Maisie had gone from being friendly neighbors to the closest of friends so quickly. Maybe it was serendipity. Maybe the Lord had known that they'd each needed someone in their corner.

All she knew for sure was that she was going to miss Maisie a lot. "When I move to Canada, you're going to have to promise to answer my calls no matter what time of day or night it is."

Maisie's bottom lip trembled before she visibly regained her composure. "I will, but only if you promise to do the same for me." She chuckled. "Don't forget that all this Snow-drop Inn business is going to be new to me. I might be able to handle the easy stuff, but a Vanderhaven family takeover just might be too much."

Vivian laughed. "Of course, but it's not the Vanderhavens you have to worry about. It's the guests who seem mild mannered and only want 'one more thing.'"

"Yep, I'm definitely putting you on speed dial," Maisie joked. She held out her hand. "It's a deal. We'll call each other all the time."

Vivian shook her hand. "That way we might both be starting over, but we won't be doing it alone."

Her friend's smile widened. "I like that. I like that a lot."

"Me, too," Vivian said. At last, she was ready to leave behind her past and move on with the future. One step at a time.

CHAPTER FORTY-THREE

"YOU'RE DOING GOOD, WILL. Keep your skates straight now."

Graham was so proud of the little guy. Will had now completed six lessons, and instead of hugging the side of the rink, he was skating over the ice with a good amount of confidence.

"You're skating good, too, Graham."

"Thank you. I was a little worried. I haven't put on skates since our visit to the rink by my parents' house."

"You told me then that you never forget how to skate. That it's like riding a bike."

"I did say that." What he hadn't added was that he was no longer a little boy who practically bounced back every time he fell on the ice. Whenever he fell down now, it felt as if every bone in his body was getting jarred. "Just think, in January, you were scared to let go of the rail, and now you're zipping along by my side."

"I'm getting pretty good!"

"Yes, you are." Graham looked at Will fondly. "You know, we can do this a lot when we're in Canada."

"That's what I told Coach Julian."

Graham slowed their pace as they turned the corner. "Are you excited about the move?"

"Uh-huh."

"Do you remember that you and your mom are going to stay with my mom for a little bit until I get settled in my new home on the base?"

"Your mom is nice," Will said. When they reached the exit, Graham helped Will off the ice and put on his skate guards. "Let's go sit down for a moment. I want to talk to you about something."

"Okay." For the first time since they'd come to the rink, Will looked worried.

Graham led him over to a wooden bench off to the side. There wasn't anyone else around at that moment, providing them some privacy. After they were settled, Graham said, "Will, your mom and I have been talking a lot about the things we want to do after we move."

"I know."

"You do?"

"Yeah. Mommy said we could go ice fishing."

"Yes. Well, ice fishing is fun, but we've also

been talking about things like the house we want to buy and where exactly we want to live."

"Mom said I could paint my room blue."

"Yep." Graham was starting to sweat. These big conversations were more intimidating than he'd realized. "We not only talked about houses and your new blue room, but about the three of us."

Will didn't say a word, only stared up at him. His blue eyes, so guileless and trusting, made Graham's insides feel like they were imploding. How was he ever going to be enough? How was he ever going to make sure that Will felt *he* was enough?

Swallowing through the lump that had formed in his throat, he soldiered on. "What I'm trying to say is that I love you and your mom very much."

"I know that."

"You do?"

"You wouldn't be wanting us to be with you all the time if you didn't, Graham."

The boy's voice was so confident and sure, Graham felt the tension in his shoulders ease. "That's right. You and your mom are my favorite people in the world to be around." He cleared his throat. He could do this. "So, um, when people love each other, they want to be a family."

"You want us to be a family, Graham? A real one?"

"I do, Will. I want the three of us to have each other. Not just you and your mom, and me and your mom. I want you and me to have each other, too." Seeing a wrinkle of confusion form on the boy's forehead, Graham knew it was time to stop messing around and say the words. "I want to marry your mom, but that's not all."

Will looked at him with a bit of trepidation. "What do you mean?"

He said a little prayer. He needed some support here. "It means that I'd like to be your new dad." When his expression didn't change, Graham added, "I mean, your stepdad."

"Then I won't have to tell everyone that my dad is up in heaven."

"You can tell people that if you want to," Graham assured him. "I'm sure your dad is up there right now looking down on us. I also know that he loved you very much and didn't want to leave you, ever. I'm certain he's watching over you each and every day and is so proud of how great you're doing. I'm also hoping that he won't mind if I step in for a time. I'd like to be your dad, too."

"So I'll have two."

Releasing a sigh, Graham nodded. "What do you think about that?"

"If you and my mom get married, that means you'll be with us forever."

"It means that the three of us will be a family." He winked. "Until you grow up and start your own family one day."

Will nodded. He stared out into the distance, obviously thinking about everything they'd just said.

Graham started to sweat again. He hoped he hadn't said all the wrong words. Maybe he should have practiced his speech a little more.

"Hey, Graham?"

"Yes?"

"I'd like that."

"Me, too." He was sure he was grinning ear to ear.

"Can we skate some more?"

"Yeah. Of course." Standing up again, he reached for Will's hand. The boy slipped his gloved one in his own and allowed Graham to pull him to his feet.

Minutes later, their guards were off and Will was skating again by his side.

When he looked up at Graham, he smiled.

That was all that Graham needed to see. Everything was going to be okay. Scratch that... it was going to be perfect.

EPILOGUE

IT WAS CHAOS. That was the only way to completely describe the scene at Gwen's farmhouse. The house was packed with people and Christmas presents and noise. Two tables were set. There must have been at least a dozen pairs of wet shoes in the front entryway. Candy, Will's taffy-colored golden retriever pup, kept sniffing them when she wasn't getting hugged and petted by all the kids.

Christmas music was playing in the background, and the NORAD Santa Tracker was on the television.

It was the complete opposite of Christmas Eve last year. Thinking about that day, and how hard it had been for her to promise Will even two days of guest-free privacy, Vivian shook her head. No wonder he'd called NORAD. He'd been desperate for their lives to change!

"How are you doing?" Graham said. He stepped behind her and wrapped his arms around her middle. "Is my noisy family driving you crazy? Do you want to escape the madness yet?"

She laughed. "Of course not. It's fun to see your family all together." Gesturing at Will, she added, "Besides, can you imagine trying to pry our boy away from here? He would fight us tooth and nail."

"He's so happy."

That was an understatement. Will was in the middle of all his new cousins, looking like he was having the time of his life.

To Vivian's relief, he'd not only adapted to their new life in Kingston with ease, but he adored his new cousins. Doug's kids always went out of their way to include him when they got together. His cousins had been all he'd talked about for the last week.

Pressing his lips to her brow, Graham said, "If you start to get tired, let me know. I can run you over to Doug and Susan's house and come back. Will won't mind. He understands that you need to take care of yourself."

Will had been ecstatic about becoming a big brother. It was only when she'd started having morning sickness that he'd become worried. Graham had told him that he was worried, too, but they could work together to help her. Vivian had been so touched that she'd started crying, which she'd blamed completely on hormones.

"I'll let you know if I need a break, but I'm fine. Really."

"Are you ready to tell everyone yet?"

She knew Graham could hardly stand it, he was so pleased about the news. She'd asked him and Will to keep things quiet until the first trimester was over. But now that she was thirteen weeks along, they were out of the danger zone. "We can tell them whenever you're ready."

His eyes lit up. "Really?"

She smiled. "Really." They hadn't expected to become pregnant so quickly. Vivian had actually thought that she might not be able to have any more children. She and Emerson had been trying for a year before he'd passed away.

Even more surprising, Graham had been the first to suspect that her constant sleepiness was something more than just a by-product of their busy life in Kingston.

"Let's tell everyone tonight after dinner," she said.

He chuckled. "After tourtière?"

"Oh my goodness…how could I forget?" In October, when everyone had gotten together for Canadian Thanksgiving, Vivian had finally worked up the nerve to tell his family about how bad their first attempt at making the meat pie had been.

Everyone, even the kids, had thought it was hysterical. Ironically, it had been Vivian's recounting of their Boxing Day tourtière tragedy that had cemented her relationship with Graham's mother. Gwen had teared up, saying that she'd never heard of a sweeter gesture.

"Dinner, everyone. Come to the table!" Gwen announced.

It took a while, but after they'd gathered together at the two tables, Doug led them all in a prayer, and then his sisters proudly brought out the four tourtière pies they'd made alongside Gwen that morning. There were salads and stewed cabbage and several vegetable side dishes, too. It was a huge Christmas Eve feast.

When everyone had finished making their plates, they all dug in. "You get to have your regular Christmas Eve meal again, Graham," Will said.

He'd already eaten two bites. "I do, and it's perfect. Thank you, ladies." Glancing her way, his smile faltered. "Viv?"

"I'm sorry!" she yelped before running to the bathroom.

With the door closed and the sink running, she heard everyone asking Graham what was going on. Vivian rested her head against the door and tried to let the next wave of nausea pass as she heard Graham tell his mother not to worry.

When she finally opened the door, she found Graham standing just outside, obviously waiting to make sure she was okay. "I'm sorry about that," she said.

"No worries," he murmured as he took her hand and led her back to the table.

"Is everything all right, Vivian?" Gwen asked.

Glancing up at Graham, looking so handsome and proud, Vivian knew there was only one reply. "Everything is fine. I just discovered that our baby isn't a real big fan of tourtière, either."

Stunned silence was followed by the scraping of chairs, loud cheering, applause and laughter. In the middle of it all, Will ran over and hugged her tight.

"We get to finally tell everyone that I'm going to be a big brother?"

She laughed. "Yep. You can share the news with whomever you'd like." Looking into his blue eyes, she rumpled his hair. "It's wonderful, isn't it?"

"It's the best Christmas gift ever."

Vivian thought this baby was a wonderful blessing indeed. But as she looked up at her husband, she couldn't help but think that nothing could beat last year's gift—after all, she'd gotten her very own RCAF sergeant on Christmas Day.

* * * * *

Get 4 FREE REWARDS!

We'll send you 2 FREE Books plus 2 FREE Mystery Gifts.

~~~
FREE
Value Over
$20
~~~

Both the **Love Inspired®** and **Love Inspired® Suspense** series feature compelling novels filled with inspirational romance, faith, forgiveness, and hope.

YES! Please send me 2 FREE novels from the Love Inspired or Love Inspired Suspense series and my 2 FREE gifts (gifts are worth about $10 retail). After receiving them, if I don't wish to receive any more books, I can return the shipping statement marked "cancel." If I don't cancel, I will receive 6 brand-new Love Inspired Larger-Print books or Love Inspired Suspense Larger-Print books every month and be billed just $6.24 each in the U.S. or $6.49 each in Canada. That is a savings of at least 17% off the cover price. It's quite a bargain! Shipping and handling is just 50¢ per book in the U.S. and $1.25 per book in Canada.* I understand that accepting the 2 free books and gifts places me under no obligation to buy anything. I can always return a shipment and cancel at any time by calling the number below. The free books and gifts are mine to keep no matter what I decide.

Choose one: ☐ **Love Inspired**
Larger-Print
(122/322 IDN GRDF)

☐ **Love Inspired Suspense**
Larger-Print
(107/307 IDN GRDF)

Name (please print)

Address   Apt. #

City   State/Province   Zip/Postal Code

Email: Please check this box ☐ if you would like to receive newsletters and promotional emails from Harlequin Enterprises ULC and its affiliates. You can unsubscribe anytime.

Mail to the **Harlequin Reader Service:**
IN U.S.A.: P.O. Box 1341, Buffalo, NY 14240-8531
IN CANADA: P.O. Box 603, Fort Erie, Ontario L2A 5X3

Want to try 2 free books from another series? Call **1-800-873-8635** or visit www.ReaderService.com.

*Terms and prices subject to change without notice. Prices do not include sales taxes, which will be charged (if applicable) based on your state or country of residence. Canadian residents will be charged applicable taxes. Offer not valid in Quebec. This offer is limited to one order per household. Books received may not be as shown. Not valid for current subscribers to the Love Inspired or Love Inspired Suspense series. All orders subject to approval. Credit or debit balances in a customer's account(s) may be offset by any other outstanding balance owed by or to the customer. Please allow 4 to 6 weeks for delivery. Offer available while quantities last.

Your information is being collected by Harlequin Enterprises ULC, operating as Harlequin Reader Service. For a complete summary of the information we collect, how we use this information and to whom it is disclosed, please visit our privacy notice located at corporate.harlequin.com/privacy-notice. From time to time we may also exchange your personal information with reputable third parties. If you wish to opt out of this sharing of your personal information, please visit readerservice.com/consumerschoice or call 1-800-873-8635. Notice to California Residents—Under California law, you have specific rights to control and access your data. For more information on these rights and how to exercise them, visit corporate.harlequin.com/california-privacy.

LIRLIS22R2

Get 4 FREE REWARDS!

We'll send you 2 FREE Books plus 2 FREE Mystery Gifts.

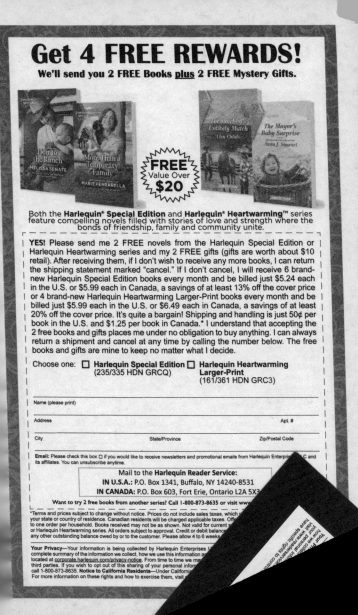

FREE Value Over **$20**

Both the **Harlequin® Special Edition** and **Harlequin® Heartwarming™** series feature compelling novels filled with stories of love and strength where the bonds of friendship, family and community unite.

YES! Please send me 2 FREE novels from the Harlequin Special Edition or Harlequin Heartwarming series and my 2 FREE gifts (gifts are worth about $10 retail). After receiving them, if I don't wish to receive any more books, I can return the shipping statement marked "cancel." If I don't cancel, I will receive 6 brand-new Harlequin Special Edition books every month and be billed just $5.24 each in the U.S. or $5.99 each in Canada, a savings of at least 13% off the cover price or 4 brand-new Harlequin Heartwarming Larger-Print books every month and be billed just $5.99 each in the U.S. or $6.49 each in Canada, a savings of at least 20% off the cover price. It's quite a bargain! Shipping and handling is just 50¢ per book in the U.S. and $1.25 per book in Canada.* I understand that accepting the 2 free books and gifts places me under no obligation to buy anything. I can always return a shipment and cancel at any time by calling the number below. The free books and gifts are mine to keep no matter what I decide.

Choose one: ☐ **Harlequin Special Edition** ☐ **Harlequin Heartwarming**
(235/335 HDN GRCQ) **Larger-Print**
(161/361 HDN GRC3)

Name (please print)

Address   Apt. #

City   State/Province   Zip/Postal Code

Email: Please check this box ☐ if you would like to receive newsletters and promotional emails from Harlequin Enterprises ULC and its affiliates. You can unsubscribe anytime.

Mail to the Harlequin Reader Service:
IN U.S.A.: P.O. Box 1341, Buffalo, NY 14240-8531
IN CANADA: P.O. Box 603, Fort Erie, Ontario L2A 5X3

Want to try 2 free books from another series? Call 1-800-873-8635 or visit www.

COUNTRY LEGACY COLLECTION

COUNTRY LEGACY

EMMETT
Diana Palmer

COURTED BY THE COWBOY

THE RANCHER AND THE BABY
Marie Ferrarella

Cowboys, adventure and romance await you in this new collection! Enjoy superb reading all year long with books by bestselling authors like Diana Palmer, Sasha Summers and Marie Ferrarella!

YES! Please send me the **Country Legacy Collection!** This collection begins with 3 FREE books and 2 FREE gifts in the first shipment. Along with my 3 free books, I'll also get 3 more books from the **Country Legacy Collection**, which I may either return and owe nothing or keep for the low price of $24.60 U.S./$28.12 CDN each plus $2.99 U.S./$7.49 CDN for shipping and handling per shipment*. If I decide to continue, about once a month for 8 months, I will get 6 or 7 more books but will only pay for 4. That means 2 or 3 books in every shipment will be FREE! If I decide to keep the entire collection, I'll have paid for only 32 books because 19 are FREE! I understand that accepting the 3 free books and gifts places me under no obligation to buy anything. I can always return a shipment and cancel at any time. My free books and gifts are mine to keep no matter what I decide.

☐ 275 HCK 1939   ☐ 475 HCK 1939

Name (please print)

Address   Apt. #

City   State/Province   Zip/Postal Code

Mail to the **Harlequin Reader Service:**
IN U.S.A.: P.O. Box 1341, Buffalo, NY 14240-8571
IN CANADA: P.O. Box 603, Fort Erie, Ontario L2A 5X3

#447 WYOMING CHRISTMAS REUNION
The Blackwells of Eagle Springs • by Melinda Curtis

Horse trainer Nash Blackwell's life-altering accident was...well, just that. He wants to rebuild. The first step is winning back his ex-wife, Helen Blackwell. Can trust once broken be regained?

#448 THE CHRISTMAS WEDDING CRASHERS
Stop the Wedding! • by Amy Vastine

Jonah Drake's grandmother will marry Holly Hayward's great-uncle—unless Holly and Jonah can stop them! The family feud is too unyielding for peace now, even at Christmas. Working together is their only option...but love brings new possibilities.

#449 THE DOC'S HOLIDAY HOMECOMING
Back to Adelaide Creek • by Virginia McCullough

Jeff Stanhope's focus is family. He's the new guardian to a teenager—and trying to mend things with his estranged sister. The last thing he needs is to start falling for her best friend, single mom Olivia Donoghue.

#450 A COWBOY'S CHRISTMAS JOY
Flaming Sky Ranch • by Mary Anne Wilson

Caleb Donovan needs Harmony Gabriel. The event planner can throw his parents a wedding anniversary like no other, though she shows up for the job with her baby girl. Caleb has all the family he needs...but soon he *wants* more.

HARLEQUIN
PLUS

Announcing a **BRAND-NEW** multimedia subscription service for romance fans like you!

Read, Watch and Play.

Experience the easiest way to get the romance content you crave.

Start your **FREE 7 DAY TRIAL** at www.harlequinplus.com/freetrial.